NO
GOOD
DEED

VICTOR
GISCHLER

NO GOOD DEED

FORGE®

A TOM DOHERTY ASSOCIATES BOOK
NEW YORK

This is a work of fiction. All of the characters, organizations, and events portrayed in this novel are either products of the author's imagination or are used fictitiously.

NO GOOD DEED

A Forge Book
Published by Tom Doherty Associates
175 Fifth Avenue
New York, NY 10010

www.tor-forge.com

Forge® is a registered trademark of Macmillan Publishing Group, LLC.

The Library of Congress Cataloging-in-Publication Data is available upon request.

ISBN 978-1-250-10669-8 (hardcover)
ISBN 978-1-250-10670-4 (ebook)

Our books may be purchased in bulk for promotional, educational, or business use. Please contact your local bookseller or the Macmillan Corporate and Premium Sales Department at 1-800-221-7945, extension 5442, or by email at MacmillanSpecialMarkets@macmillan.com.

First Edition: September 2018

Printed in the United States of America

0 9 8 7 6 5 4 3 2 1

For my wife, Jackie

NO
GOOD
DEED

PROLOGUE

It had all happened so fast.

A party. Champagne. They'd done it. The algorithm had worked. The AI element had been the key, and the son of a bitch had worked like a charm. Marion Parkes had to admit the kid threw a good party. Parkes wasn't much of a party guy, but he'd met the girl, someone from one of the downstairs offices, and yeah, okay, it had turned into a pretty damn good party.

But the algorithm. Holy shit, the algorithm worked!

He'd forgotten all about the algorithm when the police had kicked down his door the next morning. Confusion and shouting as they pushed him face-first onto the floor, then the handcuffs, and Parkes all the time yelling, *What's going on?* and *I didn't do anything!*, and then they'd found the drugs hidden in a baggy in the back of the toilet, and where the hell did *they* come from?

And then the words that stunned him to silence, the cop telling him, "You're charged with aggravated rape."

What?

The girl from the party, he found out later.

This was all a huge, enormous, terrible mistake.

"Tell it to the judge," they'd said.

It still all seemed like a blur, Parkes finally snapping awake when the judge's gavel had banged him into the joint.

A clang on the bars, and Parkes's head spun around to see the inmate who wheeled the cart from the prison library around the cell block, a porky little pig-faced guy who didn't talk much. He handed a magazine in through the bars, and Parkes took it. He handed back a carton of cigarettes. The inmate made the carton vanish into the book cart and ambled on to the next cell.

Parkes took the magazine to the back of his cell so none of the other inmates could see. Or the guards. Or anyone.

He opened the magazine to find it there as expected, a piece of folded clean white paper. He began unfolding, hoping it was big enough. Butcher's paper. Not quite as big as he'd hoped, but big enough for what he wanted to do. For the first time since he'd been sent up, he smiled.

You're not the only genius in the world, kid. Marion Parkes would get his licks in. Even if it was the last thing he ever did.

He spread the butcher's paper on the floor between the end of his bunk and the toilet. He wondered how many cartons of cigarettes for a proper drafting table and laughed. If his parents could see him now.

His mom and dad had both been scientists in North Korea, had sacrificed everything to smuggle the three of them out and get to America. They'd taught him everything. Other kids had been playing blocks or choo-choo trains, and Parkes had been memorizing the periodic table.

But his parents' field of study—nuclear reaction—left him cold. So yesterday. So Cold War. Even when they were building computers bigger and bigger, Parkes knew the future was making computers smaller and smaller. They'd be in everything. They'd run the world.

And Parkes had been right.

AI would be the next thing. In fact, Parkes had constantly scrambled to keep up with the latest advances. So many young bucks in the field now.

Like the kid.

Yeah, it had been the kid who'd lured him away from the university.

Every semester, Parkes offered a sort of recruiting speech in all the introductory-level computer classes. He used layman's terms to excite the undergrads, especially when talking about AI. What if a computer program could not only think but be intuitive? Could computers have gut feelings? Could that be simulated? Imagine a program that's been asked to cooperate with a completely foreign program or system it has never encountered before. Imagine you're a traveler and you meet another traveler who speaks a different language. You cooperate, learning a bit of his tongue, he a bit of yours.

Of course. Not difficult to understand such a process at all.

But now imagine instead of meeting another traveler you meet a bear. Or a goat or a bird or a salamander.

Or a rock or a stream or fog.

What was needed was a computer program that could say to itself, *What you did last time isn't going to work here. You need to try something completely different.*

It had been one of the kid's people who'd seen the lecture on YouTube. Then a series of interviews. Then four months later, Parkes had found himself moving into a new office in Silicon Valley, working for the kid.

Parkes bent over the butcher's paper, painstakingly recalling the algorithm from memory. He wrote with a pencil, small neat script. He took his time. He'd only been in stir a week, but he'd learned quickly there wasn't a lot to do. The most popular thing to do with time was to kill it. Likely he'd have invented some project for himself anyway. But this wasn't just killing time.

It was revenge.

He used the bottom of his shirt to wipe the sweat from his brow. He didn't want to drip onto the butcher's paper. He stopped several times to flex his hand. He didn't want it to cramp up. He went on like that for three hours, then had to stop for lunch, falling in line with the other inmates for the cafeteria. Prison food had not been as bad as he'd anticipated.

Although it hadn't been especially good either.

Then exercise in the yard. Parkes kept to himself and watched for anyone coming at him. He figured the kid would have him finished in here. All Parkes asked was time to finish copying the algorithm before they came for him.

It would have been nice if he'd figured it out sooner.

Parkes had already been sentenced and was awaiting transfer to the big house when he'd read about Dr. Patel's death in the newspaper. Suicide. Patel had worked with Parkes on the project for the kid. He'd recently been divorced, but Parkes had never thought the man capable of taking his own life. He'd recalled his last conversation with the man.

"I'm leaving to go back to India next month," Patel had said.

Parkes had expressed surprise. Patel had been successful in America, was making great money even with an ex-wife leeching away half. What Patel said next surprised Parkes even more.

"Don't tell anyone I'm leaving, okay?" Patel had said. "Especially not the kid. I want to keep at least one contact here, and I trust you, but otherwise I need to slip away quietly."

Patel had even said it again. *Don't tell the kid.*

Strange but . . . okay.

A day later, a coworker friend had come to bring him some things—deodorant, toothbrush, magazines. "Did you hear about Nancy?" he'd asked. "Damn. I still can't believe it."

Parkes had been stunned.

"Fucking drunk driver," his coworker had told him. "Like a

quarter mile from Nancy's house. Can you believe that shit? Look, Marion, you hang in there, okay?"

What an absurd, tragic thing to happen. That Nancy Kenner would accidently be killed within days of Patel's suicide . . . well, what were the odds? It was a crazy, messed-up world.

And to think, Parkes had mused. *With Nancy and Patel gone, that just leaves me as the last member of the core team who could reproduce all the research.* Sure, there were various techs and grad assistants who'd done some grunt work, and yeah, the kid had all the data under lock and key, but if they ever wanted to reproduce the entire process to duplicate the results . . .

Parkes had gone cold.

Patel's words had rung in his ears. *Don't tell the kid.* Patel was splitting the country and didn't want the kid to know. Did Patel know something? He was dead. So was Nancy Kenner. That left one guy who knew the algorithm, its application, everything.

Marion Parkes.

A frantic call to his lawyer. A rushed meeting. It had been difficult to make the lawyer understand all the technicalities, but he'd been all for anything that might be grounds for an appeal. All Parkes had to do was sit tight in his prison cell and keep his nose clean during the months it would take to process the appeal.

That's when Parkes had known he was a dead man.

The kid would be able to arrange it. No doubt. If he could contrive Patel's suicide and see to it Nancy was killed by a drunk driver, then he could certainly arrange for Parkes to meet his untimely demise in the clink. Parkes had paced his cell for three days, his brain grinding for a way out of this mess, all the time looking over his shoulder, waiting for someone to drag him into a shadowed corner and end him forever.

Maybe he could write letters, go to the newspapers. But the kid had been clever. Who would believe a junkie rapist?

That's when something rose up within him, a sort of cold fury that he should suffer such an injustice. Probably Parkes would not be able to save himself.

But, by God, he'd have the last laugh.

Parkes bent over the butcher's paper, writing in his tight, neat scrawl until his fingers and back and neck ached. He glanced at his watch. Lights out in ten minutes. He could just finish if he paid attention.

He finished with thirty seconds to spare. He stood, looked down at his accomplishment. There it was. The algorithm. Of course, there would need to be some other components to make it work, but this was the key. From what was on that butcher's paper, any postdoc could extrapolate the rest.

"Lights out!" called the guard walking the cell block. "Lights out!"

Parkes rapidly began folding the paper. His hands shook. He took a deep breath, let it out slowly. A second later, the lights went off. He lifted his thin bunk mattress and tucked the folded piece of butcher's paper under—

Wait! He'd almost forgotten.

He flipped the folded wad of butcher's paper over. In the corner, he scrawled a seven-digit number. Directly beneath it, he scrawled a second seven-digit number. And then a third seven-digit number below that.

Parkes would need help getting the algorithm into the right hands, and the three seven-digit codes were the price for that help. A price he was happy to pay, as a matter of fact.

Certainly less than what he'd paid his crappy lawyer.

He tucked the butcher's paper under his mattress and lay back on the bunk. He felt suddenly profoundly exhausted. Maybe it was that he was at the end of it all at last. He had one bullet to shoot, and he was about to pull the trigger. After that . . . well, whatever would happen would happen.

He closed his eyes.

But sleep wouldn't come. The hours dragged by, but every time he started to doze, some cold dream he could never remember jolted him awake. Soon dawn crept in through the bars, and Parkes gave it up, rolled out of his bunk, splashed water on his face, dressed.

And waited.

At last the porky inmate pushed the library cart to his cell. Parkes handed the magazine back to him, the butcher's paper and delivery instructions folded inside. The inmate stuck the magazine into the center of a pile of magazines and pushed the cart onward, his slack-jawed expression never wavering.

Parkes heaved a heavy sigh. It was out of his hands now. He felt an odd blend of emotions. Satisfaction mixed with a vague sense of anticlimax. He realized he might be feeling this way partly because he hadn't had more than forty minutes of sleep all night. They would come to march the inmates off to the showers soon. Standing under the cold spray would bring him around in time for some runny eggs and toast in the cafeteria.

He fell into line like a zombie, towel over his shoulder, and shambled to the showers.

Parkes wasn't sure how long he'd been standing under the spray when he started awake. Dead on his feet. He closed his eyes, lathered up, rinsed.

When he opened his eyes again, he couldn't see anyone in his peripheral vision. The inmates on either side of him had moved away. Had Parkes lost track of time or—

Oh hell.

Just when he'd figured it out, he felt the shiv enter his side from behind, a blinding flash of pain that took his breath away. His mouth fell open to yell or call for help, but just this dry croak came out, and then the shiv was in him again and a third time, and then he was on the floor, the shower spray still stinging his back.

Parkes caught a glimpse of a naked leg, the inmate turning slowly and leaving him there. Parkes struggled a moment to lift his head and get a look at the guy, but what good would that do? Who would he tell? What would it change?

He had to hand it to the kid. He worked fast. Barely behind bars a week, and already he had a man on the job. But Parkes would have the last laugh. He'd arranged everything, was even proud of how he'd figured it, who would deliver the package. The icing on the cake. The kid would hear about Parkes's death and figure he'd put a lid on the algorithm, that he owned it outright. The only people who could reproduce it again were dead. If the world wanted the algorithm, it would have to go through the kid.

Maybe that had been his plan all along. The kid was all about the long-term plan. The big picture. But if Parkes's plan worked, then he'd just fucked the kid straight in the ass.

Parkes laughed, but it turned into a hacking cough, blood flecking his lips. He coughed and coughed and then stopped. The shower spray mixed with the blood, swirled down the drain.

The screws found him like that, wet and pale and shriveled and rubbery, drained of blood, a slight and mysterious smile on his face.

1

Movement. Noise.

Something down the hall woke Francis Berringer from an awkward dream in which he was late for work.

He blinked at the alarm clock. It wasn't a dream.

"Shit."

He scrambled out of bed, trying to untangle himself from the sheet, failed, and tumbled to the floor.

"Shit!"

The sounds again. Somebody rattling around in the kitchen.

"Enid?"

Francis heaved himself to his feet, glanced at the other side of the bed. Enid wasn't there.

"Enid," Francis called.

No answer.

He went down the short hall, yawning and scratching himself, and found her in the tiny combo kitchen-dining area. She had her earbuds in. No wonder she hadn't heard him. There was a suitcase open on the table, and she was tossing clothes into it without folding them.

"Enid!" he said louder.

She turned abruptly, startled, took out one of the earbuds. "Did I wake you?"

"You should have earlier. The alarm didn't go off."

"Did you mix up A.M. and P.M. again?"

He didn't know. Maybe? It was hard to think before coffee. "Did you start the coffee maker?"

"You know I'm off caffeine."

Oh, yeah. She'd made so many changes lately, going vegan and dumping coffee. So many self-help magazines. She had at least a half-dozen subscriptions. They were all over the little apartment. Francis subscribed to a single magazine, *Adventure Travel*, hikes up Machu Picchu, that sort of thing. They'd had a special all-dining issue last month about eating exotic bugs and things all over the world. Enid made fun of him for that. Adventure and Francis didn't go together.

He had to admit he was unlikely to eat bugs. He'd have to be really hungry.

He went to the kitchenette and started the coffee maker. Dark roast.

Francis went to the cramped bathroom, still wiping sleep from his eyes. Stockings and a bra hung over the shower curtain. He urinated, flushed, yawned. He put toothpaste on his toothbrush, started brushing, mouth foamy. He looked up and locked eyes with himself in the mirror.

Wait. He'd missed something.

He spit, wiped the toothpaste from his mouth as he bolted from the bathroom back toward the living room. Toothpaste still dribbled down his chest.

Francis blinked at the suitcase on the table. "Are you going somewhere? Are you packing?"

"I told you I got a job," Enid said. "I told you last night."

He tried to remember the conversation. He'd been dog-ass tired when he'd dragged home last night. "I thought you picked up another shift."

"Not a *shift*," Enid said. "A job."

Like a thousand other actresses, she waitressed between jobs. Since Francis had known her, she'd done a whole lot of waitressing and not much acting. A play at some converted place in SoHo and a part in an independent film where she played the corpse of a dead prostitute.

"Well, that's . . . good?" Francis eyed the suitcase. "Where is it?"

"Chicago."

"Chicago?"

"Yes."

"Chicago, Illinois?"

"Yes."

"You didn't tell me this last night."

"Yes, I did," she insisted. "I said I got some work."

"I thought you were picking up another shift at the Patty Melt," Francis said. "Don't you think leaving town is a sort of important detail that you left out?"

"You know how I am about confrontations," Enid said. "I was going to leave you a note."

"A note?"

"It seemed simpler."

"When are you coming back?"

"Yeah, about that." Enid zipped the suitcase shut. "I'm not. It's a tour company, starting in Chicago and then going to the West Coast. This is big for me."

"What? You were just going to leave without saying . . . *anything*?"

"See? You're upset."

"I'm . . . but . . . well, what the hell? How did you think I would react?"

"Thus, the note." Enid's face softened, and she put her hand gently against Francis's cheek. "Look, it was good for a while. But

my career is dead here, and I'm not doing any more crappy waitress shifts in that crappy diner. I smell like grease all the time, and
since I've gone vegan, the smell of bacon makes me ill. You're nice,
Francis, but you're not give-up-my-career nice. Take care."

She turned, dragging the suitcase toward the door on its little
wheels.

"Wait!"

She opened the door, went out without looking back.

"Enid!"

Francis started after her, realized he was in his underwear, ran
back to the bedroom, grabbed a pair of sweatpants off the floor.
He danced back down the hall, trying to get his legs into the
sweats. He caught his toe in the fabric and went down, smacking
his head hard against the open door.

"Fuck!"

He blinked the stars out of his eyes, stood, pulled the sweats on
carefully, then dashed down three flights and out the front door of
his building.

Just in time to watch Enid's taxi pull away.

"Damn it."

Francis trudged back upstairs, caught sight of the clock.

"Damn it!"

He was definitely going to be late, but there was still a chance
he could slip into the office without Resnick noticing. There was
usually a ten- or fifteen-minute grace period, people hanging up
jackets, pouring cups of coffee, clicking on computers, and checking voice mail. If he hurried, Francis could make it.

He peeled off the sweats, put on charcoal-gray slacks, black socks,
wing tips. He grabbed two shirts off the floor. He smelled the white
one. *Ugh.* He tossed it aside and put on the blue one. He grabbed
a mustard-yellow tie. Tied it. The skinny part was longer than the

wide part. *Oh, come on.* He tied it again. The skinny part was still too long. *Screw it.* He tucked the skinny part inside his shirt.

Coffee. Francis still needed caffeine. He threw open the kitchen cabinet with the to-go cups. There were at least a dozen. Not a single cup matched a lid. How was that possible? He grabbed the biggest, filled it, and headed for the door.

Francis hit the street ten seconds later, fast-walking toward his subway station, hot coffee spilling over his fingers.

"Ouch. Shit."

In the back of his mind, he was still thinking about his tie. Francis wondered if he were OCD. Not for the first time. He didn't actually know the clinical definition of OCD. He just knew he hated loose ends, small tasks inappropriately or halfway done.

Fussy, Enid had said. She'd had a way of boiling things down. Not that he was fussy about everything. He had no problem leaving dirty clothes on the floor or dishes in the sink. She'd yelled at him about *that* too.

There's no pleasing her. Probably better off she's gone.

But Francis didn't feel it in his gut.

He glanced down at his wristwatch. Yeah, he was going to be late. And he was dangerously close to crossing from *buffer-zone* late to *noticeably* late. He walked faster.

The putrid smell hit him like a fist. Francis walked past the mouth of an alley with an enormous pile of garbage. Why did they let it pile up like that? Maybe there was another strike. He took a deep breath and kept walking.

Then stopped.

He didn't have time for this, but he couldn't help it. He had to go back and see if he'd seen what he saw.

Francis went back and looked. It was a suitcase, perched atop one of the trash piles.

And it was open.

He stood there looking at it and realized what had caught his attention. A few things, actually. First, it was clean. Not just the suitcase, but the contents too. Women's clothes—silk blouses, fashionable skirts, and *lots* of underwear. He reached in tentatively and plucked out a pair of panties—lace, a soft pink. The tag still dangled from them and read THE SMART SHOPPE. The suitcase was full of panties, never worn, perfectly folded, tags still on.

An old man walked by, giving him the stink eye from under a porkpie hat. Francis tossed the panties back into the suitcase like he'd been burned.

In addition to the suitcase's contents, Francis noticed something else. It wasn't like a normal suitcase, not like Enid's black one with the zippers and wheels. Francis always wondered about such cookie-cutter suitcases. All black, all the same size to fit into airline over-head bins, all looking exactly the same, so people put stickers or string on them so they could find them on the baggage carousels.

The suitcase atop the garbage pile didn't look like Enid's at all. Not black. No little wheels. It looked like something from a 1940s movie, big and square, some kind of alligator skin or probably fake. Brass clasps. Except it couldn't be from the 1940s because, like its contents, it was obviously brand-new.

There was something else inside besides clothes. A small, soft leather case. He took it and flipped it open. It was a case for business cards and held about twenty of them, white with a simple typeface:

GhostGirl@unlimited.net

He took one of the cards and put it in his shirt pocket, tossed the rest back into the suitcase.

Just leave it. Resnick is going to have your ass on a plate.

Francis moved quickly before he could change his mind, slamming the suitcase closed and clicking the brass latches into place. He double-timed it down the sidewalk, coffee still sloshing. The suitcase was built solidly, and he listed to one side with the weight of it. This wasn't going to work, not on a crowded subway and not when he was trying to move fast.

He schlepped it another half block and turned into the Patty Melt.

Just as he'd hoped, Francis knew the woman behind the counter, a fifty-something world-weary veteran of New York greasy spoons, named Amanda. Sharp tongue, heart of gold, sore feet.

"Enid don't work today, Francis," Amanda told him. The way she said it made it clear Amanda didn't know Enid had weighed anchor for good.

Francis thought it an inopportune time to set the record straight and asked, "I hate to ask, Amanda, but is there a place I can stash this? I'm already late."

Amanda frowned but said, "In the cooler, I guess. But you need to get it after work. I can't leave it overnight."

"You're the best."

Amanda took the suitcase, and Francis was already out the door, hoofing it hard down the sidewalk.

"Can I see you in my office, Mr. Berringer?"

Francis had almost made it to his desk, thought he would actually slip by unseen, and then Resnick leaned out of his office door and called him in. A sigh leaked out of Francis, and he headed for Resnick's door, shoulders drooping.

Resnick's secretary, Naomi, sat at her desk outside of Resnick's door, some kind of *Mad Men* throwback with too much makeup and hair piled on top of her head. She held a coffee mug that said WORLD'S GREATEST AUNT. She mouthed *sorry* at Francis as he passed.

Francis shrugged.

Inside, Resnick told him to shut the door.

Francis shut it.

Bart Resnick was Francis's section manager. He sported a Johnny Unitas buzz cut, pink clean-shaven cheeks, a striped tie with a short-sleeved shirt. You could slice salami with the crease down his pants. He was always squinting, like he was trying to see something in you he could exploit. He looked at Francis that way now, fidgeting with a rubber band on his desk, seeing how far it would stretch without breaking. A USMC coffee cup on his desk filled with pens and pencils.

Francis was pretty sure a casual study of everyone's coffee mug in the office would tell him all he needed to know about these people.

"How long have you been a purchasing agent here at McGyver & Roth, Mr. Berringer?" Resnick asked.

"About a year?"

"Fourteen months."

Yeah. That's about a year. Dick.

"And," Resnick pressed, "how many times in that span have you been late for work?"

"I guess at least three or four times."

"Eleven times."

Shit.

"That's not going to work, Mr. Berringer," Resnick said. "It's not shipshape."

"No, sir."

Shipshape was new. Resnick usually favored other expressions. He was insistent that everyone on his floor *have their ducks in a row* and that all his people should do everything *according to Hoyle.*

"You're on McGyver & Roth time. When you come in late and take a paycheck, you're stealing from McGyver & Roth."

"I understand."

"I don't think you do," Resnick said. "Are there mitigating circumstances that might explain today's tardiness, Mr. Berringer?"

I set the alarm wrong, and my girlfriend left me, and I found a suitcase full of panties. "No, sir."

Resnick held up a single finger. "One more chance, Berringer. After that, I have to refer you to HR." He shrugged, tried to look sympathetic, but it came off as gassy. "After that, it's out of my hands."

"I understand, Mr. Resnick."

Resnick rose, came around to Francis's side of the desk. "I'm glad you do." With one hand, Resnick opened his office door. With the other, he gave Francis's shoulder a fatherly squeeze. "You know I don't want to be the bad guy here. I'm your pal."

Francis felt his face go hot.

"Just straighten up and fly right, and we won't have any problems."

Straighten up and fly right was back in the rotation. Great.

"Yes, sir. Thank you."

And a second later, Francis was standing next to Naomi's desk with a sick feeling in his gut. He glanced over at her, hoping for a sympathetic look. That was her specialty, a sympathetic look or a squeeze on the arm. *Never mind Mr. Resnick. You know how he can be. It's nothing personal.*

But she hadn't noticed Francis. She frantically shuffled through the papers on her desk.

"Oh, shit." Her voice a hoarse whisper. "Shit, shit, shit."

2

"You okay?" Francis asked.

Naomi's face was bleak with stress. "I've lost the damn zip codes for this week's direct mailing." She opened every drawer in her desk, slammed them closed again, shuffled through the same pile of papers she'd just shuffled a moment earlier. "They were on a yellow Post-it on top of all the paperwork that went down to marketing. It'll take me an hour to look them up again, and they want them *now* before the deadline."

"The Post-it note on the papers I took to the copy room yesterday?" Francis asked. "Five zip codes?"

"Yes!" Naomi looked at him hopefully. "Have you seen it?"

"Get a pencil."

"What?"

"Get a pencil and write this down," Francis told her.

She eyed him with curiosity but grabbed a pencil and a pad.

He said, "70806, 70808, 70812, 70815, 70836."

She scribbled them down, her eyes coming back up to pin Francis. "These have to be right or I'm screwed."

"Francis doing his trick again?"

Naomi and Francis both turned to look at the lanky guy talking to them across the top of his cubicle divider. Marty Clarke had been at the company about as long as Francis, good-natured and nerdy, Clark Kent glasses and a nose like a beak, thinning black hair.

"It's not a big deal, Marty," Francis said.

Another head popped up from the next cubicle over from Marty's, freckles and red hair and bright green eyes. He couldn't see it from where he was standing, but Francis could picture her Hello Kitty coffee mug. Becky had been hired only six weeks ago and was still learning the ways of the office.

"Francis does a trick?" she asked.

Francis frowned at Marty. "It's not really a trick."

"He can remember numbers perfectly," Marty said.

Becky's eyes widened with interest. "Oh, like a photographic memory?"

"Not really," Francis said.

"Francis, are you sure these numbers are right?" Naomi was urgent about it. "I have to take these down right now."

"Can you read a book and then, like a year later, recite it back?" Becky asked.

Francis shook his head. "It's not like—"

"Not photographic memory," Marty said. "More like the genius on that nerd show. *Eidetic* memory."

Naomi grabbed Francis's arm, insistent. "Francis!"

"The numbers are right, Naomi," Francis said. "I promise. I'm never wrong about—"

Naomi was already fast-walking toward the elevator.

"Can you count cards?" Becky asked.

"I bet he could totally take down a casino," Marty said. "We should pool our money this weekend and hit Atlantic City."

"Guys, no, really," Francis said. "It's not like any of that. I just remember numbers. If they're in a row or a column. I remember the order. It's nothing more than that."

"Can you add up all the numbers in your head like a human calculator?" Becky asked.

"No."

"Oh." Becky looked vaguely disappointed before sinking back down into her cubicle.

"Well, I think it's cool," Marty said. "You could probably cobble together some kind of vaudeville act. The Numerical Memory Man!"

Marty's raw enthusiasm drew a weak smile out of Francis. "Maybe. Right now, I'd better get back to my desk."

Francis wandered into the cubicle maze, zigzagging toward his desk at the core of the humbling gray malaise. His desk was a small, tiny rectangle of metal with two drawers and a five-year-old desktop computer. He turned the computer on. It hummed a dirge, booting up. The morning email included the usual repetitive corporate directives. There was also something from Naomi about leaving food in the break room fridge over the weekend.

He scanned his in-box, hoping to see some final word from Enid, maybe a change of heart and a promise to come home soon. There was no such email. Francis pushed back in his chair, sighed.

He remembered the business card in his shirt pocket, took it out, and squinted at it.

He clicked Compose, entered the email address, and wrote *Suitcase* in the subject line.

Dear Ghost Girl,

Yeah, he felt dumb typing that.

I found your suitcase on a pile of trash. Must be a mistake since everything inside is brand new. Would be happy to arrange a good time and place to return it to you.
Francis Berringer

Francis read over the message. Wow, was he really that boring? But what else was there to say? He could arrange to leave the suitcase with the reception desk in the lobby downstairs, and Ghost Girl could pick it up in the morning. If she even replied at all.

He glanced at the two photos taped to the bottom of his computer monitor.

The first was from a back issue of *Adventure Travel*. It was a picture of some people in a big inflatable raft going down some river rapids. There was an article about a place in Colorado on the other side. It had been the only adventure vacation in which Enid had ever shown any interest. Francis remembered being surprised, because she hated getting her hair wet. He'd been setting a bit aside from each paycheck for the trip.

Francis pulled the magazine page down, folded it, and stashed it in his shirt pocket. Maybe he'd still take the trip on his own next summer. He tried to picture himself setting out alone on an adventure vacation but couldn't.

The other photo showed Francis and Enid in Central Park. It had been a bright, spring day, and they'd stopped a woman walking her dog to ask if she'd take the picture. They both looked so ridiculously happy, Francis hugging Enid from behind, her twisting to kiss the point of Francis's chin, but her eyes coming back to the camera. They'd had hot dogs and then caught a bargain matinee of *Mamma Mia!*, which Francis had liked and which Enid had thought cute that Francis had liked it.

It had been a good day.

Abruptly, Francis snatched the photo off the monitor and made to rip it in half. He stopped himself. There was no point to such a dramatic gesture. Who would see or care? He tossed it into the top drawer of his desk with the paper clips and Post-it notes. A quick glance around his cubicle depressed him suddenly. With the photo of Enid in his desk drawer, there was not a single thing to identify the tiny space as his. He'd refused to invest in a self-identifying coffee mug on the grounds that he would *not* be in this place the rest of his life. It could have been the cheerless cubicle of any other cog in the corporate machine.

Francis sighed long and loudly and ran his fingers through his hair. He pushed away from his desk and stood.

He walked four cubicles down, took a deep breath, and leaned against the flimsy cubicle wall, attempting nonchalance, crossing his arms, trying to look cool or casual or something, knew instinctively it wasn't working but couldn't quite stop himself.

"So, hey, Rhonda." *Say something smooth.* "Whassup?"

Idiot.

Rhonda didn't look up at him. Her gaze was fixed on the compact mirror in her hand. She traced a line around the edge of her lips with a makeup pencil. Rhonda was one of those women put together so perfectly that Francis found himself a little short of breath around her. A designer skirt cut just above the knees, stockings hugging perfect legs and stiletto heels. A sheer cream blouse. Pearls. Blond hair like she'd just stepped out of the salon. Her perfume made Francis a little dizzy.

Almost everyone agreed there was something about Rhonda that didn't quite fit in with their little cubicle community, like she was just biding her time until a rich-enough guy came along to marry her away from this place. In a city of doctors and lawyers and stockbrokers, it was only a matter of time.

She switched to eyeliner, still watching herself closely in the little mirror. "Hello, Francis."

"Have a good weekend?"

Rhonda made a small noise in her throat, which Francis took to mean her weekend had been adequate and ultimately not really any of Francis's business.

"I was wondering . . . I mean, I was thinking . . ." Francis cleared his throat. He was suddenly so thirsty. "I was thinking we could grab a drink after work today. There's that wine bar across the street." In college, Francis had been more of a beer and chicken wings sort of guy, but Rhonda had *wine bar* written all over her, and Francis had taken strides recently to mature himself. He'd purchased a book on wine etiquette and was halfway through it.

Rhonda's eyes slid to Francis, held his gaze a moment before returning to the mirror. "You're nice, Francis."

"Oh. Uh, thanks."

"I don't do nice."

Ah.

Francis opened his mouth, shut it again. He turned around and walked back toward his own cubicle. He thought he heard snickering from Marty's direction. Francis should have known better. The thin cubicle walls offered only the illusion of privacy. Everyone could hear everything.

Francis went back to his desk, sat, cheeks burning.

Oh, yeah, that wasn't embarrassing at all.

And anyway, such an obvious approach to forgetting Enid wasn't exactly Francis's style. He'd had other girlfriends but couldn't for the life of him remember anything he'd done to get them. They seemed to come and go of their own accord with no relation to Francis's intent. They'd sweep through his life and carry him along for a time before moving on. Enid seemed no different now that he thought about it. He should have known.

A blinking red flag on his computer monitor caught his attention, a message in the in-box.

I have your office address. I'm coming for the suitcase.
Do NOT contact me via this email again.
Ghost Girl

He sighed. *You do have a way with the ladies, Francis.*

3

The morning crept by.

Processing purchasing orders tended to make the day drag. Francis spent the morning stifling yawns and traipsing back and forth to the break room to refill his paper coffee cup. He'd been too rushed to pack a sandwich, so when his lunch hour rolled around, he sat alone at a break room table, eating a bag of vending machine corn chips. At one point, Rhonda entered the break room, saw Francis, turned on her heels, and sashayed right back out again.

Francis returned to his desk, leaden and listless, and mindlessly crossed tasks off his to-do list. Twenty minutes before the end of the day, Naomi asked Francis to take a stack of papers down to human resources. Francis welcomed the errand. He could run out the clock meandering downstairs and then take his time coming back, shut down his computer, and go home.

Not that he was eager to return to his empty apartment. Maybe he'd stop at the wine bar himself and try out some of the stuff he'd learned from the book.

Francis dropped off the paperwork, took the elevator back up to his floor, and walked the hall slowly, hands in pockets. Thai food. He'd get takeout on the way home instead of the wine bar maybe. He'd avoided Thai because of Enid's peanut allergy, but now—

Something grabbed him by the collar and jerked him back into another room. The door slammed him into darkness.

Soft, thin fingers covered his mouth.

"Don't talk." A woman's voice.

He didn't. It was hard to tell much about her in the darkness. She smelled like soap with a little vanilla.

They stood that way a moment. Francis could see only the vague outline of her in the darkness, but it seemed as if her head was cocked, listening. A few seconds later, she blew out a sigh, seemed satisfied, and flipped on the light switch.

"I need my suitcase."

She wasn't what Francis had pictured.

Maybe two inches shorter than he was, slender, Francis's age, maybe a year or two older. Glowing white skin a sharp contrast to red lipstick so dark it was almost black. A gold ring in her left nostril, multiple studs in both ears. Her neck was long and slender, with a tattoo of a Celtic cross just under her right ear. Her faded jeans were torn at the knees, and she wore a dark green Che Guevara T-shirt under a creased and cracked leather bomber jacket. The scuffed combat boots gave her another inch.

Francis liked her hair the best. Shaved close up the back and sides with a huge mop of what he thought used to be blond hair now dyed lime green on top. It fell in front of her eyes.

She blew it out of the way. "You still with us, champ? Hello?"

"Uh . . ." Francis rallied himself. "Um . . ."

"You Berringer or not?" She pulled a folded piece of paper from her jacket pocket, shook it open, and held it up next to his face. It was a blown-up photocopy of Francis's driver's license photo. "Francis Berringer."

"Yes. Yeah, that's me."

"Give me my suitcase."

"I don't have it."

"You said you *did* have it."

"I do. I mean I did. Not *with* me."

"Jesus, why the fuck didn't you tell me that? I took a risk getting here."

"You said not to write you back."

"Shit."

"Look, it's okay," Francis said. "I'll bring it in tomorrow morning and—"

"Where is it?"

"A place near my apartment. It's perfectly safe. In the morning—"

"I can't wait that long."

There was a coiled intensity about the girl that put Francis on edge. Her cold blue eyes flashed a manic energy. Francis felt a stab of fascination with her, and it surprised him.

The door slowly swung open.

The girl took half a step back, tensed, one low hand forming into a tight little fist.

Rhonda stood in the doorway, one eyebrow arching into a bored question.

"Do you mind?" the girl said. "We'd like a little privacy."

"Privacy?" Rhonda's expression downshifted from boredom to disdain. "I just need a hole punch."

The girl grabbed Francis by the belt and pulled him into her hip. "We're going to screw in here. My man needs a taste or he gets the jitters. Come back later."

Rhonda's mouth fell open. Francis could not remember ever seeing her speechless.

The girl shut the door in Rhonda's face.

"Suitcase," she said abruptly, turning back to Francis.

"I'll take you to it after work."

"Now."

"It's only like a few more minutes until I clock out."

"Then they won't miss you. Come on." She grabbed his wrist and tried to tug him along.

"What's with you?" Francis asked. "Are you wanted by the cops or something?"

"It's a long story."

What the hell have I gotten myself into?

And yet the girl's eyes pierced him, cool and insistent, and something in her gaze shifted subtly, less brusque command, some of the grit leaking away from her. It almost seemed like *please*, almost felt like *I need this*. Almost. Some message her eyes weren't meaning to send, but it was there.

"I need to go to my desk."

The grip on his wrist tightened.

"My apartment keys are at my desk."

A hesitation.

She opened the door a crack, eyes darting up and down the hall. When she was satisfied, she opened it wider and gestured him out. "Just hurry."

Francis left the supply closet, heart thumping in his chest as he fast-walked back toward the cubicle maze. He regretted ever stopping to look at that stupid suitcase. Why did he have to be so curious?

He headed into the labyrinth of cubicle space and passed Rhonda on her way out. She eye-shot daggers at him. Without meaning it, a wry smile quirked across his lips, and he winked at her. She did a double take, kept walking, and Francis felt an unexpected surge of self-satisfaction. It was petty and juvenile, and he really didn't have time to care what Rhonda thought about him with a crazy person in the supply closet, but there it was. Not quite pride, nothing like redemption, but something. He felt the smile grow on his face.

At his cubicle, he grabbed his keys, turned to leave, and almost walked right into a man in a tweed jacket.

"Francis Berringer?"

"Me?"

The guy grinned. "You."

Francis took him in at a glance. A big square head with a matching jaw. A thick bunch of red-blond hair, combed back, and matching sideburns. He smiled, showing big Charlton Heston teeth. Brown tweed jacket, black shirt, tan slacks, and gleaming brown wing tips. He looked like a used car salesman, but an upscale one—Audis and BMWs.

"I'm sorry, who are you?" Francis asked.

"Benson Cavanaugh," he said. "*Detective* Benson Cavanaugh. My associates and I are looking for somebody."

At the word *associates*, Francis's eyes took a lap around the office. A man in a black suit, with brown shaggy mustache and thinning hair, wandered through the maze, peeking into individual cubicles. Beyond him, blocking the hallway out to the elevators, was another guy, beefy and bald with ruddy checks, fitting awkwardly into a slightly too-small maroon jacket, jeans, and ankle boots.

Cavanaugh dipped two fingers into a shirt pocket and came out with a color photo, showed it to Francis. The hair was purple and a little longer in back, but it was definitely the girl in the supply closet. "Have you see this girl?"

Francis opened his mouth and froze. *Tell him. That crazy chick has done something. Probably drugs. Who knows? The guy is a cop. Tell him. This isn't your problem.*

But Francis said, "Why would I know her? Did she do something?"

Cavanaugh grinned wider, horse teeth looking like they could chomp Francis in half with one bite. But the grin didn't touch the man's eyes. They looked right through Francis, those eyes like hard, dark stones as if saying, *We both know you're full of shit, kid.*

"We have some reason to believe you've had contact with her," Cavanaugh said. "If you can help us out, we won't take up too much of your time. Otherwise, we might have to continue this conversation at the station."

How did he know? Had Francis been seen with the girl? Rhonda had seen them together in the supply closet, but even if she'd told somebody, the police could not possibly have made it to Francis's office so fast. Something was wrong here, and Francis sure as hell did not want to go anywhere with Cavanaugh.

"Look. Okay." Francis cleared his throat. "Just to be official here, maybe I should see a badge or something."

The hesitation was so slight, Francis almost missed it, but in a heartbeat, the grin sprang back into place on Cavanaugh's face.

"Sure. It's right here."

Cavanaugh's hand went into his jacket pocket, and Francis saw a flash of metal when it came back out again. A split second later, Francis felt something hard in his ribs. He looked down to see the little automatic pistol. It was small and silver and didn't look like a cop's gun at all. More like something an Atlantic City pool hustler would carry.

Like you know what a cop's gun looks like, idiot. From what, Hill Street Blues *reruns?*

"Okay, kid, now we have to do it like this. Happy now?"

Francis swallowed hard.

Cavanaugh pitched his voice low. "We're going to walk out of here nice and slow. You stick close. Everything's normal. You get me? Let's not cause a scene. That goes bad for you. Understand?"

Francis nodded.

"Say it."

"I understand."

They walked together out of the cubicle and through the maze. Francis felt cold sweat on the back of his neck. When he passed Marty's and Becky's cubicles, he glanced in each time, trying to catch someone's eye. But both of his coworkers were hunched dutifully over their computers, tying up loose ends before end of day. Francis thought he might call out to somebody or make a break for it.

The thought of the little pistol stopped him.

Which was obviously the point of it.

Naomi barely glanced up as he passed her desk. "Cutting out a bit early, Francis?"

"Yeah. Just . . . need to run a couple of errands." Francis's voice came out dry and hoarse.

"Uh-uh." She scribbled in a daily planner, clearly uninterested.

Come on, Naomi. Take an interest in current events.

But Cavanaugh herded Francis past Naomi's desk toward the hall leading to the elevators. Then they'd go down to the lobby, out of the building and . . . where? Some abandoned warehouse where they'd tie him to a chair and beat the information out of him like in the movies.

Just tell him the girl's in the closet. You don't owe her shit.

Francis opened his mouth.

Bart Resnick's office door slammed open, and Resnick blustered out. "Jesus H. Christ, Berringer, where in Sam Hill do you think you're going?"

Thank you, Bart Resnick, you cranky old son of a bitch!

"You've got nerve, Berringer. You walk into *my* office late, and now you're trying to sneak out early? Not happening. Not on my watch."

"Stand down, pal," Cavanaugh said. "This is police business."

Resnick blinked at the man. "What?"

"I got this under control," Cavanaugh said. "I'm a cop."

Resnick looked the man up and down. "Bull-fucking-shit."

Cavanaugh sighed, took one step forward, and swung his gun arm from the hip in an upward arc. The barrel of the silver automatic slammed into Resnick's balls. He went red, mouth falling open, a rough, strangled noise caught in his throat. Slowly, Resnick sank to his knees. In other circumstances, the look on Resnick's face would have been comical. In Resnick's world, he was the one who did the ball-busting.

Naomi gasped, stood up at her desk.

Cavanaugh swung the gun on her. "Quiet. Step back from that phone. Just stay calm and—"

A lime-green streak sped past Francis.

The girl held a fire extinguisher in her hands and swung it hard. It cracked loudly across Cavanaugh's wrist. He yelled in pain and dropped the pistol. The girl swung the extinguisher the other way into his gut, and Cavanaugh grunted and doubled over.

The girl tossed aside the extinguisher, grabbed Francis's hand. "Come on!" She dragged him back toward the cubicle maze.

Francis hesitated. "But the elevators are back—"

"No elevators!" She dragged him along.

Francis risked a glance back.

The beefy, bald guy still stood in the hallway, blocking the way to the elevators. His hand came out of his jacket with an enormous automatic pistol.

Shit.

He let the girl drag him into the cubicle maze.

"Where are we going?"

"Stairs!"

They came to the crossroads at the center of the maze, and the guy with the shaggy mustache leaped at them, smashing into Francis and grabbing him in a bear hug.

Marty emerged from his cubicle, eyes wide. "Holy cow. What the hell is—"

Shaggy Mustache grabbed Marty's face with a huge hand and shoved him back into his cubicle. "Shut it, nerd!"

Francis wriggled out of the man's grip, began to run.

Shaggy Mustache leaped at him, tackling Francis around the knees. Both men went down hard, grunting on impact and rolling into one of the flimsy cubicle partitions. Heads appeared over the cubicle walls, eyes wide with curiosity or alarm. The maze buzzed with speculation.

Francis tried to kick away from the man without success.

Shaggy Mustache had Francis's legs in a death hold. "I got him! I got him!"

The girl rushed back, kicked Shaggy Mustache in the face with the heel of her combat boot.

The guy grunted pain, eyes flashing rage. "You little bitch! When I get ahold—"

She kicked him again, harder. A crack of cartilage, and blood exploded from both nostrils, dripping gunk from his shaggy mustache. He screamed and let go of Francis's legs, rolling away and holding his nose, ragged whimpers leaking out of him.

"Get up!" the girl shouted at Francis.

Francis staggered slowly to his feet, wincing, favoring one knee. "I think he twisted my—"

An earsplitting crack of thunder shook the office. Everyone screamed, ducking back down into the imagined safety of their cubicles. Another shot, and Francis felt a violent tug at his sleeve. A quick glance showed the bald one holding his automatic in a two-handed shooting stance.

"Run, idiot!" the girl yelled.

Francis followed her at full speed, ignoring the twinge in his knee. More shots rang out behind him. Screams and shouts. Francis ducked his head, heart in his throat, waiting to feel a bullet in the back.

Francis followed the girl out the other side of the cubicle maze and around the corner. They ran down the narrow hall, past the water fountain and restrooms to a door marked STAIRS. The girl flung the door open, and Francis stayed right on her heels.

It was the first time Francis had ever stepped foot into the stairwell. There'd never been a need before. The walls were bare cinder block, harsh fluorescent light. They flew down the stairs three at a time. It was ten floors to the bottom, and Francis almost tumbled twice, twinges in his knee nearly taking him down.

At the bottom, the door opened into another hall Francis had never seen before. The girl sprinted ahead as if she knew exactly where she was going. Fourteen months Francis had worked in this building. He went to and from his desk, with an occasional stroll down to HR. The rest of the place was a foreign country to him. He had no idea where he was. Not a clue.

"Are you just running randomly?" he asked.

"I hacked into the computer archives of the architect who designed the building," she said. "I like to know how to leave a place."

He followed her out the door to the sidewalk. A relatively quiet side street, a scattering of pedestrians.

"Just wait a second," Francis said, panting. He rubbed his knee. It ached, but would be okay.

A minute later, she grabbed him again. "Okay, you've had your rest. This way!"

They moved fast down the sidewalk. Francis recognized where they were now and thought they were headed toward a subway station. And then what? Where was she taking him? If she thought he'd just blindly accompany her to—

The squeal of tires and the roar of an engine drew Francis's attention. His head snapped around to see a black sedan rounding the corner behind him. It gunned the engines again, bearing down with alarming speed.

"Run!" The girl sprinted ahead, not even waiting to see if Francis followed.

He chased after her without thinking, pain flaring in his knee. He ignored it, but the howl of the engine filled his ears as if the sedan were right on his heels.

The girl cut right suddenly, blazing down a narrow alley, and Francis almost tripped over himself trying to keep up with her.

They fled together past trash barrels and high brick walls.

Francis chanced a glance over his shoulder. More squealing tires as the sedan fishtailed into the alley. It was a narrow fit, about six inches of clearance on each side of the car. The sedan smashed into the trash barrels, *crunch-popping* them out of the way. A stab of fear spurred Francis faster. When was the last time he'd run this fast? High school gym, maybe. The sedan was close enough; Francis could see it was the bald one driving. In five more seconds, the sedan would run them both down.

They sprinted past a large Dumpster. Even with death bearing down on him, part of his brain noticed something odd about the way the Dumpster sat, an odd angle, like the back of it had been jacked up or something.

The girl reached for a thin length of rope dangling from the Dumpster's side and shouted, "Keep going!" right before giving it a yank. There was a metallic *tunk*, and the Dumpster began to roll. Francis ran past just in time to avoid getting clipped.

The Dumpster rolled into the path of the sedan. The car slammed on the brakes but too late. It plowed into the Dumpster, the impact making Francis flinch, a calamity of mangled metal. The Dumpster and sedan made a wedge in the narrow space. The car revved its engine, tires smoking, trying to bully its way past the Dumpster, but it was stuck tight.

Francis realized he was just standing there, gawking at the spectacle. The girl was still running, almost at the far end of the alley. Francis sped to catch up. At the end of the alley, he spotted the subway stop across the street.

Instead of heading for the crosswalk, she dodged cars, horns blaring, and made it to the other side, Francis still in tow. They flew down the stairs and through the gate, hitting the platform right as the C train was pulling into the station.

"You still live at a that place on 105th?" she asked.

"Yeah."

They boarded the train heading uptown.

Francis latched on to a pole, chest heaving as he sucked breath, his shirt pasted to him with cold sweat. "What the fuck?"

The girl didn't offer a reply.

"You know where I live?"

"Yes."

"And where I work?"

"Yeah," she said.

"I don't even know your name."

"Yeah," she said. "Probably better that way."

4

Cavanaugh sat at the back table of a dank saloon with his two bruiser sidekicks. He held a ziplock baggy of crushed ice on the wrist the bitch had cracked with the fire extinguisher. That shit fucking hurt. He couldn't bend the wrist for an hour.

The one with the shaggy mustache sat with his head back, wads of torn paper napkin shoved up each nostril. Dried blood caked his mustache.

"Jesus, Ike, what the fuck are you shooting for?" Cavanaugh said to the bald one. "That brings the authorities ten times faster. You know that."

"I didn't want him to get away."

"Idiot."

Ike shrugged and took a swig of beer.

"You need to stop telling people you're a cop," said Shaggy Mustache. With the busted nose, it came out *You deed do dop delling beople dou're a gop.* "And definitely don't use your real name, for Christ's sake."

Cavanaugh frowned. "Fuck you, Ernie."

"Not cool, man." *Nod cool, ban.*

"Damn it, we were so close," Cavanaugh said.

"She's slippery." Ike waved at the girl tending tables to bring him another.

It was a local place, and the after-work crowd had been slowly filtering in since Cavanaugh had arrived. They'd abandoned the stolen sedan, disappeared into the subway, and come back up to sunlight eight stops later. They'd slipped into a nondescript watering hole where Cavanaugh had thrown back three shots of Wild Turkey in ninety seconds, trying to numb his hurt wrist from the inside. Ike had chugged a beer, and Ernie had just sat there and groaned, prodding delicately at his flattened nose.

"Shit, shit, shit," Cavanaugh said.

Neither Ike nor Ernie commented. Cavanaugh's outburst could have meant anything. Maybe he didn't like the décor of the saloon, or maybe they were on the verge of nuclear holocaust. Who knew?

"I'm going to have to call him," Cavanaugh said.

They still said nothing.

Cavanaugh took out his phone and stared at it without dialing. He did *not* want to make this call. It would basically be saying that he couldn't handle the job. But if he waited and then shit got out of hand, it would be much worse. Better to eat a big slice of *I fucked up* pie now than face the chop later.

"Yeah." Cavanaugh sighed. "Yeah, I definitely need to call him."

"Then fucking call him." *Den fugging gall him.* "That's Bryant's job to coordinate us."

"I don't mean Bryant," Cavanaugh said.

Ike froze, his beer mug halfway to his face. "No, man, don't. Come on."

Cavanaugh shook his head, started dialing.

Ernie groaned.

Cavanaugh didn't have the kid's direct number, so really he did have to call Bryant after all.

Technically, Reggie Bryant was always on duty. If the call came in the middle of the night, an alarm would buzz him awake, and he'd roll out of bed and take his station in the next room.

His "station" was an enormous semicircle of a desk, surrounded by twenty computer monitors.

Reggie Bryant was plugged into the world like nobody else in history.

Okay, maybe the NSA. Or the Pentagon. Maybe. He could surely give those agencies a run for their money. Why not? Reggie Bryant had the best equipment money could buy. The best access money could buy. The best influence money could buy.

It helped that it wasn't Reggie's money. Oh, yeah, he was paid well.

But not *that* well.

So at anytime, anywhere, Reggie Bryant was on call. He'd been promised the budget to train an assistant to take the overnight hours, but the enterprise hadn't yet progressed that far. For now, Reggie was the whole show.

And what was Reggie's job?

To assimilate and coordinate the entire world into information that was useful to his boss, to route it to those who could most effectively use it to his boss's benefit. He was the gatekeeper of the information superhighway, the traffic cop at the intersection of ten billion avenues of data.

So, yeah, no stress at all.

Although in truth, the computers did most of the work. The new algorithm was a miracle to behold. When the calibrations were complete and the parameters fully in place, the system might not actually need Reggie at all.

Not that Reggie would mention this. He liked job security.

By all normal ways of measuring, Reggie was a genius, but the team who'd developed the algorithm were in a completely differ-ent category of brainpower. They'd integrated the algorithm with all the other analytical software. It was almost intuitive, teaching the other programs how to talk back to it, how to recognize what it valued and facilitate the flow of information and analysis that the algorithm required. It was almost as if the new algorithm enslaved all other programs, but not through any kind of brute force one usually associated with hacking and infecting.

It was more like a seduction.

Reggie's old Caltech computer professors would have frowned and *tsked* at such fanciful notions, but the next generation of programmers would need to think this way. Creativity and imagination would need to blend with cold logic. The entire industry was on the cusp of a major innovative shift.

Already the corporation's stock acquisitions were 17 percent more profitable. The analytic programs were predicting the movements of nations with startling accuracy.

The phone rang, and Reggie saw who it was from the caller ID. Not all of Reggie's tasks, alas, boasted the gravitas of predicting global events.

"What do you need, Cavanaugh?" Reggie said into the phone.

"We missed her," Cavanaugh said.

"I practically served her up on a silver platter," Reggie told him. "The Ghost Girl email was flagged, and we traced it. You knew exactly where she was going to be. How could you botch it?"

"Hey, shut up, okay? She's smart. She knew we were coming."

"Well, she hasn't used that email again or any of the other ones we're tracking," Reggie said. "She hasn't used any of her credit cards either."

"What we need is more boots on the ground," Cavanaugh said. "I know some guys."

"I don't have the authority to authorize anything like that."

"I know," Cavanaugh said. "I need you to patch me through to him."

Reggie hesitated. "You know he likes to keep a certain distance between himself and . . . field operations."

"Look, hey, we're all professionals, okay?" Cavanaugh said. "We got a job, and we want to get it done. This will all go faster if I can talk to the kid direct."

Reggie sighed. "Okay, then. Stand by. But if you want a word of advice, don't call him *kid*."

"Ten minutes, Mr. Middleton."

Aaron Middleton looked up from his magazine at the pretty young blond production assistant who'd stuck her head into his dressing room. The magazine was the latest issue of *Tech World*. Middleton's picture was on the cover, big, innocent blue eyes, shaggy mop of brown hair making him look even younger than he was, an old T-shirt. He wished they'd taken one of him cleaned up. A haircut and a slick new suit. But they didn't want the corporate professional.

They wanted the Silicon Valley boy genius. That was the draw. The interior story had been mostly fair and complimentary, but there was always that undercurrent, the usual question. *When will this blow up in his face?* The whiz kid had come so far, so fast, surely he was due to crash and burn.

Don't hold your breath, naysayers.

Middleton smiled at the production assistant, and that made her blush.

"Thank you," Middleton said.

"Someone will be in soon to double-check your hair and makeup," she said. "Although I think you look just fine."

"Understood. Thanks."

The production assistant lingered a moment as if trying to

think of something else pertinent to say, smiled again, and backed out, the door clicking shut behind her.

A sigh from the corner of the room.

Middleton's gaze shifted to Meredith Vines, perched atop a stool and tapping at a smartphone.

Without looking up, she asked, "Do you ever get tired of it?"

"Tired of what?" Although he knew full well what she was asking.

"Being a young, handsome, eligible billionaire."

"Oh, that." He thought about the production assistant, maybe twenty-two, brimming with youth and energy and a raw need to please. "I don't really have time for much."

"The good thing about being a powerful billionaire," Meredith told him, "is that girls like that are usually willing to accommodate your busy schedule. There certainly are enough of them. They could take shifts."

"Meredith, if I didn't know better, I'd say you sound jealous."

And now she did look up, frowning and narrowing her eyes. "*Not* in my job description."

Middleton laughed.

Meredith had come to him via Harvard and Stanford with an MBA and a stack of recommendation letters from various bigwigs, CEOs, congressmen, and whatnot. Short and slight, but with such a striking presence, she owned any room she entered. Her red hair was pulled back tightly against her skull. Sharp, angular features made more severe by makeup applied with the precision of a Nazi rocket scientist. Gray suit, skirt just above the knees, pumps giving her a little more height but not much. Eyes such a pale blue they were almost ice.

Meredith was a year younger than Middleton's thirty, and

he'd long ago set aside his attraction to her. She was far too valuable as his chief of staff. Aaron Middleton ran TomorrowCorp, and Meredith Vines ran Aaron Middleton. A hundred small but vital tasks clicked exactly into place each and every day thanks to her dogged ministrations, freeing Middleton to focus on the big picture. A few months ago, Meredith had taken off two days to attend a sick sister, and Middleton had barely been able to dress and feed himself.

Okay, maybe I'm exaggerating a little. But only a little.

"Are we still on with the chamber of commerce after I finish this interview?" Middleton asked.

"No, that's pushed to next Wednesday," she said, consulting her smartphone. "You need to see the marketing presentation as soon as possible if we want the launch to go off in time. That means getting all the department heads in line so they can break out and have meetings with their own—"

Meredith's smartphone began to play "Big in Japan" by Alphaville.

"Let it go to voice mail," Middleton said.

"It's Bryant," she told him.

"Answer it."

"Hello, Mr. Bryant. It's Meredith. Oh? Let me check his availability." She looked at Middleton, raised an eyebrow.

He thought a second, held out his hand. Meredith gave him the phone.

"Hi, Reggie. What can I do for you?" He listened, nodding. "I see. No, please don't worry about it. You should always use your own judgment, of course. I suppose you'd better put him through. You can secure this line, yes? I'll stand by, then."

A click and a beep.

Middleton said, "Hello, Mr. Cavanaugh. I infer progress on our project isn't all we might have hoped for."

"Sorry for that," Cavanaugh said. "And sorry to have to call you like this."

"Let's just work the problem. Reggie implied you needed additional resources."

"I just need more guys," Cavanaugh said. "It's like playing fucking Whac-A-Mole."

The makeup woman came in to check Middleton's face and hair. He held up the *Just a moment* finger, and she backed out again.

He cleared his throat, fidgeted in his chair, trying to force patience. "I understand you're being figurative, but I don't follow."

"We go where she is, and she just runs off someplace else," Cavanaugh explained. "If we got enough guys to chase her and then more guys waiting at wherever she's running to, we can nab her a lot easier. It's pretty simple, really."

"Yes, it does seem simple when you explain it like that," Middleton admitted.

"And something else."

"Please do go on."

"I feel like we're being fed the bare minimum information-wise," Cavanaugh said. "Who is this girl really? What did she do? I need to know how to track her down. I'm feeling a little hamstrung here."

Middleton opened his mouth, closed it again.

Meredith looked at him with open concern, and Middleton realized he was sitting with legs crossed, bouncing one foot nervously up and down. He made himself stop. Meredith knew him too well, his every tic and quirk.

"Middleton?"

"Excuse me, Mr. Cavanaugh, I was momentarily distracted," Middleton said. "I'll have a dossier prepared on the girl that you will hopefully find helpful. In the meantime, please submit the names of the men you wish to add to the roster so Reggie can do a background check. I'll have payment vouchers issued through the proper channels. Good day."

Middleton hung up before Cavanaugh had the chance to irritate him further.

The makeup woman entered again tentatively. "They're ready for you on set now, Mr. Middleton."

He stood. "Of course. Remind me when this will air again."

"Later tonight."

"Thank you. I'll be along in a moment."

The woman nodded and left.

Middleton headed for the door, but Meredith put a hand on his arm, stopping him.

Her eyes searched his. "Something's upset you."

He forced a smile. "You know how I am about loose ends." Middleton could be pretty anal about them, actually. The construction of his new house is Sonoma was a perfect example. Middleton had been frantic about every little detail. Meredith had basically thrown a net over him and pulled him back from the brink of madness.

But this . . . Meredith didn't need to know about this. "It's being handled."

She clearly didn't like being out of the loop but knew better than to press it. "Okay. Let me know if I can help."

"I will." Although Middleton didn't think there was really anything Meredith could do about his wife.

5

Francis emerged from the Patty Melt, spotted the girl across the street waiting for him. He frowned and shook his head. She didn't seem to like that. She pointed left, motioning for him to meet her at the corner.

He crossed at the light and they stood together, the early evening crowd flowing around them.

"Amanda wasn't there." He'd told her about the waitress to whom he'd given the suitcase.

"You said she'd stashed it."

Francis sighed. "Neither of the evening shift waitresses knew anything about it, and when I asked the night manager to check the cooler, he didn't see it. He frankly seemed a little put out that I asked."

"Maybe she took it with her."

"Maybe."

"Do you know where she lives?"

"I don't even know her last name," Francis said.

"This is bullshit!" Her frustration was at a whole new level.

"Yeah, well, I'm sorry," Francis said, his own patience thinning. People had tried to kill him today—which was new—and his knee hurt. He'd probably get fired. "And I'm not keen to discuss it here in the middle of the sidewalk. My apartment is close, and I think we need to talk about—"

"No."

"You don't want to talk?"

"I don't want to go to your apartment, and neither do you."

"I don't?"

"If they can find you at work, then they can find out where you live," she said. "And don't you think the police might have taken an interest in the little dustup at your office?"

"So wait. Who's coming to get me at my apartment? The police or the people pretending to be the police?"

"Probably all sorts of people," she said.

"Okay, then all the more reason to talk, because you'd better believe I have some questions. Let's just go to a coffee shop or something."

"No coffee." She shut her eyes tight, rubbed her temples. "I need a real drink."

"Okay," Francis said. "I know the spot."

The girl took the shot of Jack Daniels out of the waitress's hand before she'd even had a chance to set it on the table. She tossed it back, shivered, then said, "A draft beer. Whatever's light."

"Right." The waitress left to fetch it.

Francis took to his pint of Boddington's more timidly. They'd taken a table near the window so Francis could watch the street and entrance to his building. That way he could see anyone suspicious coming or going.

"It's not like they skulk around in trench coats," she said.

"Fair enough." Francis sipped from his pint. "But I can at least identify who's a neighbor and who's somebody I've never seen before. But forget all that for a minute. I don't even know your name."

"Works for me."

"Fine, I'll call you Ghost Girl the rest of—"

"Okay, stop. Emma. Just call me Emma."

It didn't suit her. But Francis thought about it and couldn't think what would.

"Amanda won't go back to work until the breakfast shift in the morning, and if I can't go to my apartment, then I'm open to suggestions," Francis said. "Maybe we can meet back at the Patty Melt in the morning. I'll make sure Amanda gives you the suitcase."

"If you think you're getting—"

She cut off when the waitress arrived with her beer. The waitress gave them both a curious look before departing but said nothing.

Emma leaned forward and lowered her voice before starting again. "If you think you're getting out of my sight before I get my suitcase back, think again. You'll get killed or arrested or something, and then I'll be stuck."

"I wouldn't want to inconvenience you by getting killed."

"Funny," she said flatly. "You're extremely humorous."

"Please remember that I was only trying to do a good deed."

The hint of a wry smile from her. "They say no good deed goes unpunished."

But Francis wouldn't be derailed. He fully intended to have his say. "No, listen. Seriously. I was just trying to be helpful. And this is what I get. I don't *owe* you anything. You know that, right? There's obviously something going on with you and something in that suitcase—probably *drugs* or something—but does anyone tell me anything? No. I get bossed around and nearly killed—oh, and my girlfriend walked out on me this morning; I know that's not your fault, but still—and I'll probably lose my job, which I hate, but I still need a job, right?"

"That's a mouthful," Emma said. "Feel better?"

"Not as much as I'd thought." He shrugged, sipped. "A little."

She put her serious face back on. "Look, I get it. You want answers. Here's the best I can do. Yeah, I've got something going on. I haven't murdered anyone. Not smuggling drugs, nothing like that. So put your mind at ease about all that. But are there bad people after me? Yes. It's a long story, and I'm sorry you got dragged into this. My manners are not at their best right now. Help me get my suitcase back, and I promise to get out of your life. Then you can go to the police, explain it wasn't you, tell them about the crazy girl with the suitcase."

"Are you in trouble?"

"I'm in trouble."

"And what's in the suitcase will help you?"

"Yes."

Francis went back to his beer, gulping this time. He stifled a burp, then asked, "Okay, so what do we do next?"

"We need to find the waitress with the suitcase," Emma said. "Before the bad guys do."

Francis rolled his eyes. "How could they possibly know a completely random diner waitress has the suitcase?"

"I have one of my new guys watching Berringer's apartment," Cavanaugh said into his phone. "What else do we know about this guy? Anyone else on the lease?"

"Somebody named Enid Bachman," Bryant said on the other end of the line.

"Give me the rundown on her."

"Okay. Hang on." The sound of keyboard tapping. "She gets her paychecks direct deposited to a local bank. She's a waitress. I have it on the map, some diner just a few blocks away."

"What's it called?" Cavanaugh asked.

"The Patty Melt."

NYPD hadn't been glad to see him.

Harrison Gunn didn't much care. As a matter of fact, he rather enjoyed it. Flash his ID, declare federal jurisdiction, and watch the locals steam. Not that he'd want to push things too far. Gunn had been an agent with the National Security Agency for eleven years, and something he'd learned early in the going was that things went a lot smoother with the cooperation of local authorities than without it.

The officer tasked with bringing Gunn up to speed was a world-weary detective sergeant in a wrinkled gray suit and scuffed shoes. Gunn disapproved of the man immediately based specifically on his appearance. Gunn realized this was a minor failing in himself, but he still took in the detective's cheap haircut, tie pulled loose, his overall sloppy appearance and pegged the man as unprofessional. It was likely not even true, but Gunn wouldn't disabuse himself of this impression until offered proof to the contrary.

By contrast, Gunn's black suit was perfectly pressed, perfectly tailored, and lint-free. His shoes had been polished to a blinding gleam. He had a standing weekly appointment with his barber, not a hair out of place. He was an intricate, precisely calibrated, well-oiled machine and looked the part.

"Everybody in the office pretty much has the same story," the detective said. "Berringer comes in and does his usual. Toward the end of the day, the girl shows up and then the guys claiming to be cops. Look, I know you've claimed jurisdiction, but people running around claiming to be cops? We can't let that stand."

"I understand," Gunn said. "We'll get them. Let's focus on the girl for a moment."

"Only one of the office workers got a good look at her," the detective said. "Most everyone went under their desks when the shooting started. She's this way."

The detective led Agent Gunn into the cubicle maze and introduced him to one of the women there.

Rhonda sat looking bored, painting her nails. "Can I go yet?"

"Soon," Gunn said. "The detective says you saw the girl in a supply closet?"

"Yeah."

"Can you describe her?"

"Green hair. Nose ring. One of those girls that thinks attitude trumps good grooming."

Yeah, that is definitely her, thought Gunn. "What was she doing in the closet?"

"She was in there with Francis. The girl rather rudely indicated they were about to . . . become intimate." Rhonda's expression made it clear she couldn't imagine why anyone would want to do anything like that with a girl like that.

Gunn and the detective exchanged *Oh, really?* looks.

"Were they a regular item?" Gunn asked Rhonda.

"I couldn't possibly guess," Rhonda said. "But he'd asked me out earlier in the morning. Seems our little Francis is something of a player."

"Uh-huh." Gunn turned back to the detective. "I want to talk to the manager now."

Resnick slumped at his desk. He looked like he'd had a rough day.

"I already told this whole story to the cops," Resnick said.

"I just want to ask a few questions about one of your employees," Gunn said. "Francis Berringer."

"Berringer." Resnick made a face like the name tasted bad in his mouth. "That fucking guy is fired."

"I'm the manager." He was fat and sweaty, thinning hair plastered flat atop his melon head. "You wanted to see me?"

"I appreciate your time," Cavanaugh said. "I'm Officer Riggs. NYPD. I'm looking for an Enid Bachman. She's a waitress here at the Patty Melt, yes?"

"Is this about the boyfriend?"

"The who?" Cavanaugh asked.

"Francis was in here earlier, looking for Amanda," the manager told him. "He wanted her last name so he could look up her phone number. Is he in trouble or something?"

"Well, it's police business."

"I knew it. Damn it, I just knew it," the manager said. "He kept asking about some suitcase, and I just knew that kid was up to no good."

"Suitcase?"

"Jesus, is he a serial killer or something?" The manager glanced around the diner as if expecting Francis to suddenly leap out with a butcher knife. "Next you'll tell me the suitcase is full of body parts."

Cavanaugh took a small notebook and pencil from his pocket. "Amanda, you say? It would really help us if you had an address for her."

6

Amanda lived in a rent-controlled building on 101st Street.

Francis and Emma climbed the six flights to her apartment. It wasn't the worst building Francis had ever seen, no graffiti or obvious disrepair, but the halls hadn't seen a new coat of paint since the Nixon administration. A vague mildew smell in the stairwell.

Francis paused in front of Amanda's door without knocking, bent to massage his knee.

Emma frowned at him. "You okay?"

"Hurt it earlier. Six flights didn't help."

"Man up, Frankie."

Francis returned her frown. "I generally prefer to go by Francis."

"Uh-huh. Knock on the door."

Francis knocked. No answer.

"I told you we should have called first," Francis said. "So we'd know she'd be here."

"Yeah, and also she'd know we were coming," Emma said. "That hasn't always worked out for me."

"That's not a surprise, actually."

"Just knock again."

Francis knocked again. This time he thought he heard movement from within the apartment, also a low mutter, a grunt.

He knocked harder. "Amanda?"

The muttering grew louder, then finally, "What?"

"Amanda, it's me. Francis."

"I didn't order any!"

"No, it's Francis. Enid's . . . I know Enid."

"What?"

"Is something wrong with her?" Emma asked.

Francis shook his head. "I don't know. Maybe we woke her up." Francis raised his voice. "Amanda, it's me, Francis. I gave you a suitcase earlier today to hold for me. Sorry to drop by announced, but I need to get it. Sort of important, actually."

A long pause.

"Francis?"

"Yes!" Relief flooded him. "Yes, Amanda, it's me. Do you have the suitcase?"

"Come in. It's unlocked."

Francis and Emma exchanged glances. Emma shrugged.

Francis turned the knob and slowly pushed the door inward on creaking hinges.

The odor that hit him was a striking mix of VapoRub, cigarettes, scotch, and something deep-fried. The little apartment was crowded with too much furniture, cheap paintings, wallpaper with a tight floral pattern faded nearly to nonexistence. Off to the right, the living room segued into a narrow kitchen with a stove and refrigerator from the 1970s. A dimly lit hall to the left led away presumably to a bedroom and bath.

Amanda lay fully reclined, in an ugly green, threadbare La-Z-Boy. The arms had been duct-taped where the fabric had pulled apart. The stand on the right side of the chair was crowded with an ashtray overflowing with butts, a crumpled pack of Basics next to it, a two-thirds-empty bottle of cheap scotch, and a Fairly Odd-Parents juice glass with two fingers of booze.

No lights had been turned on, the living room lit only by the flickering television screen, a game show on with the sound turned all the way down. The movement of the figures on the TV screen cast weird shadows over Amanda and the rest of the room.

She wore a blue bathrobe and tattered pink slippers. She was a stout woman, and when she shifted in the chair, she seemed like some ancient troll queen on her throne, the La-Z-Boy creaking and groaning like it might come apart any second under her weight. The light from the TV gave her face a haunted look.

Amanda squinted at Emma, her eyes refusing to focus. "Enid, you changed your hair."

"Amanda, this isn't—" He broke off. Forget it. Not important, and she wouldn't remember anyway. As far as Francis could tell, she'd been hitting the scotch hard and was only half-heartedly trying to emerge from her stupor.

"Amanda, I gave you a suitcase at the diner this morning." Francis spoke calmly and slowly. "You said you'd stash it in the cooler."

She blinked, thought about it. "Roy wouldn't let me."

The breakfast shift manager. Enid had mentioned him often in non-glowing terms.

"I brought it home." Her eyes shifted back and forth in her head, taking in the apartment around her like she'd never seen it before.

"We need it," Francis told her. "Can you get it for us? It would be a huge help, and then we'll get out of your way."

Amanda put her pale hands on the arms of her chair, made an attempt to push herself up. She slumped back, deciding the effort wasn't worth it. God help her if there were a fire. She waved a hand back down the hall. "You can get it."

Emma pushed past him, heading back toward the bedroom. Francis began to follow, hesitated, glanced back at Amanda. The woman was already easing her head back, eyelids drooping shut. In the morning, this would all be some fuzzy dream to her.

Francis hurried after Emma.

Amanda's bedroom was small, a single unmade bed against the far wall, a vanity that might have been an antique or maybe was just old. A closet. A lamp with a dusty shade. Light oozed a dim yellow through the dirty glass of the room's only window.

Emma went to the floor, looked under the bed, cursed when she didn't find the case. She went to the closet, began rummaging, pushing aside shoes and hatboxes. "I don't see it."

"This feels weird being in here, going through her stuff," Francis said. "I hardly know her. I bet I've only said a hundred words to her."

"You think I'm having a good time? Help me look."

Francis went to the window. Not much of a view, a rusty fire escape and another tenement across the alley. Was this Amanda's life every night, coming home to an empty, dank apartment? *Maybe I'd numb myself with the occasional bottle of scotch too.*

He turned back to Emma when he heard the racket from the closet. She was pulling everything out, throwing clothes on hangers over her shoulder.

"Stop that," Francis said. "You're messing up the place."

"It's not here!"

"That's no reason to wreck her closet. She was doing me a favor."

"Where the fuck is it?"

"Jesus." Francis shook his head, held his hands up in an *I'm done* gesture. "Okay. I'm going. We tried. But I'm not sticking around to—"

"We're not going anywhere," she said heatedly. "Not until we find—"

Before the argument could really get started, it was preempted by a knock at the front door. It was loud enough to be heard down the hall with the bedroom door closed.

Emma and Francis froze. Waited and listened.

A louder knock. Amanda woke this time, her muffled voice saying something to the person on the other side of the door. A muted voice spoke back to her. Francis thought it sounded like a man's voice, but he couldn't make out anything being said.

Emma looked a question at him. *Who is it?*

Francis shrugged. *How the hell would I know?*

Amanda said something else, and so did the person on the other side of the door. It was probably a version of the same conversation Francis had had earlier. A second later, he heard the front door creak open.

Shit.

The conversation between Amanda and the newcomer was slightly clearer now. Francis still couldn't hear the exact words, but the tone and sound of the voice was very familiar.

Emma's eyes widened with alarm. She'd recognized the voice too.

Cavanaugh.

Shit shit shit.

Francis spun to the window, tried to open it. It was stuck fast.

Emma waved her hands frantically. *Hurry up.*

Francis gestured at the window. *It's fucking stuck, okay?*

They could still hear Cavanaugh and Amanda talking in the living room.

Francis drew his arm back to bang the window with the heel of his hand and then stopped himself. It would make too much noise.

He grabbed the frame, pushed up with everything he had. It wouldn't budge. He kept pushing, face going red, gritting his teeth so hard, he thought they'd break. He leaned in, tried to get under it for the best angle. He pushed hard, arms starting to tremble. He could hear his heartbeat in his ears.

Come on . . . come on . . . come on . . .

A loud crack and the window slid upward. Francis's joy at the window's opening was blunted by the worry that the loud noise would draw attention.

"Come on," he whispered.

He swung one leg over the windowsill, ducked his head, and wriggled through the small opening. The rusty fire escape outside groaned with his weight, but he ignored it. He stuck his head back in, looked for Emma.

"Where are you?" he whispered.

Emma stuck her head out of the closet, whispered back, "I still don't have the suitcase."

Are you fucking kidding me? Fury rose up in him. "Fuck the damn suitcase. That guy is going to come fucking murder us in five fucking seconds! Now get your fucking ass out here."

She looked at him, surprised.

Yeah. He'd surprised himself a little.

"Please," he added.

Then Francis looked down and saw it.

The narrow space between the vanity and the wall near the window was almost exactly the same size and shape as the alligator-skinned suitcase. Francis had been standing over it the whole time. He reached in and grabbed it by the handle, lifted it up to show Emma.

Her mouth fell open. Surprise, relief, gratitude in her eyes.

Francis pulled the suitcase through the window, motioned for Emma to follow. *Get your ass out here!*

Emma took half a step toward him.

The doorknob rattled, slowly began to turn. Her eyes shifted to the knob and went wide. She stepped back, pressing herself flat against the wall in the space behind the door. Slowly the bedroom door swung open.

Francis whipped back out of sight, back against the bricks to the side of the window. He held the suitcase with a white-knuckled grip, held his breath and listened. He glanced over the side of the fire escape. It was rusty and rickety, and he didn't trust the railings. It would be a long fall.

A vague sense of movement from within the bedroom, shoes shuffling on carpet. Francis imagined Emma standing stock-still behind the door, holding her breath just like Francis was. He waited, expecting any second to hear Emma scream, to hear a gunshot.

The sounds faded. Silence. Francis counted to sixty. Slowly.

Cautiously, he edged back toward the window, turn his head to peek inside—

A flash of movement, and Francis's heart lurched, a scream of terror stuck in his throat. Wings flapping. The pigeon cooed as it flew away, landing on the roof of the building across the alley.

A pigeon. Jesus. Francis blew out a relieved burst of breath, turning back to the window—

Two arms shot through the open window and latched on to the suitcase.

"Gimme that fucking thing!" Cavanaugh yelled.

A surge of adrenaline shot through Francis. He put a foot against the windowsill, yanked back with everything he had, but Cavanaugh had a death grip on the suitcase.

"Let go, kid," Cavanaugh said. "Just leave it and beat it out of here. You don't want any part of this."

He was right. That was the thing, Francis realized. This wasn't his suitcase. None of this was his problem. All he had to do was let go.

He pulled harder.

Through the window's dirty glass, he saw a figure loom up behind Cavanaugh.

Emma reached past Cavanaugh, grabbed the window, and slammed it down on his forearms. Hard.

Cavanaugh threw his head back, howled like an enraged animal. He let go of the suitcase. He struggled to open the window, but it was stuck again, and he was bent awkwardly, struggled to pull himself free.

Francis tucked the suitcase under one arm and didn't look back. The fire escape swayed and rattled and creaked alarmingly as he flew down the narrow, rusty stairs. The fire escape ended ten feet short of the ground. Francis jumped. In midair, he remembered his injured knee and twisted to take the brunt of the landing with the other leg. He hit and rolled into a stack of trash bags. Some of the trash bags dislodged and fell on top of him, one leaking something foul smelling down the back of his shirt.

He pushed the bags off him, staggered to his feet, and scanned the trash pile for the suitcase. He had to dig through the garbage, but he found it, snatched it by the handle, and picked a direction to run.

Francis rounded the corner of the building, slammed on the brakes, and backpedaled. He took a deep breath, steadied himself, and then looked back around the corner cautiously.

They must have ditched the car they'd smashed up against the Dumpster and gotten a new one, another black sedan newer and bigger. Francis recognized the bald one behind the wheel.

Cavanaugh and the other one with the mustache emerged from Amanda's building, Emma walking between them and looking a hell of a lot calmer than Francis would have. Cavanaugh's right hand was in his jacket pocket, and Francis knew he was grasping that little silver automatic. The one with the mustache had dark circles under his eyes and a piece of metal fastened across his nose with white surgical tape.

They ushered Emma into the back seat of the sedan, and two seconds later, the car eased into the flow of traffic, heading uptown.

That's it, then, said a little voice inside Francis's head. *Time to go to the police, give them the suitcase, tell them everything.*

But another surprise voice piped up and said, *Do something, chickenshit.*

7

Harrison Gunn stood in the middle of Berringer's living room and scanned the place one more time, hands in pockets, rocking heel to toe and wondering how the man had even gotten involved. Berringer didn't add up. The NSA had been chasing the girl for weeks, knew her connection to Middleton, but Berringer had come out of nowhere, a completely new wrinkle to the hunt. An old college boyfriend? A distant relation? The mainframe in DC had done a search and hadn't come up with anything.

Francis Berringer was a complete nothing. So much so that it made Gunn suspicious.

"We've been over everything, sir. Twice," said the agent in charge of the forensics team. "We failed to turn up anything useful."

"I'd had higher hopes," Gunn admitted. "Agent, you don't think . . ."

"Sir?"

Gunn had been about to wonder out loud if Berringer was perhaps in the employ of some foreign entity. Russian hackers would pay top dollar. Or the Chinese. If somebody got to the girl before the NSA . . .

"Never mind, Agent," Gunn said. "Just letting my mind wander. This Berringer fellow is a sudden unknown factor, and we all know how sudden unknown factors offend my natural sense of tidiness."

The agent smiled weakly. "Yes, sir."

"You're running his prints?"

"We found two sets throughout the apartment," the agent said. "We're running them both."

"Let's put our sudden, unknown Mr. Berringer on the watch list, shall we?"

"It's already been done," the agent said. "If he so much as uses his library card, we'll know it."

Gunn looked at the agent with a mild expression of pleasant surprise. "Have you really? Already? Well, good for you, Agent. Good for you."

The black Mercedes JetVan raced up the highway toward Sonoma.

When the company had started to grow and the money began rolling in, Middleton had briefly allowed himself to be carted around in a limousine. He'd hated it instantly. First, he had the foolish feeling he was always on his way to some prom. Not that he'd actually gone to his prom. Middleton had not quite come into his own while still in high school.

Secondly, the limousine seemed an absurd waste. Not the cost. Indeed, the JetVan cost five times what the limo did after Middleton paid to have it custom made into a mobile office. A desk, leather seats, multiple monitors all showing CNN, Fox News, MSNBC, and various other feeds, all the stock markets from around the world. A mini kitchen and a lounge area. A partition separated passengers from the driver. Satellite connection.

No, it wasn't that the limousine was so much a waste of money. More like a waste of time. When Middleton began his company in a two-room office above a hardware store, his hours had been spent huddled over a computer in a small room, coding coding coding. With success came meetings and meetings and meetings.

Such long, endless, ridiculous, useless meetings. Too many people in this world loved to talk and talk and talk. This meant Middleton logged hundreds of miles a year zigzagging back and forth between meetings. The hours in the back of the limo were wasted.

Thus the mobile office in the JetVan. They had become the most productive hours in his day. The miles blurred past, and Middleton ticked items off his to-do list.

Meredith had pointed out that Aaron Middleton was a rich and powerful individual and that the vast majority of those who wanted a meeting with him would gladly make the trip to wherever Middleton happened to be. If the price of admission was to gather around a hot tub while Middleton soaked naked, sipping a piña colada, then so be it. It had been Meredith who'd made him fully realize that the word *billionaire* meant something.

But really it was too late. Middleton had already fallen in love with the mobile office. He liked the idea of being a moving target—so to speak. And although he understood Meredith had been exaggerating to make a point, the idea of an audience while Middleton soaked naked in a hot tub was unspeakably off-putting.

Winning Meredith over to the JetVan had been as simple as keeping the mini fridge well stocked.

"There's Pellegrino," she said, bending to examine the fridge's contents.

"Do you feel the interview went well?" Middleton asked.

"I do."

"So do I," Middleton said. "Let's celebrate with something stronger. Is there a Michelob Ultra?"

"Yes."

"Good. I feel like a beer."

"I'm not sure Michelob Ultra qualifies as beer." She opened one and handed him the bottle.

She selected a Diet Dr Pepper for herself.

"How is the house coming?"

"Soon," Meredith said. "They told me soon when I asked this morning."

Middleton frowned. "They've been saying that for a week and a half."

Meredith shrugged. "Contractors."

"Is Pete on-site?"

"Probably," Meredith said.

Middleton sipped beer, pulled his tie loose. "Vid him in, will you?"

"Okay," she said. "Give me a minute to arrange the secure satellite connection."

"I wonder what our own satellite would cost."

She laughed.

"What?"

"You asked me the same thing two weeks ago," Meredith said.

"I did?"

"Yes."

"Then why didn't you find out?"

"I *did* find out," she said. "And when I told you, you said, 'Never mind.'"

Oh, yeah. Middleton did have a vague recollection of such a conversation. He seemed to remember a similar conversation about buying an island. And another conversation about buying the San Diego Padres. He made a mental note to give Meredith a raise. What she saved him in outlandish impulse purchases would be well worth it.

A few minutes later, they had Pete on the closest monitor to Middleton's desk.

"Pete, my man, tell me what I want to hear."

"We're definitely in the home stretch, Mr. Middleton." Pete's smile was genuine, believable.

Pete Levin didn't know anything about building a house or landscaping or interior design. Pete was a dapper sight, with his fashionable red-framed glasses and houndstooth check jacket and bow tie and perfectly oiled hipster mustache complete with handlebars. Middleton tried to imagine the man holding a hammer and failed. But Middleton didn't consider they were simply "building a house." It was a project far more massive than that, and such an enterprise demanded Pete's organizational skills. The man ate, slept, and breathed timetables, work flowcharts, budgets, and construction regulations. He was known for his catchphrase: *Let's put a stop to all the grab-ass and make it right and hurry.*

"The former Epcot Imagineers were here this morning to oversee the installations they designed," Pete reported. "The last bit of landscaping is being watered in now. We had to get a waiver from the county because of the watering ban, but we handled it. The bureaucracy has honestly been a nightmare. It would have been simpler to build a space station."

"Uh-huh." Middleton nodded along, sipping beer.

Pete went on about various permit problems and labor disputes that had been handled with his usual cool proficiency. Middleton's attention drifted, his eyes going to Meredith.

She'd kicked off her shoes and had propped her feet up on the chair across from her. Middleton had noticed before that she almost never wore stockings or hose. Her legs were smooth, feet slender, toes pink and pedicured and perfect. The red toenail polish matched her fingernails.

He tore his eyes away from her, face blushing and warm. Aaron Middleton had never been a people person. He'd found women especially difficult, like some alien species, but he knew enough not to jeopardize a good employer-employee relationship by forcing the issue. There was almost nobody in his life he trusted the way he trusted Meredith Vines. If he made his feelings known, and Meredith found it a violation, would she leave? Demand some outrageous sexual harassment settlement? He couldn't risk it. He needed her.

He'd needed a woman once before, and she'd betrayed him. Her actions threatened him even now, threatened everything he'd built. He felt that sudden anger well up within him, that involuntary clenching of his fists. He didn't like it when the anger suddenly surfaced. He prided himself on always maintaining control, but it was a lie. So many times he was barely keeping it together. This thing with his wife was pushing all his buttons. It wasn't fair. That one person could take everything away seemed a grotesque injustice.

I won't let you take away the one thing I love. I won't let you.

Meredith sipped Dr Pepper through a bendy straw and read a copy of *Forbes.* A strand of hair had come loose, and she idly tucked it back behind an ear. Middleton could watch her forever.

"Sir?"

Middleton jerked his attention back to the monitor. "Sorry, Pete. You were saying?"

"They are still bringing all the computer and security systems online," Pete said. "They're calling it the most advanced, fully automated single-family residence in the world. *Modern Living* called again about a photo layout. The editor seemed pretty eager about it."

"Never mind *Modern Living,*" Middleton said. "When can I move *in?*"

"The trucks with the furnishings and other household items are here," Pete said. "They're waiting for the inspectors to give the final—"

"Incentivize the inspectors to hurry." Pete was a good man.

He'd know what that meant. "Grease the wheels, Pete. Tell the movers to furnish the bedroom and the kitchen if there's too much to do it all. They can do the rest tomorrow. I want to sleep in my own house tonight."

"Yes, sir," Pete said. "The movers are union. I presume it's okay to—"

"Double time. Triple. I don't care," Middleton said.

"I'll get it done."

"Thank you, Pete."

Middleton killed the connection. He glanced back at Meredith. She didn't look up from her magazine, but her mouth spread into an amused grin. The woman had respect for him, but nothing like fear. He loved that about her.

"You don't approve?" he asked.

A very slight shrug. "You're the boss."

8

Francis watched the sedan pull away and figured that was it. She was gone.

So what can you do, dumbass? Nothing, that's what. Go to the police. Tell them the whole story. They can help her. It's out of your hands.

Everything he told himself made sense. Everything he told himself made him feel sick in his stomach with failure.

And then the sedan stopped at a red light. A long, agonizing second passed as Francis felt his brain making a bad, bad decision. Nothing he could think of would talk his brain out of it.

He turned his head, looked back down the street. A taxi was coming. He ran to the curb, flagged it down. It pulled up and let him in.

The cabbie turned around and looked at him. "Where you going?"

Francis pointed ahead and said something he'd secretly wanted to say all his adult life. "Follow that car."

The cabbie looked at him.

Francis looked back.

The cabbie was a beefy guy in his midfifties, big potato nose, saddlebags under his eyes. Wide ears like fleshy barn doors. He probably had a name like Sal or Vinnie. Francis glanced at the cabbie's license. Brad. Close enough.

"Let me tell you something, mister," the cabbie said.

Shit.

"I been a cabbie in this fucking city for twenty-eight fucking years. You hear me?"

Ohhhhhh, shit.

"And finally—today—finally somebody asks me to *follow that car.*"

What?

"You just made my fucking day, buddy." Brad put the car into gear just as the light turned green. "Let's get after him."

They pulled into traffic and caught up with the sedan, two cars in between them. The traffic flowed easily around them. Francis wondered where Cavanaugh could be taking the girl. What Francis might do when he caught up to them was another serious question for which no obvious answer presented itself.

He clearly hadn't thought this through, but if he had, he probably wouldn't have been sitting there in the back of a taxi.

The cabbie's eyes met Francis's in the rearview mirror. "So what is it? You a cop? We after some asshole?"

"I'm not a cop," Francis said.

The cabbie's eyes again in the mirror. "No, I guess not. You don't look the type. No offense."

"None taken." The sedan changed lanes ahead. "Don't lose them."

"'Don't lose them,' he says. Teach your grandmother how to suck eggs?"

Francis had no idea what he'd meant by that.

The cabbie switched lanes to a chorus of blaring horns.

"So what is it?" Brad asked.

"What's what?"

"What's the deal? Who we chasing?"

"It's kind of a long story," Francis said.

"Give me the *Reader's Digest* version."

"I don't know what that means."

"Jesus."

The sedan took a left, and the cabbie had to run a red light to keep up. More horns and rude gestures.

The traffic was lighter here, and the sedan cut across two lanes and took a sudden right. The cabbie followed. The sedan took another sharp left, and the taxi squealed tires keeping up.

"They might be onto us," Brad said.

Francis fastened his seat belt.

"What about a private eye?" Brad asked. "You a shamus?"

"I'm just trying to help a friend," Francis said. "She's in trouble."

"A girl." Brad nodded liked he'd known it all along. "It's always a girl."

"You trying to fucking kill us?" Cavanaugh said. "What're you driving like that for?"

Cavanaugh and Ernie sat in the back seat with Emma between them. Ike drove, his eyes bouncing back and forth between the rearview mirror and the side mirror.

"That taxi is following us," Ike said.

"Bullshit." But Cavanaugh turned and looked out the back window. The taxi was there a few car lengths back, but New York was lousy with taxis. "Take the next turn as sharp as you can."

Ike jerked the wheel hard, and the sedan fishtailed, tires squcaling again as they took a right onto a narrow street, the back tire going over the curb, a hubcap spinning away in a metallic clamor. Ike leaned on the horn to warn a woman with an armload of grocery sacks. She had to step back quickly to keep from getting clobbered. She shouted obscenities after the sedan. Cavanaugh heard the word *cocksucker*.

All three of them in the back seat had slid across to the left and piled up on each other.

"Hey, get off!" Emma said.

"Shut up." Cavanaugh looked back. The taxi was right with them. "Shit."

"Who is that?" he asked Emma.

"Do I know? You tell me."

Cavanaugh pulled the little automatic from his pocket and pushed the cold barrel against a smooth patch of skin just under her ear. "I don't have a lot of patience right now."

Emma's upper lip curled into a sneer. "Please. You're not going to do anything to me, and we both know it."

"Accidents happen."

"You're not the only ones after what I have," she said. "It could be *anyone* back there. Hell, the Japanese offered me two million for it three days ago."

Cavanaugh open his mouth to say something, closed it again when her words sank in, and looked at her quizzically. His orders had been clear. *Get the girl. Get what she has.* The details had been sketchy.

"Holy crap, you didn't know," she said. "You have no idea why he sent you after me."

"I know plenty," Cavanaugh growled. He jerked a thumb over his shoulder at the pursuing taxi. "Ike, lose the bastard."

"Right."

Ike stomped the accelerator flat, passed a Mini Cooper on the left, and then cut back right in front of it. The Mini Cooper slammed on its brakes as the sedan took a hard right. Cavanaugh watched the taxi zig and zag to avoid the Mini, almost annihilating a bike messenger. Horns and shouts and general New York uproar.

"I'll take us through the park," Ike said, jerking the wheel again.

Cavanaugh was still watching through the back window. The

taxi was coming fast. "Whoever the hell they are, they mean business."

Francis held on to the handle over the door with a white-knuckled grip. *I am going to die.*

"They've definitely made us," Brad said. "Don't worry. I'm on him like a bad rash."

The sedan ran a yellow light, and by the time the taxi hit the intersection, the light had turned red. The ongoing sound of brakes and tires and angry horns had faded to background noise. Francis's fear of a sudden fiery death was still front and center.

The sedan turned into Central Park, and the taxi followed.

Again, Francis realized he had no idea what he'd do if they actually caught up with the car ahead of them, and his brain strained to come up with some kind of plan. When he'd hopped into Brad's taxi, Francis had envisioned the sort of stealth in which he might locate the bad guy's hideout and . . .

And then what? Hideout? What am I, after the Joker? What the hell was I thinking?

"I think we got 'em," Brad said.

Francis looked to see what he was talking about. There was a traffic jam up ahead. The sedan was slowing down and would eventually be forced to stop. And then what?

Francis reached for the door handle.

"Why are you slowing down?" Cavanaugh asked.

"Logjam." Ike gestured at the traffic ahead.

"Think of something," Cavanaugh demanded. "Right fucking now."

Ike turned the sedan onto the sidewalk and headed into the park, crawling along at ten miles per hour. Pedestrians scooted out of the way, giving them annoyed looks as they passed.

"Not cool, dude!" a skateboarder yelled at them.

"Did we lose him?" Ike asked.

Cavanaugh looked back. The taxi was twenty feet behind them. "Floor it!" he told Ike.

Ike floored it.

The engine roared, and the sedan leaped forward. People scattered off the sidewalk and into the grass and bushes. No hard stares this time, just screams and panic. The sedan came within three inches of a woman who was barely able to yank a stroller out the way.

Cavanaugh felt a stab of alarm in his gut. "Jesus, Ike!"

"You wanted fast, you got fast." Ike jerked the wheel at the last minute to avoid a man with a dog on a leash. Ike hunched over the wheel, eyes wide, sweat pouring down the back of his neck. He kept hitting the horn with one fist. "Out of the way, assholes!"

"You're going to kill us," Emma said.

Cavanaugh wanted to tell her to shut the fuck up, but to Ike, he said, "Maybe you should ease back, pal."

Rocks and trees rose up on either side of the narrow walkway. Ike said, "No, it's cool. I think I know where this comes out. If we can get to the freeway—"

The sedan rounded a gentle curve. A horse and carriage clopped past at the crossroads in front of them. Ike slammed on the brakes. The two tourists in the back of the carriage froze, terrified and wide-eyed. The carriage driver was an old man in a battered top hat, reins in clenched fists. He tried to control the horse as it reared up, whinnying panic, hooves swatting at the air.

Ike lost control of the sedan, and it went off the walkway. There was a terrific *slam-crash-bang* as the left tires went over a low boulder humped up from the ground, scraping metal before the car slammed down again on the other side. It flew headlong into the wide trunk of an old elm with a deafening *pop-crunch*. It sat there with the hood pushed in like a cartoon accordion, steam hissing from the cracked radiator.

Cavanaugh found himself on the floor, not sure how he'd gotten there. The world had blurred through the front windshield, then bumps and jerks and then tossed around like flakes in a snow globe. He inferred they'd smashed into something, but didn't know the extent of the damage.

He pulled himself back into the seat, dazed, blinking stars out of his eyes. "Ike?"

Ike didn't answer.

The bald thug had been thrown forward over the steering wheel, cracks in the windshield radiating from the point where his forehead had struck glass. A thin line of blood trickled past his ear.

"Shit." Cavanaugh's fist closed around his little automatic, and he shoved the car door open, staggered out, knees wobbly.

Something slammed hard across his hand, and the pistol went flying.

He screeched pain and drew his arm up against his chest. *Same fucking wrist.*

Cavanaugh looked up to see who'd jacked him, and a big alligator suitcase came down hard square on his forehead.

9

It was a sturdily built piece of luggage, Francis had to admit.

He watched Cavanaugh feebly pull himself along the ground with one hand, the other palm over the spot on his forehead where he'd been whacked, blood seeping between fingers and down into one eye.

Francis slammed the suitcase down hard again, this time across Cavanaugh's back. The guy flopped flat, kissing dirt.

Francis cranked the suitcase back for one more wallop, but Cavanaugh made no effort to get back up again.

The gunshot crack was so loud, Francis felt it in his teeth. He had to clench himself to keep his bowels from letting go. *I'm dead. I'm dead. I'm dead.*

He checked himself. No bullet holes.

"Hands off, ya bitch!"

Francis looked to see Emma grappling with the mustache thug on the other side of the sedan. She'd grabbed his arm, the thug's gun pointing off into the woods. He backhanded her, a crisp *smack* of flesh on flesh.

She reeled, and the thug brought his pistol around again.

Francis flung the suitcase.

It spun through the air and collided with the thug's bandaged nose. He bellowed furious agony. "Motherfuckers!"

Francis scooted around the car in a flash and arrived just as Emma regained her feet. They both leaped on him, and the three went down in a pile. They hit the ground on top of the thug, the air huffing out of him. He flailed blindly, eyes closed tight against the pain.

"Get his gun!" Emma shouted.

Francis held the thug's arm against the ground with one hand, leaning all his weight into it. With his other hand he tried to pry the thug's fingers off his pistol.

"Get the fuck off me!" the thug yelled.

Emma balled up her little fist and popped him on the bandaged nose. Fresh blood squirted from his right nostril. He screamed and thrashed but let go of the gun.

And suddenly the pistol was in Francis's hands. The weight of it surprised him. "I got it! I got it! What do I do? Do I shoot him?"

"No! Just knock him out," Emma told him.

Francis slammed the butt of the gun against the side of the thug's head.

"Fucking . . . shit." He wasn't knocked out but dazed.

Sirens rose in the distance.

Emma scrambled to her feet, grabbed the suitcase. "We've got to get out of here."

"I've got a taxi," Francis said. "Right over here—"

He pointed at the taxi just as Brad put it in reverse, the tires smoking as it backed up at full speed, fishtailed around, and headed back the way it came. Apparently, the sirens were all Brad needed to hear to decide his adventure was over.

Emma offered Francis a blank look. "You were saying?"

"Come on!" Francis ran toward the horse and carriage.

The two tourists had climbed down from the carriage and huddled off to the side, gawking at the spectacle. Skaters and joggers had stopped to look too.

The carriage driver saw Francis coming and held up a hand to fend him off. "Don't want no trouble here."

"Look, we just need to get out of here." Francis took his wallet from his back pocket, opened it. "I can give you . . . shit. Eight bucks."

Emma took a wad of cash from the front pocket of her jeans. She peeled off five crisp bills. "Five hundred dollars."

The carriage driver eyed the cash. "Get in."

They climbed aboard, and the driver clicked his tongue. The horse and carriage headed away at a fast trot. Not the speediest getaway in history, but faster than on foot. Francis looked back. The small crowd watched them go, but nobody seemed eager to do anything about it.

Francis sank into the seat, heart hammering the inside of his chest. He blew out an exhausted, relieved sigh. "That was messed up."

"We're not clear yet," Emma said. "Those sirens are getting louder, and there's plenty of bystanders who'll be happy to tell them which way we went."

"I can take you to the edge of the park," the driver called over his shoulder.

"That works," Emma said.

"And then what?" Francis asked.

"We need a place to lie low."

"I need to hit an ATM," Francis said.

"Are you an idiot?" she asked. "No bank cards. No credit cards. That's how they find you. Give me your smartphone."

He fished it out of his pants pocket and handed it to her.

She dropped it on the floor of the carriage and smashed it with her boot heel.

"Hey!"

She picked it up again and flung it into the bushes.

"What the actual fuck?" Francis said.

"They can track it."

"Okay, then, you have all the answers," Francis said. "Where do we lie low?"

She sat back, hugged the suitcase close to her like she'd found a lost child. "I think I have an idea."

10

The whole place was a circus.

Middleton had been excited at first when the JetVan had driven through the old stone gates and past the rows and rows of grapevines. The new vines were still being trained to the guide wires that ran the length of each row. Once past them, the rows of mature vines stretched out for acres and acres. The Sonoma vineyard had been producing quality grapes since the 1940s. It had been in the same family since that time, and Middleton had simply thrown money at them until they'd cried uncle.

Middleton rarely drank wine, but the idea of a vineyard appealed to him. It brought an old-world vibe to his life that balanced out all that gleaming Silicon Valley high tech.

The JetVan had then driven by the barn and the outbuildings and the main house that had come with the property. The house was done in a Californian mission style, a handsome five-thousand-square-foot structure, and had been refurbished for the family who would oversee the vineyard operations. Middleton himself had little interest in getting dirty or fooling with the minutiae involved in running a vineyard and winery.

They'd kept driving, the road now clearly new construction, back into the heretofore undeveloped part of the property to the plot of land overlooking the small lake. Middleton had picked the spot himself and hadn't been back since. The eagerness to see his finished home was a palpable thing filling up his chest.

But then they'd come through the wooded area into the clearing and saw the circus, moving trucks stuck in a half-flooded yard, dozens of people milling around, talking in little groups. Workers went back and forth with wheelbarrows. Other workers leaned on shovels, watching. None of this random activity seemed coordinated or useful.

The JetVan parked off to the side, and the driver came around to slide open the door for Middleton and Meredith.

"I thought they'd be finished." Middleton said it sort of breathlessly as he stepped out of the van, as if he found the spectacle fatiguing and intrusive.

"Just hang back," Meredith told him. "I'll find out what's happening."

She stepped out of the van, her shoe squishing into the wet ground. "Maybe a leak or something? Damn, okay. Don't worry. I've got this."

Meredith headed for the crowd, game face set in stone. Middleton didn't hang back, followed after her more slowly, each step spongy and wet. Each step also brought a growing sense of dread, but he pressed on doggedly.

He didn't really care about wet shoes. Okay, he cared a little. But he was looking past the confused throng of people at his new house beyond.

It was beautiful. Naturally he'd seen pictures as the construction had progressed, a chunk here and there, but it was different seeing it like this. It was real and right there in front of him.

Gleaming white stone, every angle so sharp you could shave with it. Wide windows stretched along most of the external surface, but they were currently covered by highly polished accordion shutters. A simple command would open or shut them. A set of metal double doors ten feet high guarded the entrance. From above, the house looked like a huge circle, a central hub from which radiated three large wings. The house was a single story except for one area perched atop the center of the hub, accessible by elevator or a narrow spiral staircase. It sat up there like a dome hunched up slightly from the rest of the building, round windows like portholes circling the entirety of it. Francis had deliberately avoided using the words *bridge of a starship* when talking to the architects. People already thought him eccentric enough. It would be his personal office, his private inner sanctum. But it would also be more than that. It would be the command center from which he would take on the world.

Middleton walked toward the house. A home. His home. It was almost as if he floated, mesmerized. The world went mute, faded into the background. His new home glowed in the light of the setting sun. His own personal sanctuary.

"Hey, you Middleton?"

The world came tumbling back down on top of him.

Middleton blinked, turned to see a big man huffing toward him, sweaty T-shirt, threadbare jeans. A ball cap that said BRUINS. Meredith's head snapped around, watching the guy with a blend of alarm and annoyance as he approached Middleton. Part of Meredith's job was to be a buffer between Middleton and the myriad of people clamoring for a piece of his limited schedule.

"I'm Aaron Middleton," he admitted, wishing briefly he could be someone else.

"Look, the guy in charge said to only unload a few rooms, but that doesn't make any sense."

"It doesn't?"

The guy shrugged. "No point in getting the trucks unstuck just to come back in the morning and get them stuck again."

"Stuck?" Middleton looked the trucks. The main effort to get them unstuck consisted of men looking down at the tires and shaking their heads.

Meredith was there suddenly, tying to subtly maneuver herself in between the guy and Middleton. "Hi there. Hello. I'm sorry, but we've just arrived, and we're just trying to get a handle on things. You are?"

"Ray."

"Hi, Ray, I'm Meredith. Just give us a minute to assess the situation, will you?"

"Okay, but we're burning daylight," Ray said. "Sooner we get started, sooner we finish."

"Don't listen to him!" someone shouted.

All three heads turned to see another man running at them, arms waving.

Ray groaned. "This guy again."

"You've already done enough damage!" The newcomer was a stick figure of a man with sharp tanned features; he wore work khakis and a wide straw gardener's hat.

"Hey, man, get off my ass," Ray said. "The guy said to back the trucks up to the house, so we did."

"Excuse me. Hello. Me again." Meredith smiled tightly, attempting to gain control of the conversation. "One at a time, okay? Who arc you?"

"Mason. I'm the assistant groundskeeper, and this idiot backed over the main waterline for the sprinkler system."

"The guy told me to back the trucks up," Ray repeated.

"The guy?" Meredith asked.

"You know." Roy waved back at the chaos behind him. "The guy."

"Fussy, slender, organized fellow with nerd glasses?" Meredith said. "Dressed like a Brooks Brothers mannequin?"

"There you go."

"Fantastic," Meredith said. "Pete Levin. That's the guy we need as fast as possible so we can straighten everything out, okay? So find him and—"

"Why were the sprinkler lines above ground?"

Middleton instantly regretted asking the question. The attention shifted from Meredith to him, all eyes like hot lasers. All of them talked at once, Ray and the groundskeeper each telling their versions of the story, Meredith trying to regain control.

There had apparently been a problem with a permit or something, and they'd had to dig up the pipes, and the moving trucks had backed over one of them and now the water was gushing nonstop, and they'd sent for the head groundskeeper, who had the only key to the maintenance shed with the water shutoff valve. Another woman—middle-aged, fashionable, carrying her shoes and splashing as she ran—complained loudly that the movers were dragging mud across tens of thousands of dollars of tile and carpet.

Ray shouted over everyone else at Middleton. "You're the boss, right? Just tell them to let us unload!"

"No!" The assistant groundskeeper was vehement.

Middleton said, "Uh . . ."

He felt dizzy, tried to shrink and disappear behind Meredith. Why were they all talking at the same time? What did they expect him to do? It had been nearly a year since he'd had a full-blown attack, had even taken himself off the medication. If these people could all just slow down and calmly explain one at a time, then maybe he could—

He found it hard to breathe. Why was it suddenly so hot? He loosened his tie, trying to make sense of the babble, the voices blending into a muffled drone. Sweat poured down his back and behind his ears.

"Pete!" Meredith waved frantically. "Over here. Thank God."

Middleton focused, saw the man dart through the crowd, rushing toward them. His hair was slightly mussed—which, for Pete Levin, was a sign of the apocalypse.

He arrived, panting, holding up his iPhone. "I'm *so* sorry, Mr. Middleton. I wanted to call immediately, of course, but my phone died. There was a problem with the impact study on the land, and they made us dig up the sprinkler pipes—"

"Pete." Meredith spoke the single syllable with such effortless command, it startled Levin.

His eyes shifted from Middleton to her. "Meredith?"

"I need you to focus, okay?"

The briefest pause. "Of course."

She kept her eyes on Levin but reached back to take Middleton's hand. She gave it a quick squeeze. Relief flooded him.

"Get somebody to bring in some planking and lay down a path to the front door," she told Levin. "Bring in a bed and some chairs, just enough to get through the night. If we can't move the trucks, then arrange transport for the movers. They can come back in the morning. Contact a cleaning crew and have them stand by. Maybe we'll need them tonight, maybe in the morning. But they need to be ready. All the rest of this"—she gestured at the flooded yard, the pipes, the throng of people—"get it fixed. Spend money. Make it happen."

Middleton had been listening to Meredith take charge of the situation, and then there were simply a few missing seconds.

Middleton realized he'd lost track of his surroundings. He drifted through the moment in time, dazed, as if the moment had been lifted from the flow of time and set on a high shelf. His feet were wet and cold. He looked down, saw the water over his ankles. He was gently being pulled along the walkway to the front door of his new home.

Meredith smiled back at him. "It's okay. Come on." Her voice sounded like it came from the bottom of a deep well.

He turned his head slowly, looking around dreamily, and caught sight of a small block building the size of a cottage. It was surrounded by new hedges, almost as if the hedges were meant to hide the building, or would eventually when the hedges filled out. He didn't remember that building from the original designs.

A door opening and closing. The outside racket muffled to almost nothing.

Deep breaths. In through the nose, out through the mouth.

The foyer had been designed to make a man feel small. The ceiling vaulted high above them, a gleaming modern chandelier overhead, lengths of metal crisscrossing at odd angles and brilliant globes. Wide hallways led off in three directions toward the three different wings of the dwelling.

Middleton blew out another long sigh and slowly sank into a sitting position on the cold tile floor. His new house felt immense around him. There was a strange reverence, almost like it was some weird temple. Everything was white and futuristic and sterile.

Meredith's soft fingertips on his back. "Welcome home."

11

"I've hacked into the rental car company's computer and removed your name," Bryant said, "and replaced it with a fake."

"Thanks," Cavanaugh said.

"How did you happen to wreck it?" Bryant asked. "You got the insurance, didn't you?"

"It's a long story."

"What about the girl?"

Cavanaugh cleared his throat. "We're working on it."

"You lost her again, didn't you?"

"I said we're working on it. This isn't like your cushy office job. What are you going to tell the kid?"

"That you're working on it, I guess."

"Good," Cavanaugh said. "Call us if you get a hit on her." He hung up.

"Pass the wine," Ernie said. It came out *Pad da wine*. In addition to the tape across his nose, he now had a bandage wrapped around the top of his head.

In fact, all three of them had similar bandages around their heads. The trio drew stares, and Cavanaugh felt like a fucking moron.

Cavanaugh filled his own wineglass from the carafe, then passed it to Ernie. They'd found a family-style Italian joint and had spent the last half hour passing around dishes of spaghetti and sausage and garlic bread. The carafe was full of a decent house Chianti.

"How many stitches you get?" Ike asked him.

"Four." The corner of that fucking suitcase had caught him just right on the forehead. It had hurt like a bitch. "You?"

"Thirteen."

"Jesus," Cavanaugh said. "Although it did look like you smashed the shit out of the windshield."

"I don't even remember it," Ike said. "One second I'm driving, then the next thing I know, you guys are dragging me through the park."

"FYI," Ernie said. "You're heavy."

They ate, drank wine.

When the coffees arrived, Cavanaugh sat back and said, "Guys, we need to talk."

"So talk," Ike said.

"I'm serious," Cavanaugh said. "Just us three. Okay?"

Ike and Ernie exchanged looks.

They understood what he meant. Cavanaugh had hired on some additional muscle for this job. Some of them were watching Berringer's apartment, others his workplace. More following up on other leads. Footwork that probably wouldn't amount to much, but they needed to cover all bases. They were solid guys with references, but they weren't inner-circle material.

Ernie, Ike, and Cavanaugh went back a ways. Cavanaugh had met Ernie in stir when doing a stretch for protection. When they got on the outside again, Ernie introduced him to Ike. So when Cavanaugh said he had something for the ears of the inner circle only, they sat up and paid attention.

Cavanaugh asked, "You like our current boss?"

By mutual understanding, they never used Middleton's name. You never knew who could be listening.

"Never met the guy," Ernie said.

"Just . . . okay, fine," Cavanaugh said. "I'm not talking about him *personally.* I'm talking about our current employment situation."

"Oh." Ernie sipped Chianti, shrugged. "Yeah. I mean hand-holding is easy money. I mean not this particular job we're on at the moment, but usually it's low stress and the money is good."

Hand-holding was what they called jobs they did for the mega-rich. Men like Middleton—ridiculously powerful and influential billionaires—always attracted problems. They had legions of people at their disposal to handle these problems: lawyers and accountants and private detectives and security guards. But often there were times these people simply couldn't get the job done. A very pregnant bimbo who needed to be "persuaded" to drop a paternity suit. Newspaper reporters who needed to be "convinced" there was nothing really newsworthy where they were poking their noses and should move on. Business rivals who needed to find another business.

The rich and the powerful had become accustomed to getting their own way. Bending the rules? Don't be ridiculous. They paid men like Cavanaugh to bend the rules for them.

"We ain't been working for him that long," Ernie pointed out. "He seems pretty clean."

Cavanaugh didn't mention what he'd arranged to happen to Marion Parkes in the joint. Even the inner circle didn't need to know everything. The fewer ears that heard things meant the fewer loose lips to squawk. But maybe he would tell them after all. The kid had a ruthless streak in him that wasn't obvious, but it was there. The kid could be dangerous. But he wouldn't mention it to the boys unless he thought it would help him make his pitch.

"Finding this girl is the first real test," Ernie said. "If this sort of thing is typical . . ."

"Then I'd want a raise," Ike said. "Supposed to be an easy gig for easy money, remember."

"He does pay us good," Cavanaugh said.

Ike shrugged. "Yeah."

"So, okay, you say easy work for easy money," Cavanaugh said. "So what's the easiest work of all?"

"Slapping hookers for a pimp?" Ernie said.

"Jesus, what? No." Cavanaugh rolled his eyes. "Try to class it up a little, will ya?"

"You tell us, then," Ike said. "What's the easiest work?"

"Not working at all," Cavanaugh told them.

"What are talking about?" Ernie asked. "Just becoming a hobo or something?"

"Fuck that," Ike said. "I have a kid at Dartmouth."

"No, idiots, I'm talking about retirement. What if your biggest concern every day was deciding what flavor margarita you wanted while lounging on some tropical beach?"

"I burn too easy for the beach," Ike said. "I got Irish skin."

"Whatever." Cavanaugh waved his hand impatiently. "Sucking back some beers on the porch of your trout-fishing mountain cabin. Whatever you like."

Ike looked doubtful. "I don't know. Cabin in the mountain sounds like I'd be in for a lot of snow. I don't like snow."

"Jesus, whatever you want is what I'm saying," Cavanaugh said.

"I'd play a shitload of golf," Ernie said. "I'd need new clubs."

"There you go." Cavanaugh was talking to Ike but gesturing at Ernie. "Whatever your perfect idea of a permanent vacation is. Easy living."

"Well, I guess you'd need to bank some serious cash for that," Ike said.

Cavanaugh thrust a professorial finger into the air. "Exactly."

The light came on in Ernie's eyes. "The Japanese."

Cavanaugh tapped the tip of his nose. "This guy's catching on."

"Well, I'm not," Ike said. "The Japanese what?"

"You were busy driving and didn't hear her," Ernie said. "The Japanese offered her two million for it."

Ike shrugged and spread his hands in a *What are you talking about?* gesture. "Two million for *what?*"

"Hey, hey, keep it down," Cavanaugh said.

Ike leaned in, lowered his voice. "Two million for what?"

"Getting the girl is only half the deal," Ernie reminded him. "Also she's got something. Intellectual property and property . . . uh . . . propinary . . ."

"Proprietary technology," Cavanaugh finished for him.

"Right," Ernie said. "That."

"Two million three ways is a pretty damn good payday," Ike said. "But I don't smell retirement."

"I'm just saying, if the Japanese will pay that much, then maybe the Russians will pay more? The Chinese?" Cavanaugh shrugged. "Big crime isn't armored car heists anymore. It's all this cyber shit and high tech and industrial espionage. My guess is that our employer would pay the most of anybody just to keep it from the competition."

"If we crossed him, I *doubt* he'd be our employer anymore," Ike said.

"That's why we have to make sure the payment is big enough," Cavanaugh said. "We do this, there's no going back."

Ernie stared into his coffee cup. It had gone cold. "I'm sitting here with a broken nose and a bandage around my head. Playing golf every day sounds pretty good."

———

The first place didn't work out.

The second place was willing to do it cash only, no questions asked. Emma peeled enough hundreds from her bankroll for the entire night. The pay-by-the hour hotel in Queens was called the Wayfarer's Retreat, and at least three hookers came in and out of the lobby while the bored guy at the front desk handed Francis and Emma their keys.

The lobby had likely not been refurbished since the hotel had been built in 1970-whatever. The halls were dim and gray. There was a faint smell like stale beer. The muffled sounds of adults at play came from some of the rooms they passed. Francis walked on, looking straight ahead and feeling embarrassed.

The room itself was surprisingly warm and inviting if a bit garish. The burgundy wallpaper had a fake velvety texture. Paintings in ornate gold-painted, wooden frames depicted nude Rubenesque ladies reclining on overstuffed chaise lounges. A king-sized canopy bed. Lots of tassels and extra pillows. A flat-screen TV hung on the wall opposite the bed.

"I need to pee." Emma went into the bathroom, the door clicking shut behind her.

Francis sighed heavily and flopped on the bed. His wallet dug into his hip. He fished it out of his back pocket and put it on the bedside table next to the phone. He kicked off his shoes. Francis realized he was utterly exhausted, wrung out like an old dish rag. Nonstop stress and fleeing danger and fearing for your life would do that, he supposed. Various aches began to seep into every limb and joint. But the bed felt so good. The mattress was cheap, but he didn't care. He felt his eyelids sag.

The bathroom door opened two inches, and Emma put her face against the crack. "I want a shower. You need to get in here first?"

"Go ahead."

The door clicked shut again. Then the sound of running water.

Francis thought to check his email, remembered his phone had been boot-stomped and tossed into the bushes. He sighed.

He reached for the remote, flipped on the TV. Apparently, the cost of the room included full porn privileges. He kept flipping channels until he found a local newscast. He watched, thinking maybe they'd mention the car chase and wreck in Central Park, but sleep tugged at him again, and in seconds, he dozed.

His eyes popped open. Had it only been a few seconds? Francis realized the water shutting off in the bathroom had woken him.

Emma emerged from the bathroom in a cloud of steam, a fluffy oversized towel wrapped around her, hair wet and slicked back.

Francis averted his eyes back to the television, began flipping channels. "Listen, eventually we're going to need some plan to—"

"Wait! Shut up. Go back to that."

Francis blinked. "Go back to what?"

She crossed the room in two quick steps, holding her towel closed with one hand and snatching the remote away from Francis with the other. She backtracked a couple of stations until she found what she wanted, thumbing the volume up a few notches.

It was some sort of interview show. A smartly dressed Megyn Kelly type sat across the desk from a young go-getter in an expensive suit. They were already in mid-conversation.

"—pretty much always happens that way," the go-getter was saying. "We go through long periods of steady technological advancement, but then *wham*, we stumble upon a discovery or an invention that takes us forward exponentially. I feel we're on the verge of something very similar in the computing industry, especially in the way we sort and analyze data."

"And you claim you're going to lead this charge?" the journalist asked. "Some might say that's a pretty big boast. Especially from someone so young."

Polite laughter from the go-getter. "I get that a lot. Trust me."

"In fact, some call you 'the kid,' yes?"

Francis noticed a slight twitch in the go-getter's left eye. More polite laughter. "Well, it's not a nickname I encourage. I feel my accomplishments have and will continue to speak for themselves, and eventually my youth won't be an issue."

Francis climbed out of bed and left her to watch the interview. In the bathroom, he unzipped, urinated. Her clothes hung on a hook behind the door. When he washed his hands, he glanced over and saw Emma's panties and socks hanging on the towel rack. They'd been rinsed and wrung out and hung to dry. Francis felt a surprise pang of disappointment that the panties were simple and white and in no way alluring.

What are you doing here? Are you insane?

He dried his hands and went back out.

Emma was still watching the interview.

The go-getter was still talking. "Imagine a smart system that runs your whole house, controls the environment, turns the lights on, and—"

"But computers can do that already, can't they?" interrupted the interviewer.

"They can only do what we tell them," the go-getter went on patiently. "The trick is a computer recognizing when to stop doing something or to change what it does. I mean, yes, you can program it with detailed parameters and contingencies, but if next-gen artificial intelligence worked more like human intuition? What if a computer could sense your mood and put on some music you might like? I mean, we're years away from that, but we've already started working with software that doesn't just give you what you want . . . but what it thinks you *might* want. What it thinks you *need*."

"That's amazing," the interviewer said. "You say it could somehow sense mood. But . . . but how would it *know*?"

The go-getter smiled widely. "Exactly."

Emma stared at the TV without blinking.

"Who is that?" Francis asked.

"That's my husband."

12

Francis's eye popped open, and it took him a few seconds to remember where he was. He'd fallen hard into long, deep sleep, curled all the way to one side of the bed.

Emma had taken the other side of the bed, still wrapped in a towel. When Francis had broached the subject of what would happen next, she'd claimed to be too exhausted to think clearly. All she'd wanted was sleep, but she'd promised to hash it all out in the morning. She'd even go with Francis to the police and explain everything if Francis insisted. He'd been mollified. They'd slept.

He rolled over, looked. Emma wasn't there.

Francis sat up slowly, rubbed his neck. Various pains still ached his body. He needed to exercise more, maybe join a gym.

He staggered into the bathroom, yawning. He splashed water in his face. He looked up at the towel rack. The panties and socks were gone. It took Francis a moment to realize what that might mean. He jerked his head around, saw her clothes were no longer on the hook.

Shit shit shit.

He ran back into the other room, eyes frantic.

No suitcase. No girl.

"Shit! Fucking dumbass idiot!" How could he have been so stupid? Of course she was gone. She'd said pretty clearly she couldn't go to the police. What had Francis thought? That he'd won her over somehow?

His hand went automatically to his back pocket. His wallet

was gone. No, wait. He'd taken it out last night. He checked the nightstand. It was there. Right next to it was his American Express gold card. Next to that was a stack of crisp hundred-dollar bills, and next to that was a short note scrawled on hotel stationery. He snatched it up and read.

> I had to use your credit card. I left enough cash to cover it. Sorry. Had to go.

Francis counted the money. Fifteen hundred dollars.

Credit card? It didn't make sense. He remembered her warning. *That's how they find you.* She'd been pretty serious about it. It was specifically why they'd found a hotel that would take cash only without a credit card or identification. What could she have needed so desperately?

Francis flipped the credit card cover and dialed the toll-free number on the back. He navigated through the automated options until he found himself talking to a live human being on the other end.

"I just need to confirm a recent transaction," he told her.

She confirmed that his most recent transaction was for two first-class airline tickets leaving from New York's LaGuardia Airport flying to Los Angeles, California. She rattled off the airline and details of the flight.

"Did you say two tickets?"

"Yes, sir."

"Can you confirm those names for me, please?" Francis asked.

"Absolutely," she said. "Emma Middleton and Francis Berringer."

Francis glanced at his watch. He had fifty-seven minutes to make the flight.

———

"We assembled a team to meet her at LAX as soon as the computer flagged her," the agent told Gunn over the phone. "There's an interrogation facility nearby, and our California office has good relations with local law enforcement and airport security. Plus we'll have ample time for the team to set up at the gate. We thought it a better plan than trying to take her at LaGuardia or diverting the flight."

"Agreed," Gunn said. "Arrange a government jet for me. I want to be there when she disembarks. I'll take command of the team."

Gunn grinned. The girl had messed up this time. They all do eventually. You can't run from the federal government forever.

Bryant sat at his control station, monitoring the traffic from Manhattan to Queens. Cavanaugh and his goons would never make it, but they had to try. The new software had immediately picked up the NSA chatter and the reception they were planning for the girl at LAX, so getting ahead of her there was out. Cavanaugh's only chance was to try to catch her at LaGuardia.

But . . . well . . . just no. It wasn't going to happen. The bridges were a mess, and anyway, they'd never get through security in time. Cavanaugh's only chance was that the girl's flight might be delayed. Considering they were talking about LaGuardia, the odds weren't really so bad.

Middleton would not be pleased to hear the government had beaten them to his wife. Not pleased at all. Aaron Middleton looked about as benign as a man could on the outside, bland and pale, a computer nerd straight from central casting, but Bryant had glimpsed some streak of menace lurking below the surface, ready to be triggered. He could almost hear the kid ticking whenever they were in the same room.

A dulcet chime alerted Bryant that the computer had something to tell him. He brought it up on the central monitor. The program had been slowly getting better at anticipating the user's needs, making mistakes at first but then correcting them with little or no input from Bryant. It knew they were searching for the girl. It had been the program that had not only flagged the girl's name on an airline reservation—which was simple enough, really—but also had identified the NSA activity as directly related to her.

Apparently, the program now had something else it thought Bryant wanted to know.

Information scrolled across the screen. Emma Middleton's life story unfolded before his eyes. Every pay stub from every job, every place she'd ever paid rent or had mail delivered. Names and addresses of relatives. Every scrap of information that had ever been collected and digitized.

Again, this was not beyond the capabilities of intelligence programs already in existence. It was exactly how the NSA's mainframe had tracked the girl. But as Bryant watched the computer monitor, he realized yet again he was seeing something different. The program was sorting the information, discarding some bits of data, rearranging others. It was doing the work normally done by a human analyst who sifted the raw data to come up with educated guesses and likely scenarios.

The program knew what Bryant wanted and traveled down informational back alleys, linking together unlikely scraps of information that might not be obvious to others. It had its guess and showed it to Bryant.

Bryant picked up the phone and dialed Cavanaugh. "You'll never make it to LaGuardia in time to catch her, but I'm arranging a charter flight for you and your men. I know where she's going."

Francis gulped for breath. He'd run all the way to the gate. They were still boarding when he arrived. He spotted the suitcase first, registering a fraction of a second later it was Emma carrying it. She fell into line with the last few stragglers boarding the plane.

Francis ducked into the magazine shop across from the gate. Emma obviously wanted to be shed of him, so she could still bolt if he surprised her before boarding. He pretended to browse the magazines, keeping one eye on the gate.

He spotted the new issue of *Adventure Travel*. On the cover was a gorgeous woman in a bikini, snorkeling underwater with a spear gun. The water was an impossible blue, and colorful fish swarmed around her. The issue would eventually arrive at his apartment, but it was a long flight from New York to Los Angeles, so he hastily paid the cashier, then jogged to the gate.

The door was just starting to close when Francis arrived. The gate attendant frowned at him but took his boarding pass and waved him through.

The flight attendant in the first-class cabin looked him up and down. He remembered he was wearing yesterday's outfit, clothes he'd actually slept in. He probably wasn't coming off as first-class cabin material, but his boarding pass spoke for itself. She managed a welcoming smile and gestured toward his aisle seat four rows back.

Emma sat in the window seat, pensively looking out the little portal.

In his head, Francis had rehearsed a few different ways to do this. He hadn't had a lot of practice making an entrance, and the best he could come up with was to flop down into the seat next to her and say, "I've never flown first class before. Kind of makes multiple near-death experiences all worth it."

Her head snapped around, eyes shooting wide. Surprise instantly turned into acute annoyance. "What the hell are you doing here?"

"Apparently, I have a ticket."

"Idiot."

"You know, I did chase you down in a taxi when those guys grabbed you," Francis said. "I'm not saying I rescued you just to be thanked . . . but it would be nice to be thanked."

"I *was* thanking you, dumbass. Why do you think I bought you a plane ticket? When the credit card flags what we're doing, they'll stop looking for you in New York because they'll think you're flying with me to California. Except now you *are* flying with me to California. Sort of undermines the whole strategy."

Ah.

"Well," Francis said. "I . . . uh . . . did not know that."

She crossed her eyes at him. "Duh."

"You still could have said something," Francis insisted. "Waking up to find you gone was . . . disconcerting."

"Disconcerting?"

"Very."

"Probably I was trying to avoid this exact conversation."

"Yeah, well, that's not cool." He remembered Enid saying something similar about leaving a note so she could avoid an awkward conversation.

Emma considered him a moment, softened her voice, and said, "Listen, Frankie—"

"I don't really go by—"

"—the thing is I'm sorry if this isn't *cool*," Emma said. "You seem like a decent regular guy. I got you into something you didn't want to be part of. I get it. But as I think you've noticed, this hasn't been exactly *cool* for me either. Quite obviously, I have some shit going on. I did my best to get you out of it, but you fucked that up. Okay, so I didn't let you in on the plan, and that's on me too. But I have very important life-and-death shit on my plate right now, and I don't have time to babysit you."

"Who's helping you?" Francis asked.

"I don't need anyone's help."

"We've already seen that's not true," Francis said. "Here's a radical idea. Yeah, I didn't ask for this, but here I am. So maybe you tell me what's going on, and I can help. Look, I help you, I help *myself*, right? If you just vanish, God knows how I explain myself, but if I help you solve whatever this is, then that clears you to come explain to the police that I'm just some dumb schmuck who found a suitcase in an alley. How about that?"

She shook her head, laughing in that way people do when nothing at all is funny. "Forget it. I'm talking to a brick wall. Just sit back and relax, okay? It's a long flight."

"Fine with me." Francis showed her the copy of *Adventure Travel*. "I have a magazine."

13

The light in the room rose to 15 percent. Enough to see but not enough to jar the sleeper's waking experience. The sound of rain and flowing water rose very gently and slowly in volume through hidden high-definition speakers. Climate control brought the interior temperature up two degrees.

Gently, Middleton's eyes opened.

Memories seeped back slowly. He'd suddenly felt so exhausted, so overwhelmed, like the entire world was squeezing in on him tighter and tighter. He didn't want to go back on the medication, but maybe he'd have to. He would have shut down completely if Meredith hadn't been there.

She'd taken over the decision-making process, told the movers to bring in *all* the furniture and to set it up. If it took all night, then so be it. She hadn't wanted them to come back and create a whole new clusterfuck—her word. The movers had worked fast, and Meredith had taken Middleton to the one room that didn't need any furniture.

The indoor pool was huge. The glass ceiling could be tinted almost opaque or slide back completely to allow natural sunlight. In the corner of the pool complex was a large, built-in whirlpool bath. Meredith had rapidly brought the whirlpool up to temperature, and Middleton had sat on the edge, shoes and socks off, trousers rolled up to the knees, and let the warm water soothe him.

And Meredith had talked. Not about anything important. Siblings. Old college roommates. The time she nearly bowled a three hundred game. Most importantly, she asked him no questions, made no conversational demands on him. Her voice washed over him as soothing as the warm water swirling around his ankles. Everything about her—her light touch, musical voice, the faint smell of citrus from her shampoo—was a balm to him.

Eventually, the text came that the movers had completed their task. He had only the vaguest memory of Meredith taking him by the arm and leading him to his new bedroom, pulling the covers up to his chin. Blissful silence and darkness and he'd closed his eyes and left the chaos of the day behind him.

Now he sat up and took in his surroundings. The lighting came up another 10 percent.

The walls were perfectly white and smooth. A modern easy chair sat in one corner, his suit jacket thrown over the back. He got out of bed. The carpet was soft and comfortable under his bare feet.

He walked toward the bathroom, which sensed him coming. The lights came on. The heating coils beneath the floor brought the tile up to a comfortable temperature. *These are the system presets*, Middleton realized. As he lived in the house and got the feel of it, he would tweak all the automated systems to suit him.

Middleton used the bathroom. Showered. Again, the water temperature was factory preset. He decided to leave it for now.

The door to his walk-in closet had been designed to seem just another stretch of wall. It slid to the side as he approached. The closet was the size of a two-car garage. Everything was perfectly organized—suits, casual wear, shoes, underclothes, and socks. He approached a rack of tracksuits. Middleton despised exercise, but found the suits comfortable. He selected a black one with white stripes down the sleeves and pant legs. Sneakers. Ankle socks.

Something bothered him, and he wasn't sure what.

"What time is it?"

"It is 9:39 A.M., Pacific standard time," said a disembodied voice. The voice was male, a calm, nonthreatening baritone. Another factory preset. Yes, that would need to be changed as soon as possible. Middleton didn't like that guy at all.

He figured it out. Usually by this time in the morning, there were already a dozen things that needed his attention. Meredith must still be keeping the hordes at bay for his benefit.

He got momentarily lost trying to find the kitchen, but the fresh aroma of hazelnut drew him on. He found a white ceramic cup in the cabinet next to the dispenser, placed it under the nozzle, and pushed the button. It dispensed a cup of fresh black coffee. He sipped. Perfect.

"What's your name, computer?"

"Adam."

"Is that factory preset too?"

"Adam is the default start mode name assigned to your household system."

Marion Parkes had designed the system for him, and Middleton felt a quick stab of regret, thinking of the man. But it had to be done, hadn't it? Parkes and the others? He couldn't control what they might do, who they could speak to. Middleton felt the old panic start to rise up again and immediately put Parkes out of his mind. That was the past. This was the here and now. He focused exclusively on his coffee, sipped, enjoyed the aroma.

"Adam, where is Meredith?"

"Biometric identification has yet to be calibrated," Adam said.

Okay, so he'd find her the old-fashioned way. The house wasn't *that* big.

Except it was, and was designed to *seem* even bigger, hallways curving in such a way to foster a sense of many areas, ceilings vaulted or slanted in such a way to emphasize space. He passed spare bedrooms and a library. He found an enormous atrium, sunlight flooding in from above, and circled around it, finally finding the formal living room. Grotesquely expensive modern art covered the white walls. Middleton lacked appreciation for most art. The paintings here had been chosen for their rigidly symmetrical patterns and unobtrusive color palettes.

Meredith curled on a white leather couch, her shoes on the floor. She must have been equally exhausted, he realized. Constantly being the buffer between him and the rest of the world in its entirety would likely drain anyone.

He turned to leave her in peace.

"It's okay." She sat up slowly, pushing loose strands of hair out of her face. "I'm awake."

"There's coffee."

"Good. Can you show me where the kitchen is?"

"Follow me."

In the kitchen, she sat on a stool at the big island, sipping coffee and tapping like mad at her smartphone. "I've canceled everything nonessential and told them we'll get back to them about rescheduling when we can. Your morning board meeting has been pushed to after lunch, but if you want to video in, then you won't need to leave—"

"Hey."

She looked up at him, the question in her eyes.

"It's okay. You can just drink your coffee," Middleton said. "You don't have to hit the ground running just this once."

Meredith laughed.

He smiled too even though he didn't get the joke. She had the best laugh. "What?"

"I don't think you understand my job," she said. "It's easy for you. All you have to do is be a genius."

His smile faded. "I make it hard, don't I? Your job would be plenty tough enough with anyone else, but it's something extra with me, isn't it? Probably not what you bargained for at all."

"Oh no, I . . . I mean, I'm not complaining. Please don't think . . . I mean—"

"I know. I just mean I *get* it. I want you to know I couldn't do it without you. Thank you. Now, am I the boss or not?"

"You're the boss."

"Then I say you can enjoy a cup of coffee and put work on hold. You don't even have to drink it fast. Then when you're finished, you can go back to being a frantic crazy person."

With exaggerated slowness, she set aside the smartphone, her eyes still on Middleton. Then she took up the coffee cup and slurped loudly.

"You're very funny."

She smiled, craned her neck to look around as if seeing the kitchen for the first time, white except for the gleaming stainless steel appliances. "Everything is so white."

"Blank."

"Blank?"

"I don't really think of it as white," Middleton said. "I think of it as blank. I didn't want to live in a place that felt . . . cluttered."

"Do you like it?"

"Like what?"

"Your new house."

It was such an obvious question that Middleton felt stunned by it. The house hadn't been built to be liked but to serve his specific and peculiar needs. Wherever possible, the house had been automated. No live-in servants. People would come to clean or make repairs when he was out. They would be gone before his return. Likewise, he would find his kitchen magically restocked when he wasn't looking. Gourmet meals would be assembled elsewhere and stored in his walk-in freezer and prepared with all the ease the most technologically modern kitchen could provide.

All so Aaron Middleton would not have to see or talk to or interact with any other human being he didn't want to.

That he might like the house would be a bonus, he supposed. But the point was to preserve as much of his sanity as possible.

"I think I like it," he told Meredith. "I'll need to live with it a little while."

She sipped coffee.

"Two things."

She raised an eyebrow.

"First, arrange to have Mable brought out. I should have thought of that before now, actually."

"Of course." Meredith reached for her smartphone.

"*After* you finish your coffee."

She jerked her hand back dramatically, refocused her attention on the coffee cup.

"Second, I believe I saw some kind of blockhouse across the lawn on our way in last night."

"Ah. Yes. Well. I've been assured you won't be able to see it at all once the shrubs fill in."

"That's not really the point."

"It's not?" That innocent look on her face, so cute.

But Middleton refused to be diverted. "I don't remember authorizing that."

"Oh no. No, no. You did." She started reaching for her smartphone again as if it were a security blanket but stopped herself. "You don't remember?"

"I do not."

"Well, you know. You maybe didn't notice." She squirmed on the stool, not looking at Middleton now. "I mean, there was so much stuff, so much paperwork for this house and permits and everything, it was probably just stuck in with a bunch of other stuff and you signed it without even realizing."

"I see."

"This coffee is really good." She sipped.

"What's it for?"

"The blockhouse?"

Middleton frowned. "What have we been talking about?"

"It's for the security guards."

Middleton felt the rising anxiety like a knot in his chest.

"There is a path on the other side of the blockhouse that leads to a separate parking area," she said hastily. "You won't even see them come and go."

"Why do they need to be there at all?" He'd spent millions of dollars to get away from people only to discover there was a building full of them across his front lawn.

Meredith sighed. "You still don't understand who you are. Do you know what happens to the corporation's stock if something happens to you? And the insurance company won't sign off on our keyman policy unless you have appropriate security."

Middleton still couldn't believe how fast it had happened. Founding the company with almost no start-up capital, incorporating, going public. He'd been on magazine covers. Television. The public knew his name now alongside Gates and Jobs.

Too much. Too fast. The knot in his chest twisted. So much

that could be taken away. It had all been so much simpler when he'd had nothing.

Meredith lay a cool hand on his forearm. The stress leaked out of him.

She squeezed. "You are okay."

Yes. He was okay. The blockhouse and the security guards were nothing, really. As Meredith had explained, he would never see them, or, if he did, then that meant he had bigger problems, right? It was the idea that he hadn't known. That it was out of his control.

But Meredith had explained. She was right. She was always right. If he had her, he'd be fine. *She must never leave me*, he decided. Never. He made a mental note not to say that out loud in exactly that way. It would come off a little creepy. Still, it was true. His world would cease to function without her.

But she wouldn't leave him. Middleton trusted her as he trusted no other person on the planet. Others had betrayed him. Even those closest to him. Meredith never would.

"Well, then," he said. "Maybe I'll just have another cup of coffee."

That crooked smile, the one when she was being playful. "Maybe more caffeine's not what you need right now, champ."

14

They arrived for their layover on time in Minneapolis. Emma walked ahead of Francis as they disembarked, a tight grip on the alligator suitcase.

Francis scrambled to catch up. "The connection is the other way."

"Knock yourself out, Frankie," she said. "I'm going this way." She followed a sign that said GROUND TRANSPORTATION.

"I don't understand," he said. "I thought we were going to Los Angeles."

"And that's what everyone else will think too," she said. "I chose the flight based on the layover."

"Wait, so you're not getting on the next flight?"

"What a good listener you are."

He followed her through baggage claim and out to the sidewalk at the loading zone.

Emma turned on him abruptly. "This is where we part ways, Frankie."

"Just like that?"

"Like I told you," she said, "you weren't supposed to come with me. Go home. Tell the police your story. They'll see you're harmless enough. They'll believe you. I'm sorry I got you into all this. Really. Go home."

She turned and walked toward long-term parking and didn't look back.

Francis stood a moment, thinking she might turn around, not

even sure if he wanted her to. He tried not to feel foolish and failed. He'd made one bad decision on top of another, starting with a suitcase that was none of his business and ending with trying to help someone who didn't want to be helped.

Francis slowly lowered himself onto a nearby bench. *Every man secretly yearns to be called harmless*, he thought sarcastically. *She's right. Just go home.*

To what? Enid was gone. Emma was probably right that he'd be able to explain himself satisfactorily to the police, but what about work? Would Resnick fire him, and if he did, would that be better or worse? There was not really so much to go back to after all.

A rumble of an engine. A car pulled up and parked right in front of Francis's bench. It was an automobile from the early 1980s, an ugly green, the word *Oldsmobile* on the grille. The window was down. He looked inside. Emma sat hunched over the wheel, looking straight ahead. She glanced reluctantly at Francis, then looked forward again, shaking her head. She sat like that a long ten seconds.

She looked back at Francis finally, sighed, and said, "Well, shit. Get in, then."

Francis didn't need to be asked twice. He jumped in and closed the door. "I didn't know you were from Minneapolis."

"I'm not."

"Why is your car here?"

She put the Oldsmobile into gear and pulled forward. "Not my car."

Oh . . . just . . . hell.

"What do you mean they weren't on board?" Gunn stood in the number 5 terminal at LAX. He'd expected his agents to be coming toward him with the girl and Berringer in handcuffs. Instead, he was on this irritating phone call.

"They weren't there," said the agent on the other end of the line. "Agents boarded the plane to double-check. A quick call to the ticket desk at MSP International confirms they didn't board the connecting flight."

Gunn cursed a blue streak inside his head. *Stupid, stupid, stupid.* There was no excuse. He'd been foolish and lazy. When the girl had booked the flight to California, Gunn had naturally assumed she was on her way to address unfinished business with Aaron Middleton. Gunn thought that in her haste, she'd finally slipped up. But he was the one who'd botched it. He didn't intend to let it happen again.

"Find them," Gunn said. "Check into anything she might be doing in Minneapolis, but obviously she could be headed anywhere. Check the bus and train stations and all the car rental places. Just *find* them."

The 1982 Oldsmobile Cutlass Supreme glided down Highway 169 to Highway 60 and took a turn west on Interstate 90 toward Sioux Falls. Stops had been quick—bathroom and fast food.

"Because older cars are easier to hot-wire," Emma had explained.

"Oh." It had occurred to Francis that if a person had decided to take up auto theft, then why not steal something that was actually a little more stylish? Or at least comfortable. The Oldsmobile rattled loudly. The AM/FM radio didn't work. A vague odor of old cigarettes.

In Sioux Falls, they took Interstate 29 south. Lots of farm country. Cows.

Francis dozed.

122 • VICTOR GISCHLER

The car hit a bump and jostled him awake sometime later. They'd left the interstate far behind, and the Oldsmobile now rattled down a dirt road. Trees had risen up on both sides of the road.

Francis sat up, rubbed his eyes. "Where are we?"

"Almost there."

The road ran alongside a stream that was almost big enough to be called a river, but not quite. Another dirt road even narrower and bumpier broke away from the stream, and Emma followed it into the forest, poking along under ten miles per hour. This went on for a few minutes until the road curved, then opened into a wide clearing. There was a two-story clapboard house with a wrap-around porch, a large barn with faded red paint beyond. To one side of the house was a line of junk cars, rusted from the decades, weeds growing high around deflated tires. An assortment of hubcaps leaned against one side of the porch, and on the porch itself was the husk of an old motorcycle, either half-stripped or half-assembled, depending on your point of view.

Emma parked in front of the house and got out, taking the suitcase with her.

Francis stood a moment, taking in his surroundings. "This isn't what I was expecting."

Emma rolled her eyes. "Really? What were you expecting, exactly? The Waldorf Astoria? Sorry we can't all be sophisticated New Yorkers like you." She headed for the house, shaking her head.

He sighed, following after her. "I'm from Ohio."

15

Francis and Emma followed the porch around the corner to a side door, stepping over motorcycle parts as they went. She pulled a single key from her jeans pocket and unlocked the door, led Francis into a large kitchen.

It felt stuffy and still, like a place uninhabited for a long time. Mismatched appliances, an iron potbellied stove next to a range from the 1980s and a fridge ten years older than that. Kitchen table with lighthouse salt-and-pepper shakers in the middle. Lots of Formica. Last year's calendar showing an old-time sailing ship. It was stuck to the side of the fridge with a SEE ROCK CITY magnet.

Emma walked straight to a cabinet over the sink, opened it, and pulled out a half-empty bottle of Wild Turkey. She opened it and titled the bottle back, gulping loudly. She coughed, wiped her mouth with the back of her hand. Her eyes slid to Francis's face. "Long drive."

"A long couple of days," he said.

She thought about that, nodded. "Yeah." She held the bottle out to him.

"I'm really more of a cabernet sauvignon kind of guy." A weak smile, half joking.

"Could you just not be a pussy right now, please?" She thrust the bottle at him again.

Francis took it. He hadn't much experience with hard liquor. Maybe if he just gulped it quickly, he could get it over with. He tossed back a mouthful, then swallowed, but it went down wrong, scorching the back of his throat. He spasmed, almost coughing it up, but clamped his lips tight to keep from spitting it all out. Doing that made him gag and choke, and he coughed it out through his nose instead. It *burned* and splashed down his chin and the front of his shirt mixed with mucous. He coughed and coughed until he finally got control of himself, then wiped the whiskey snot from his chin and lips with his shirtsleeve.

Emma stared at him with her mouth hanging open. For a second it could have gone either way.

Then she threw her head back and laughed loudly and long. It was the first time Francis had seen her like this, carefree, all the pent-up stress leaking from her. Not a prissy, demure laugh. Full-throated and uninhibited. She wiped tears from her eyes, blew out a long cathartic sigh.

"You really know how to wow a girl, Frankie."

"Francis."

"Listen, there's no delicate way to put this," she said, "but you stink."

"You mean that literally, don't you?"

"Don't take it personally," she said, "but you slept in those clothes, and I think you know I'm right."

He looked down at himself. "Yeah, I can't really argue with you."

"There's a shower down the hall. You look like you're about Dwayne's size, so we can get you some clean clothes. His room is next to the bathroom, and you can help yourself."

"Dwayne?"

"The guy my sister started seeing when she left her husband," Emma told him.

"Is this somebody who's going to walk in while I'm trying on his clothes and beat my ass?" Francis asked. "Because I'd like to avoid that."

"No," Emma said. "He's dead."

"Oh. I'm sorry."

"Don't be," she said. "He was an asshole. Towels on the rack over the sink."

Everything in the bathroom was old—chipped pedestal sink, small toilet, and a clawfoot tub with a floral shower curtain that circled the whole thing. The pressure was good, and the hot water stung his skin in the best way possible. Francis hadn't realized how gross he'd felt before until he was suddenly clean.

He dried off, wrapped the towel around himself. He opened the bathroom door a crack and peeked out. Then he felt self-conscious about being self-conscious. He'd seen her in a towel, after all, so what was the big deal? He still felt self-conscious.

He darted quickly from the bathroom to the bedroom with the dead man's clothes.

It was a small room with two windows that overlooked the barn. As in the rest of the house, the furnishings were old without quite being antiques. A double bed, neatly made with a patchwork quilt. A scuffed and scratched desk covered with baseball trophies ranging from high school to someplace called Kilian Community College. Posters, cheaply framed in plastic, hung on the wall, generic scenes of various natural wonders, the Grand Canyon, Monument Valley, Yellowstone.

There was also a framed eight-by-ten photo of a couple in their early thirties sitting together on a Harley-Davidson. Maybe it was the motorcycle now in pieces on the front porch. Francis assumed the guy on the Harley was the asshole. Dwayne. You couldn't tell it from the picture—a big smile, hands gripping the handlebars, close haircut, three-day stubble. Maybe a couple of years older than the woman who had a reasonable resemblance to Emma. The sister, Francis guessed. Yellow sundress hiked up, flip-flops. One hand went around Dwayne's waist, the other up for a shy wave. But compared to Emma, there was something softer in the face, the eyes less intense, as if she were still willing to give the world one more chance. There was some kind of drive-in burger joint in the background, and Francis felt like this photo was maybe taken on some vacation.

He went through Dwayne's dresser and small closet for clothes. Faded Levi's jeans, white socks, and Nike sneakers. Emma had been right. He and Dwayne wore the same size. Finding a shirt was a bit more of a challenge. Dwayne *really* liked flannel. Francis didn't. There was also an assortment of black shirts with various hair metal bands. He couldn't bring himself to wear a Poison or Ratt T-shirt. A guy had to draw the line somewhere.

And then he found it, all the way to one side in the closet. An unworn western shirt, the tag still on it. It looked like something from a Brooks & Dunn music video. Black with red piping and red embroidery on the shoulders and cuffs. Mother-of-pearl snap buttons. It was terrible.

Francis couldn't resist.

He slipped it on, felt himself grin as he buttoned it up.

His eyes slid to the door. Hanging on a hook on the back was a leather jacket. He took it down, looked it over. Francis guessed this might have been Dwayne's pride and joy, that he knew just exactly how cool he looked zooming down the road on his motorcycle with the jacket on. It was just worn enough to look cool, a simple collared jacket with a zipper up the middle. He shrugged into it.

A knock at the door. "Decent?" Emma's voice from the other side.

"Yeah. Come in."

She entered and was about to say something but stopped when

she saw him. A warm smile spread on her lips. "You don't look like you."

"I'm afraid to ask if that's a compliment or not."

"You look less . . . forgettable."

"Please. Stop. All this flattery is going to swell my head."

She'd changed too. Francis realized she wore the same yellow sundress from the photograph. Except with combat boots. On her it worked. Angry punk girl goes on a picnic.

"Come on," she said. "I need your help."

Francis followed her down the hall, past a myriad of family photos on the wall. Some were more pictures of Emma's sister and Dwayne. Others were old and faded, previous generations and distant relations. One of the photos caught Francis's eye, a broad-shouldered man in an army uniform, buzz cut and sergeant's stripes. Two little girls stood on either side of him, waist high.

"Was your dad in the army?" Francis asked.

She glanced back without stopping. "Yeah."

The door at the end of the hall opened on a narrow stairway that twisted down into a basement. At the bottom of the stairs, Emma groped above her head in the darkness until she found a pull string and yanked on the single bulb. The walls were bare natural rock, floor smooth and wooden, thick beams crossing the ceiling overhead. A threadbare easy chair, a small desk, a single bed. Cave-like but livable.

"My sister said I could stay as long as I wanted after Dwayne died," Emma explained. "She travels a lot. She's in Mexico with some new guy right now. Anyway, I don't get mail delivered here or anything, so it's not likely I can be tracked here. Not yet anyway."

"Can't they find you through your sister?"

"Maybe, but not so far. She didn't divorce her first husband, just ran off. Found Dwayne and moved in with him, not getting legally married or anything, no paperwork at city hall. When Dwayne choked on a chicken bone, she just buried him in the woods out back of the barn. Dwayne's disability checks are direct deposit and all the bills are on auto pay, so she just let it ride."

Francis waited for her to say she was joking.

She didn't.

"Help me with this." She headed for a lump against the far wall, covered by a blanket. "It's heavy."

She flung the blanket back and revealed a large footlocker. It was shut with a sturdy-looking combination lock. She grabbed the handle on one end. "Get the other side, will you?"

She hadn't lied. It was heavy. They muscled it up the stairs and back down the hall, pausing in the kitchen to set it on the table.

Francis said, "I hope you appreciate I've traveled halfway across the nation and am now lifting this heavy-ass box of lost Nazi gold or whatever it is, and that I've been gentleman enough not to pester you for a lot of details about where we are, where we're going, what it is you're trying to do, why a suitcase full of underwear is so important, why thugs want to kidnap you, and why the government wants to arrest you."

"Well, Frankie, if you recall, it was your idea to tag along, not mine."

"Francis."

She opened the refrigerator and pulled out a six-pack of Coors Light. She broke one off and handed the can to Francis. "Empty that can, please."

"But—" He shrugged and took the can, popped it open, and sipped.

"Jesus, gun it, will you?" She popped one for herself, titled it back, and chugged it until it was empty. "Like that."

Francis took a deep breath and began chugging the beer. He finished, turned his head and burped, tried to stifle it, and it came out his nose. "Damn. Again." It didn't burn as badly as the Wild Turkey, but it still made his eyes mist up.

"Okay, grab your end of the footlocker again," Emma said. "And bring the empty can."

She put the rest of the six-pack on top of the footlocker, and they carried it outside. They set it on a wide stump near the line of rusted cars. She broke off another can of beer and handed it to him. "Go."

He balked. "Uh . . ."

Emma rolled her eyes. "Geez, okay, I'll help."

She popped it open and guzzled half, then handed the rest to Francis, who finished the can. She took the three empties and headed for the cars. She lined them up on the hood of a pickup truck from the early sixties, the Chevy logo prominent between the headlights. When she came back, she bent and spun the combination lock until it popped open.

She opened the footlocker and came out with a pistol. Francis looked past her and into the locker. Guns. Lots of them.

"What is that?" He nodded at the pistol in her hand.

"Sig Sauer P-250 subcompact .380."

"Oh, that's . . . Is that good?"

"We'll see."

She reached into the footlocker for a magazine, checked to see if it was full, then slapped it home into the butt of the pistol, chambered a round, and spread her legs into a shooter's stance. She flipped off the safety and squeezed the trigger.

The sharp crack of the gunshot made Francis flinch. He looked at the beer cans. They hadn't budged.

Emma's lip curled into a snarl. "Shit."

She spread her legs another inch apart, squeezed one eye shut tight, sighted down the barrel with the other. She took a deep breath and let it out slowly. The pistol bucked in her hands, and the first beer can spun away off the truck's hood with a metallic *tink*. She fired twice more quickly, and the other two cans leaped into the air.

"That's more like it." Emma reached for another Coors Light. "We need more cans."

She and Francis finished the six-pack, and Emma blasted them off the hood of the truck without missing a shot. She went and picked them up and lined them across the hood again.

When she came back to Francis, she offered him the pistol, butt first. "Your turn. Get a fresh magazine out of the footlocker."

Francis didn't reach for it. "I'm not sure how to work the thing."

She made a trigger-pulling motion with one finger. "Pull the trigger here." She gestured toward the end of the barrel. "Death comes out that end."

Francis wasn't convinced.

"Hold on." She went back into the footlocker and came out with a revolver. "Smith & Wesson .38 police special." She swung out the cylinder to check the load, then snapped it back into position with a flick of her wrist. "You just cock the hammer back and then shoot. Revolvers are a bit simpler for rookies." She handed it to him. "Just make sure you keep it pointed downrange."

He took the gun tentatively. As with the pistol he'd held briefly in Central Park, Francis was surprised by the weight of it. The gun was old but obviously well cared for. He spread his legs a little, trying to copy Emma's stance, and held the revolver out with both hands. He aimed for the middle can, thinking if he missed a little, he still might hit one of the others.

The gun kicked when he squeezed the trigger, an unexpected adrenaline rush of pleasure surging through him.

He missed the cans.

And instead shot out the headlight of the next junk car over, a mint-green Buick Skylark with plenty of body damage.

Emma gave him the side-eye. "You were aiming for that, right?"

Francis smiled weakly. "Yes?"

He shot until he'd emptied the gun, sometimes digging up the turf in front of the pickup, other times the shots going high and vanishing forever into the forest. Emma reloaded the revolver for him, advised him on his stance, breathing, grip. Francis shot an entire box of ammo and never hit a can.

"For crying out loud, don't they have guns in Ohio?"

Francis shrugged. "It wasn't exactly a hobby in my family."

"Let's try something else." She went to the Ford and reached into the tall grass between junk cars. She came out with a rusty paint can and set it on the pickup's hood amid the beer cans.

Emma came back and said, "Okay, first thing is a bigger target." She knelt in front of the footlocker. She removed the top shelf, revealing a compartment underneath. With the shortened barrel and folding stock, the shotgun still barely fit into the footlocker. She took it out and began thumbing in double-aught shells.

"That's a little big, isn't it?"

Emma grinned. "Nothing exceeds like excess." She handed him the shotgun. "This is a Remington Model 870 Express twelve gauge with a six-plus-one-shell capacity."

"*Yadda yadda numbers* and *blah blah* is what I just heard."

"Pay attention," she said. "Pump a shell in, and then thumb the safety forward to fire. *F* for forward and *F* for fire if that helps you remember."

"Got it."

"Brace it against your shoulder firmly," she said. "It kicks like a son of a bitch. Take a couple of steps forward."

He took three steps toward the paint can.

"More."

Francis took two more steps.

"Now aim," she told him. "People think you don't have to aim a shotgun, but you do. Squeeze the trigger, don't jerk it."

Francis squeezed.

The explosion made the earlier pistol fire seem like popcorn farts, the kick pushing him back a step. The paint can erupted in metal chunks and paint, spinning and splattering the pickup white.

Emma came up behind him, patted his back. "That's your weapon. Aim directly for the middle of your target's torso. If you're off a little, you'll still hit something."

"Something?"

Emma shrugged. "An arm?"

"I don't want to shoot anyone."

"You're a nice guy, Frankie," she said. "Whoever's trying to kill you probably won't be."

16

The charter flight landed in Sioux Falls with a dozen of them—Cavanaugh, Ike, and Ernie plus the extra gunmen Cavanaugh had hired on for the gig. Bryant's information had been incomplete, but he'd told Cavanaugh that what they *did* have was solid.

Bryant had tried to explain how some computer program something something certain parameters and something something narrowing a search radius. Bryant had sounded very impressed with what he was saying. Cavanaugh wasn't.

"Just cut to the chase," Cavanaugh had told the man.

According to Bryant, the girl had a sister in Elk Point, South Dakota. She left the usual footprint on the grid—credit card charges, mail delivered to a small ranch home, checking account, phone bill, the works. Then about fourteen months ago, everything went dark. Like the sister fell off the face off the earth.

Her final week on the grid included multiple ATM withdrawals in Canton, South Dakota, leaving her checking account balance at $1.56, two meals at Laurie's Café on Sixth Street, a fill-up at a gas station three miles north of town. She'd also used her Visa to buy $144.78 worth of cleaning supplies at the area Walmart.

Okay, you don't buy that much cleaning stuff if you're on vacation, Cavanaugh thought. And there were closer Walmarts and gas stations to Elk Point. So that begged the question: Why Canton?

And so Cavanaugh and his crew found themselves in a three-car motorcade, heading south on I-29. Bryant had purchased a sedan and two SUVs through a dummy corporation to avoid messing with a rental car company again.

An hour later, while Ike and Ernie questioned some of the shop owners on Main Street, Cavanaugh found himself in Laurie's Café, talking to a haggard woman in jeans and a South Dakota State Jackrabbits T-shirt. A name tag said BRENDA. She leaned on the lunch counter, considering the photos Cavanaugh had given her, chewing her gum like she was trying to punish it.

It was between lunch and dinner, and all the tables behind him were empty. The only patron was an old-timer in a feed cap, three stools down at the counter. He nursed a cup of black coffee and read a newspaper, a pair of half-glasses perched on the end of his nose.

"I don't know this one." Brenda tapped the photo of the girl. "Maybe the other one. Picture's not too good."

"Yeah, it's a few years old," Cavanaugh said. The photo of the sister had been a not-very-good driver's license photo. Did anyone ever really like their driver's license photo? "Take another look."

Brenda squinted at the picture with renewed effort.

Cavanaugh's crew had copies of the photo and were showing it around other places. Cavanaugh had a good feeling about the café, so he forced himself to be patient.

"I think yeah, maybe," Brenda said. "But not for a while. I don't remember ever having a conversation with her or anything."

"About how long ago?" Cavanaugh asked.

She *tsked*. "I dunno. Not recent. Gary, look at this fella's pictures."

The old-timer grunted without looking up from his newspaper.

Cavanaugh moved down the counter next to Gary. He laid the pictures next to each other near his cup of coffee and tapped the one of the sister. "Brenda says she's been in here."

Gary glanced quickly at the picture, then back to his newspaper. "Never seen her."

Cavanaugh frowned. "Maybe take a better look, huh, friend?"

"I looked enough. Never seen her."

Shit.

Cavanaugh looked down at his watch and wondered if the others were having better luck. The longer they putzed around, showing pictures to the yokels, the longer the girl would have to run off to wherever she wanted. Sure, maybe she was holed up somewhere. Or maybe she was halfway to Mexico. Maybe anything.

"Seen the other one, though."

Cavanaugh's head jerked up again. "Excuse me?"

"Weird hair and the nose ring and all," Gary said. "Don't see a lot of that around here. Sort of left an impression."

"Sir, this is really helpful," Cavanaugh said. "It's important I find her. Anything you can tell me would be greatly appreciated."

Gary sipped coffee, still didn't look up from the newspaper. "You police or something?"

"Nothing like that." Cavanaugh had learned his lesson and had prepared a story. "I work for a law office in Sioux Falls. The girls are sisters, and their mother has unfortunately passed away. We're trying to locate them before the reading of the will."

Gary shook his head. "Sad stuff. Sorry to hear it."

"Can you tell me how you know her?"

"Wouldn't say I *know* her, but I saw her when I was delivering furnace oil down at Dwayne Truman's place. She was there. Like I said, sorta stood out."

"Could I get that address?"

"Not really an address kind of place," Gary said. "They live in the sticks down near Newton Hills."

"Newton Hills." Cavanaugh pulled his notepad and pen from his jacket. "That's a town?"

"State park," Brenda said. She was at the other end of the counter but still listening.

"Could you show me where it is?" Cavanaugh asked.

"Draw you a map, I guess," Gary said.

"That would be fantastic." Cavanaugh flipped over a paper place mat. "How about this?"

Gary took Cavanaugh's pen, paused before he began to draw. "Might ought to be worth a slice of pie, wouldn't it?"

"Brenda, bring the man a slice of pie on me," Cavanaugh said. "And I'll have one too."

The four men in the blockhouse were all cops. Guard duty was easy work. These rich guys, all of them thought they needed protection. Because the universe revolved around them, right? And 99 percent of the time, nothing happened, and Ron Kowolski could simply catch up on his reading. He liked novels with guys wielding swords and wizards and all that junk. Anything that was an escape. After twenty-five years on the force, he wasn't in the mood for realism.

The other three guards were all still serving. The guard duty gig was a bit of moonlighting. They were younger and unmarried and stashing away some extra cash. Ron had never married either, and while extra cash was nice, it was just good to get out of the house and do something.

Just not something strenuous.

The blockhouse setup was pretty simple. Three rooms. A lounge with chairs and a TV. That's where the other three guys were now. A bathroom. And the monitor room where Ron sat now. He'd read a few pages in his novel, then look up at the security monitors that showed various areas around the property, and then go back to his novel. Repeat until one of the other guys came to take a turn.

Ron glanced at the monitors and saw the JetVan entering the main gate. He watched a moment, knowing there were only two ways through. Anyone pulling up to the gate could call. Ron—or whatever guard was on duty—would answer the phone. If the visitor was on the list, they got through. If not, then not.

The list was god emperor general grand pooh-bah of who got through the gate. If the pope showed up and wasn't on the list, he didn't get through. Not rocket science.

Or if the car had the right kind of electronic thingy, the gate would open automatically. People who were supposed to be here had the electronic thingy. There was technically a third way through the gate. Next to the phone was a keypad, and if somebody had the right code, they could get through. But the codes were only for people who had been approved for an electronic thingy and were waiting for the thingy to be installed, and according to Ron's list, there was nobody waiting to have a thingy installed.

The gate opened, and Ron watched the JetVan pass through. He followed it from monitor to monitor as it passed the vineyard and finally rolled up to the big house.

It let out the primary resident—Middleton—and that woman who was his sidekick. Ron snapped his fingers, trying to remember her name. Meredith Vines. Yeah, that was it, real ball-breaker. Those young female corporate types were all ball-breakers, trying to prove whatever they were trying to prove. They all bent over backward to look nice, but if you mentioned it—*whack*—broken balls.

The Vines woman paused in the driveway as Middleton headed into the house. She took out her phone and began to punch in numbers. A second later, the phone rang next to Ron.

He picked it up. "Security."

"Hi, this is Meredith Vines. May I ask to whom I'm speaking?"

"This is Ron." He watched her on the monitor. She tapped a little impatient foot.

"Just a couple of items, Ron. I need you to add two people to the list of permanent residents. They're allowed through at any time."

Ron cradled the phone against his shoulder, picked up a pencil and clipboard. Vines told him the names, and he jotted them down.

"I'll log these," Ron said. "And I'll make sure the other shifts know."

"I appreciate that," Vines said. "And the other thing just quickly. A quick reminder to please use the back path only coming to and from the parking lot. It's imperative to Mr. Middleton to preserve the illusion of solitude."

Ron rolled his eyes. "No problem, ma'am. I'll make sure the boys remember."

"Thanks," Vines said. "You have a good evening."

Ron hung up, shaking his head. Fucking rich people.

17

Francis checked his pockets before shoving his dirty clothes into the washer. He'd decided to make himself useful while Emma was out. He found the picture of the white-water rafters with the magazine article on the back in his shirt pocket. He stuffed it in his back jeans pocket. Well, not *his* jeans. Dwayne's.

He tossed in Emma's clothing on top of his, detergent, then started a cold-water wash.

Francis turned, scanning the rest of the basement, and his gaze landed on the suitcase.

Yeah. The suitcase. The alligator-covered beacon of regret that had kicked off all his misadventures.

He'd come this far, risked his life. Didn't he have a right to know? He went to the piece of luggage and thumbed open the latches. Slowly he lifted the lid, looked inside. He saw only the same clothing items as before when he'd first found the suitcase in the alley. He searched, making sure to look between each garment for anything he might have missed.

Okay, so . . . what? Microfilm? Was this a spy thing? Somehow Emma didn't strike him as KGB. It occurred to Francis that the KGB might not actually be a thing anymore.

I'm definitely in over my head.

He plucked a pair of especially frilly pink panties from the case and held them up, trying to imagine Emma in them. They were completely different from the plain white underwear Francis had seen hanging in the bathroom back in the adult hotel. Neither those nor these seemed right for her. He picked up another pair, red, thong cut, which would have left nothing to the imagination.

"I don't think that's the right look for you."

Francis spun around, shoving the panties behind his back.

Yeah, that doesn't look stupid and guilty at all.

She came down the stairs, a morbidly pleased look on her face at having caught him.

Francis smiled weakly, tossed the panties back into the suitcase. "Sorry. How did it go?"

"I parked the stolen car a couple of miles away at a pump station," she said. "When they do their normal maintenance or whatever, somebody will find it. It was an easy walk back."

"Okay, good." Francis nodded. "That's good."

"You know, I don't make a habit out of stealing cars," she said. "I don't know why, but I wanted you to know that."

"No, I get it. Circumstances. Although the fact you can hot-wire a car . . ."

She laughed. "My dad was in the army. All the shooting and guns, that was him. He taught me. When he died, my mom hooked up with a completely different kind of guy. It was almost like she didn't care anymore. Like nobody would ever be as good as Dad anyway, so what did it matter? Anyway, this new guy taught me a few shady skills. I always wanted to learn things. To find out, to know things."

"Your stepdad was a career criminal?"

"Not stepdad, technically, but close enough, I guess. He came and went a lot. Kind of an asshole, really. Actually, the women in my family have a rich tradition of assholes."

"Like the guy on TV you said was your husband?"

Something deflated in her, a sadness slowly creeping across her face. "I guess you could say that."

"It's none of my business. Sorry." Except it was. Francis was here, now. He'd made it his business. Maybe that was wrong, but it's what was happening.

Emma looked at the open suitcase. "You want to know, don't you?"

"Yes, please."

She sighed, then bit her thumbnail. "Okay. But in order to understand, you need to know from the beginning."

"I'm listening."

She crossed the basement to the old, beat-up wardrobe and opened one of the doors. On the back of the door, there was a collage of newspaper clippings and photographs. Francis looked but couldn't understand what he was seeing.

"I met Aaron at Berkeley," Emma said.

Francis's face scrunched into a question.

"Aaron Middleton," Emma clarified. "The guy from TV."

"Oh. Right."

"He taught an undergrad computer programming course, and that's how I met him," she said. "Even then, he was starting up his own company in a friend's warehouse, but he was living on ramen noodles and adjunct pay in the meantime. I'd gotten a scholarship to the university, and that was back when I thought going anywhere for any reason was better than being stuck in flyover country with the rest of the bumpkins. I was way ahead of the other students in the class, so that's why he noticed me, I guess. We were married a year later."

"Divorced?"

"Separated."

"Why?"

She chewed her thumbnail again, thinking, then said, "He got weird."

Francis didn't know what to say to that. When in doubt, keep your mouth shut.

"His business took off *fast*," Emma told him. "Investors were tripping over each other to give him money. But the more successful he got, the more people crawled out of every dark corner who *wanted* things from him. I think it touched off some latent psychosis in Aaron. He became suspicious and paranoid. I tried to let him know, tried to help him, but that just made him distrust *me*."

Francis shook his head. "But it's over, right? It's done. Why would he be *after* you?"

"I'll get to it."

Francis gestured for her to continue.

"See this guy right here?" She tapped one of the pictures tacked to the inside of the wardrobe door.

Francis leaned forward and looked. An Asian man in his midthirties. "Yeah?"

"When Aaron really got things going, he needed to bring in the smartest people," Emma said. "Look, Aaron is a super genius about computers, but he still needed help. Thousands and thousands of man-hours went into the big project they were working on. There were a dozen teams working on things just to support the main team, and the head of the main team was this guy. Marion Parkes."

Francis squinted at the newspaper article taped next to the picture. "He's dead?"

"They're *all* dead." Emma waved at the pictures. "Because Aaron had them murdered."

Francis was shaking his head now, not understanding. "This says he died in prison. A dispute with another inmate."

"Aaron *arranged* that."

"Oh, come on."

"He's a multibillionaire," Emma said. "He gets what he wants. All he has to do is spend enough money."

"The guy I saw on TV didn't look so badass," Francis said.

"He's not badass. He's worse," Emma said. "He's afraid. He's like a little fluffy bunny that's been afraid of everything all his life. And then somehow the bunny gets a machine gun, and for the first time ever, the bunny can make anything that frightens him go away by pulling the trigger. That's Aaron. He's afraid, and that makes him dangerous."

Francis let his eyes wander over the pictures and the articles. "I don't understand why."

"Control," Emma said. "Marion and the others on the team could reproduce the work. There was always the chance they could sell it to another company or another country. He couldn't trust them. You don't understand what he's capable of. What he did to *me* was—"

She stopped talking, like maybe she'd crossed a line she hadn't meant to. Her eyes drifted back to the suitcase.

"Marion figured out what was happening to him," she said. "Too late to save himself. He knew his days were numbered, but he could get revenge. He was the keyman on the team, had come up with the main algorithm that made the new software special. If he could get it out into the world, then it would fuck up everything Aaron had worked for. The secret he'd killed to keep would be out there. There would be nothing he could do about it."

"And Parkes gave it to you," Francis said.

Her eyes slowly came back from the suitcase and met his. "Yes."

"And it's in that suitcase."

She nodded. "Yes."

"And it's not panties."

In spite of the grave mood that had descended over the basement, her mouth quirked into a smile. She tried to fight it for a
second, then gave up. "It's not panties."

She went to the suitcase and dumped the clothing on the
floor. She dug at the corner of the lining, and Francis heard a rip-
ping sound as she pulled it loose. She reached underneath and
then came out with a folded wad of paper, the kind of paper somebody might use to wrap ground beef or pork chops in a butcher's
shop.

She handed it to Francis.

He unfolded it.

He wasn't impressed.

"No, dink, the other side," Emma said.

He turned the paper over, and his eyes widened.

The diagram—what had Emma called it? An algorithm?—was
hand drawn, but intricate and precise and used every square inch
of the paper. If Francis had a hundred years, he would not have
been able to figure what it was for or what to do with it, but it was
obviously highly technical. And if he understood Emma correctly,
it was the key to the future of computing.

Or maybe it was a circuit for a really kick-ass toaster, and the
girl standing in front of him was batshit crazy.

"So why don't you post it on the internet or something?" Francis
asked. "Or sell it to a competitor?"

"And that's exactly what I'll tell him will happen," she said.
"Unless he cooperates. I'm hoping he'll trade."

"Trade for what?"

Her back straightened, and she lifted her chin. Something in
her eyes went hard. "He has something that belongs to me."

Francis understood instinctively that further questions along
this path would hit a dead end. She'd just opened up to him big-

time, but there were limits. There would be a time to push those limits, but it wasn't now.

Francis gently set the algorithm back into the suitcase. "So when do we go?"

"It's my concern, not yours," Emma said. "You don't have to go anywhere you don't want to."

"Oh, I agree. Fully," Francis said. "But I can't stay *here* forever, and while I understand ditching the stolen car was probably smart in the context of a criminal enterprise, it begs the question how we're going to leave. My guess is Uber doesn't come this far out."

And just like that, her face softened—not a lot, but noticeably. She fought off another smile, but Francis could see it was there right below the surface. It some acute way, Francis realized this was part of her appeal. In the short time he'd know her, he'd seen her annoyed and angry and afraid and exhausted, but there always seemed room for a shift in mood, a sudden smile as if she were eternally open to something better, refusing to cling to the negative.

"Come with me," she said. "I want to show you something."

Ike slammed his hands against the steering wheel, shifted the sedan into park, and said, "That map is bullshit."

Cavanaugh pored over the place mat map Gary had drawn. "Give me a fucking break already, will you?"

The problem with Gary's map was that while he may have been diligent about labeling things, that didn't quite translate to reality. For example, he'd drawn a crooked line and labeled it *Newton Creek*, but one stream looked fairly like another, and there was never a sign saying NEWTON CREEK or SOME OTHER DAMN CREEK, so as a point of reference, it was pretty much shit.

"Come on, Ernie."

Ernie and Cavanaugh climbed out of the vehicle and looked at the front tires stuck in the mud. They'd been lost for an hour, turned down yet another unmarked dirt road, and gotten stuck in the mud for a second time.

Cavanaugh and Ernie circled to the front of the car, placed their hands against the front, hunched over ready to push.

"Put it in reverse," Cavanaugh called. "Ike, give it some gas."

Cavanaugh and Ernie pushed. The wheels spun at first but then found some traction, and the car lurched backward. Cavanaugh stumbled forward, almost found his footing, but then tripped on a root and went down, splatting face-first in the mud. He stood again, spitting curses. His entire front dripped with mud.

Cavanaugh looked at Ernie, who was looking back at him.

"Not a word." Cavanaugh pointed at Ernie. "Not one fucking word."

Ernie held up his hands in a *No problem here* gesture.

Cavanaugh squinted at the sky. Night would fall very soon. If they had trouble following the map in daylight, then he doubted they'd have better luck in the dark. Even more to the point, he was just fed up. "We're going to try this fresh in the morning. We're going to bring everybody, and we're going to get this done."

"Works for me," Ernie said.

Cavanaugh wiped mud off his face. "Now let's see if we can find a drink somewhere in this backwater shithole."

Emma led Francis from the house to the barn. Dusk had slipped into night. It struck Francis how utterly dark it was here. It was never truly dark in New York City in the same way it was never completely quiet. Here in the wilds of South Dakota, the darkness was implacable, the silence total.

Except it wasn't really.

Gradually, Francis tuned into the night. The wind in the trees, the distant babble of running water, some stream, probably the one they'd passed coming in, twisting its way through the shallow valley. There was light also. He paused, looked up. The sky blazed with stars. He couldn't see them like this in the city.

The creak of the barn door brought Francis back to earth.

He followed her inside. There was a brief moment of fumbling while she groped for the light switch. She found it and flipped it on, and rows of industrial light fixtures hanging from the two-story ceiling cast the interior of the barn in stark illumination.

Against one whole side of the barn was a long row of motorcycles, all in various states of repair. Mostly dirt bikes, but Francis spied a couple of Harleys in pieces and something so ugly it was almost beautiful with the word NORTON on the gas tank. Hubcaps and handlebars and engine parts hung on the walls. There was also a very old tractor, although not as old as the one gathering rust and weeds outside. There were other lumpy things under tarps and a not-too-beat-up Ford F150 from the mid-1990s.

The place smelled like old, wet hay and grease and dust.

Emma went to the closest tarp, grabbed it with two hands. "Our chariot, milord."

She yanked the tarp off in one smooth motion. The vehicle beneath the tarp was not another rusty heap. Far from it.

Francis's eyes widened. "What is it?"

"Behold the 1968 Pontiac GTO," Emma said. "Four-hundred-cubic-inch V8 engine, all fully restored, candy-apple red. Dwayne's pride and joy. He was a bona fide son of a bitch, but he knew his metal."

There had not been a single moment in Francis's life he'd even come close to being a gearhead. He'd bought a $500 junker his junior year of high school just to get around and had coaxed it along enough to get through Wright State. And when he'd moved to Manhattan, it had been a relief not to bother with a car.

But this . . . this was something different.

The car gleamed perfection, not a scratch or ding. It looked muscular just sitting there, like maybe it wanted to roar out of the barn and eat a Prius. Francis felt something stir within him as if seeing the car tapped into some deeply buried, hidden reservoir of testosterone. He wanted to get behind the wheel, feel the rumble of the engine in his bones as he thundered down the open road.

"I feel like I want to eat a rare steak and then drink whiskey all night long," Francis said.

18

There was no steak.

The house had stood empty for a while, and there was no fresh food at all. But there was spaghetti and a jar of sauce and canned green beans. Emma had even produced a bottle of Chianti. They sat at the kitchen table, and Francis descended upon the meal like a starving castaway.

Emma refilled her wineglass. "Not really a wine girl, but I guess it goes better with pasta than Wild Turkey."

"I like wine," Francis said. "Seems more . . ." He groped for a word.

"Stuck up?" Emma suggested.

Francis laughed. "I was going to say *civilized*. I've been reading about it."

"You're a fancy lad, aren't you, Frankie?"

"Francis. But in this shirt, yes, I feel quite fancy." He refilled his glass too.

They ate. They drank.

Finally, she pushed her plate away and said, "I'm pulling out in the morning. I've already packed the trunk of the Pontiac. I can drop you at a train station or bus stop or whatever. Or if you wanted, you could come with me, but if you did that, I'd want to know why. Because if you thought there was some way you'd get something out of it, you'd probably be wrong."

"I'm not trying to get anything from you," Francis said.

"Then why?"

A half shrug as he sipped wine. "What I said before was true.

Yes, I can go to the police and explain everything, and it would *probably* work out. But I'd rather you were there to tell them I had no idea what was going to happen when I found that suitcase and contacted you."

"But there's something else too." The way she said it wasn't a question.

Yes. There was something else too, and Francis tried to think of a way to explain it, knew that he'd be explaining to himself as much as to her.

Francis picked up the lighthouse saltshaker, turned it over in his hands. Along the bottom it read ST. AUGUSTINE, FLORIDA. He recalled the posters from Dwayne's bedroom. "Did Dwayne like to travel?"

Emma shook her head. "My sister. Dwayne just went along with it. Dwayne preferred just hanging around the house, tinkering with an engine or watching baseball on TV. He was an asshole, but he did indulge my sister's love of travel. I guess I at least need to give him credit for that."

Francis took the magazine page from his back pocket, unfolded it, and set it on the table between them. Emma looked at it, then looked at him.

"I subscribe to *Adventure Travel*," Francis said. "Every month I look at pictures of other people having some amazing good time, an African safari or whatever. I thought white-water rafting would be fun. I've been saving up to go."

Emma's face remained blank. Maybe Francis was boring her. He pressed on anyway.

"Listen to this one part of the article." Francis flipped the page over and read, "Your Open Spaces Trek guide will take every precaution to make your wild river ride as safe and as comfortable as possible."

Emma emptied the rest of the Chianti into her glass. "So?"

"I don't think I really understood what the word *adventure* meant," Francis said. "If it's so safe and comfortable and prepackaged, does that even count? I'm not saying it wouldn't be fun; I'm just saying that maybe it wasn't ever offering what I thought I would be getting."

Emma set her wineglass on the table without drinking, frowned. "And if you come with me, then what? That's a *real* adventure?"

Francis was already shaking his head before she'd finished asking the question. "No. I'm not explaining myself right. I don't think I ever really wanted an adventure at all. I certainly don't want people trying to kill me. But I think I was trying to make my life mean something, or that something I did mattered. When those guys grabbed you and I followed in the taxi, I mean, look, I don't know. I'm not sure what I'm really trying to say. If I'd thought about it for another second, I probably would have come to my senses, but I didn't. I went after you, and now if something happened, and you got killed, then it would be like I never saved you at all." Francis blew out a heavy sigh. "I guess I just don't want to see the only good deed I've ever done get fucked up because I wasn't there to help."

She looked at him for a long moment. Francis himself hadn't even known exactly what he was going to say until he started saying it. He was even less sure about how Emma would take it.

She picked up her wineglass, titled it back, and drained it in three long swallows. She stood, circled the table to Francis's side, and pushed the little kitchen table out of the way.

Francis opened his mouth to say something.

She put two fingers on his lips. "Don't."

Right.

She swung one leg over, straddling him, and lowered herself into his lap. Francis thought his heart might beat straight out of his chest, but he made himself breathe steadily and let her do just exactly as she pleased. He didn't touch. He assumed nothing. He let her take the lead and trusted it would be good.

Emma placed a hand on each side of his face and lowered her lips to his. At first, she just mashed hard, holding him like that as if making some bold statement that she'd decided to do this and it was happening. Then she pulled away slightly, his bottom lip between her teeth. She bit, not hard, just enough to send a sharp thrill through his entire body.

Then she began kissing in earnest, lips parting, tongue sliding into his mouth, her fingers going up into his hair. He kissed back, head spinning. His arms went around her and pulled her tight against him. He went stiff beneath her, and she began to grind.

They went on like that for a bit, Francis hoping she'd start whatever was supposed to happen next because he was too timid.

She pulled open his shirt, the snaps giving away with ease, and rubbed her hand across his chest. His hands slid down to her backside, gripping and pulling her down against him. A small moan from her, barely above a whisper, her head going back, eyes closed. Francis kissed a trail from her chin down her throat.

Emma stood abruptly. "Come on."

She took his hand and led him down the hall to the bedroom.

Frantically, they pulled at each other's clothing. Her fingers went to his zipper. He pulled her shirt up over her head, then reached around for the bra clasp, was pleasantly surprised to unclasp it on the first try. One of her slim hands went to the back of his head, grabbed a fistful of hair, and brought him down to a pert breast. He licked the nipple, then sucked it hard enough to make her gasp.

They kicked off their shoes and shucked their pants.

She pushed Francis back on the bed, then took him into her mouth, head bobbing until he was fully hard. Then she climbed on top, lowered herself slowly until he was completely inside, a ragged grunt coming out of her.

Francis thought he might pass out.

He noticed the tattoo of a stylized sun around her navel, heat waves blazing in all directions. He wondered what other tattoos she had, hoped he would find them all.

She rocked back and forth on top of him, throwing her head back, the grunts getting more and more urgent. He filled his hands with her behind, pulling her along with the rhythm she'd set. He didn't think he could last too much longer.

"Do you have . . . I mean, do you take a pill or . . ."

"No," she said. "You'll have to pull out, but . . . not yet. Not . . . yet."

She rode him wildly now, the bed threatening to rattle apart. Francis bit the inside of his own lip, hoping to distract himself. Her whole body shuddered, and she groaned and went stiff. She climbed off him, grabbed his length and stroked hard three times, and he cut loose.

Emma scooted up to curl next to him, panting, a lazy hand on his chest. Francis felt like his heart was going to break right through his chest. His whole body hummed, remembering the experience.

"I didn't mean to go so fast," she said. "It's been a while. I think I was overdue."

Francis hadn't realized until now how perfunctory sex with Enid had become. He'd forgotten what it could be like when it was all new and exciting. "That was *way* better than white-water rafting."

She laughed.

They lay tangled together awhile, not talking, just enjoying each other's warmth. Then Emma reached under the covers and worked Francis ready again. This time they went slowly, exploring, a less urgent but more earnest effort. He found a tattoo of a dolphin on her ankle.

Another tattoo down at the bottom of her tailbone. A hovering Tinker Bell.

At last they finished, spent and satisfied, and dozed in the dark.

Sometime later, in a quiet voice, she said, "I did that because I wanted to. That's the only reason. Not because I felt I owed you or that I could get you to do something or anything like that. This was what it was, and it's not connected to anything else."

"Okay," Francis said.

"There's a train station about an hour from here," she said. "When we leave in the morning, I'm going to drop you there. You can go wherever you need to, but I'm heading on to California. Without you."

Francis tried to object, but she hurried on with what she was saying, wanting to get it all out before Francis could derail her.

"I haven't told you everything. You know that," she said. "But what I've got to do is something very personal. It's on me. Nobody else. Earlier, you said you didn't want your good deed messed up. I get that. And it's why you can't come. This is my good deed. Keeping you out of the mess I'm about to get myself into. And if I seem like the kind of person that's not going to let anyone change her mind once she's made her decision, then you're right. So really, anything you think you're going to say, just don't, because I'm not going to change my mind. I like you, Francis. Maybe another place and another time. But this isn't another place or time."

And then she turned over, her back to him, and scooted all the way to her side of the bed, and that was the end of the conversation.

19

It was maybe 4:00 A.M. when Francis heard Emma get out of bed, slip on her T-shirt and panties, and leave the room. He thought maybe she'd gone to sleep elsewhere, but a moment later he heard the toiled flush down the hall, and then she slipped back into bed again. She burrowed beneath the covers and was breathing steadily again in seconds.

Francis couldn't get back to sleep, thoughts tumbling in his head. It took him a minute to remember which state he was in.

South Dakota. How the hell did I end up in South Dakota?

There was no Open Spaces Trek guide to tell him what to do.

Over coffee, Francis would change her mind. He'd explain . . .

What? Emma had every right to want to handle her own business herself. The fact that Francis had just had some of the best sex in his life simply wasn't pertinent. And he couldn't say, *You're a weak little girl, and you need a man around to look after you.* She'd laugh. Or kick his ass.

But the idea of Emma going out of his life tomorrow made his chest tighten. In a week or a month? Maybe. But not tomorrow. Not before he'd had the chance to see if this could be something good, that maybe the boring doofus who worked in a cubicle and the wild-haired girl with the alligator suitcase could actually mesh.

He mentally rehearsed what he'd say to her, but it all sounded so feeble.

Slowly, a gray, grim light leaked through the blinds. The dawn was still a ways off, but the beginnings of a predawn glow edged the horizon, a bleak and timid preview of the sunrise to come.

Francis rolled out of bed, trying not to make any noise, and gathered up his clothes and shoes. He carried them into the hall and dressed there. In the kitchen, he started a pot of coffee. He looked out the kitchen window over the sink. The landscape had been enveloped by a dense gloom.

He stepped out onto the front porch. The air was pleasantly chilly without being cold. A thick fog had rolled in. From where Francis stood, he could see neither the tree line nor the barn. The row of rusted cars was close enough to appear as a line of dark shapes humping up from the tall grass.

There was something hypnotic about the morning's utter silence. Everything was so still. He could have been on a soundstage. Odd how the fog transformed everything, made his surroundings seem artificial. He stepped down from the porch, ventured across the wet grass toward the barn.

A form congealed in the mist to his left and startled him. He realized it was the old tractor. He'd forgotten it was there. He paused, looked back at the house. He'd only walked a few dozen yards, but already the house was nothing more than a dark outline, the kitchen light in the window a fuzzy orange beacon.

The snap of a twig. A frantic flutter of bird's wings.

The sounds were sudden and loud in the silent fog. Francis strained his eyes, trying to catch sight of whatever startled the bird. He knew nothing of South Dakota wildlife. Did they have coyotes?

When Francis saw them, his breath caught.

They came through the fog like ghosts, five of them or maybe six, although he sensed more beyond the range of his sight. They advanced toward the house, stepping lightly and slowly. Most of the men were merely vague silhouettes in the gray soup, but the closest was visible enough to see details. At first, Francis thought it was Cavanaugh, the same general build. But it was a younger guy with an enormous automatic pistol in his fist. Other than the occasional crunch of gravel under a shoe, they were keeping it quiet. If Francis had still been sleeping in bed, he would never have known they were coming.

Emma! Oh, shit, what do I do?

Shouting a warning was obviously a bad idea. It would only draw attention to himself. They'd have him, and then there wouldn't be a thing he could do to help Emma.

It dawned on Francis that if he could see them, then they could see him. Their attention was fixed on the house, but they had only to turn their heads to see him gawking there like an imbecile.

Francis shrank back against the tractor, slowly lowering himself and scooting around to crouch behind a big tire. He watched, feeling helpless and stupid.

Two of the men climbed the steps to the porch. The others circled around.

Francis forced slower breaths before he hyperventilated. He felt sick and nervous and sweaty behind his ears. This is what Emma had meant, Francis realized, what she'd wanted to spare him. This wasn't white-water rafting. These were men with guns, and they wouldn't hesitate to kill him. In fact, he'd made it easy for them. They could dump his body in the woods, and nobody would ever know. All he could do was cower there and watch.

No! Use your brain, dink. Think of something!

He looked over his shoulder back at the barn. Going toward it would put him deeper into the fog and out of sight, but it wouldn't last forever. As the sun rose, the fog would burn off. Whatever he was going to do, he needed to get on with it.

He turned slowly and quietly, duck-walking toward the barn.

Cavanaugh paused in front of the front door, Ike and Ernie right behind him. He motioned for the new guys to circle the house. The last thing he wanted was the girl and the kid running out the back. He was in no mood to chase those fuckers around in the fog.

He gave Ike and Ernie the eye. *You ready?*

They nodded and drew their pistols. Cavanaugh already had his little automatic out. Everyone had been instructed on how to handle this. Shooting Berringer was fine—they'd probably have to dispose of him sooner or later anyway—but the girl had to be taken in one piece. She was their payday. They'd make her talk, make her think it was the only way to save herself.

Of course, she'd probably need to disappear too. Cavanaugh was making up a lot of this as he went along. He was usually the guy carrying out somebody else's plan, not coming up with the plan himself. Soon those days would be over, and nobody would boss Cavanaugh but Cavanaugh.

He put a hand on the doorknob, paused. Were they sure this was the right house? The map really was crap, and they could have missed a turn in the fog.

Fuck it.

He turned the knob slowly. It was unlocked. He pushed the door inward, wincing at the slight creak of the hinges. They entered, clicked the door closed behind them.

A very small foyer. It opened to a small living room, a threadbare couch, fifteen-year-old TV, rough stone fireplace. It led the other way to a small dining room, round table and four chairs, a doorway beyond which Cavanaugh assumed went to the kitchen. A hallway ahead of them.

Cavanaugh motioned Ike toward the dining room and kitchen, indicated Ernie should follow him into the hallway. They paused at a bathroom, found it empty, and kept moving. The door to the bedroom was already open. Cavanaugh peeked around the corner, saw a lump curled under the covers in the double bed. The other side of the bed looked like maybe it had been slept in also. Cavanaugh raked the rest of the room with his eyes and wondered where Berringer might be.

He went to one knee and looked under the bed. Nobody.

Cavanaugh opened the closet door—

She leaped out at him, swinging something down at him hard. It would have hit him square in the forehead, but he flinched and turned aside and took the strike on the collarbone. He screamed in pain as she pushed past him, making a run for it.

Ernie filled the doorway, blocking her. She swung again— Cavanaugh could see now she was wielding a baseball trophy like a club—but Ernie caught her by the wrist and twisted. She yelped and dropped the trophy.

She punched Ernie in the jaw, but he just grunted and grabbed her. She struggled, trying to wrench loose, and he turned her around, grabbed her around the waist, and lifted. She thrashed, bare feet churning the air.

"She's like some fucking rabid wolverine!" Ernie shouted.

Cavanaugh rushed forward to help subdue her.

"Motherfuckers!" She kicked out hard, caught Cavanaugh in the gut with her heel.

Cavanaugh double over and *whuffed* air. "Damn bitch!"

Ike burst into the room. "What the fuck?"

"Get her legs!" Ernie shouted.

Ike grabbed her legs, taking several kicks to the chest in the process. Eventually, he had her by the ankles, and Ernie held her under the arms. It was tough going as she wriggled and cursed them. She twisted around a couple of times, trying to bite Ernie.

"Get her on the bed," Ike said. "Then hold her down."

They tossed her on the bed, and Ernie put a hand on her chest between her breasts, leaned all his weight into it, pinning her against the mattress. She reached up and clawed his cheek, drawing three red welts.

"Jesus!" Ernie shouted. "Do whatever you're going to do already!"

Ike pulled something from his jacket pocket. "Stand back."

Ernie stood back just as Ike reached in and touched the object to the girl's bare thigh. There was a blue flash and a crackle and pop. The girl went rigid a moment, then limp. She tried to lift her head but couldn't, eyes going glassy and unfocused.

Cavanaugh rubbed his gut. "What the hell was that?"

"Stun gun." Ike held it up, thumbing the trigger. Blue fire leaped between the two contacts.

"Where'd you get that?" Cavanaugh asked. "I didn't know you had that."

Ike shrugged. "Mail order."

The girl moaned, her limbs making jerky motions as she tried to move.

"I hope you didn't brain damage her," Cavanaugh said. "We need her to talk."

"She'll come out of it in a few minutes."

Cavanaugh grabbed a lamp from the bedside table and yanked out the power cord. He used it to tie her wrists. "Get something for her feet."

Ernie found a belt in one of the dresser drawers and cinched it tight around her ankles. "I'm getting tired of this little girl kicking the crap out of us." He dabbed at the scratches on his face, and his fingertips came away wet and red. "I need to find Bactine or something." He left the room, muttering about his various injuries.

"Ike, get out there and tell the rest of the boys to comb the entire place for Berringer," Cavanaugh said. "And tell them to take their time, no stone unturned and all that. I want time to question her without anyone around. Remember, just me, you, and Ernie on this."

"Right."

Cavanaugh went to the bed, loomed over the girl. "You gave us some trouble there, didn't you? Led us on a merry chase."

She worked her mouth, struggling to make words. "Fuh . . . fug . . . you."

"You're a real spitfire," Cavanaugh said. "But I know ways to take the piss out of you real quick. And we can make this an all-day thing if you want. Just try me. I'm a patient man, but you've used up just about all of it. Test me and see."

Francis ducked inside the barn and made sure the door was completely closed before switching on the light. He remembered what Emma had said about already packing the Pontiac's trunk and hoped it meant what he thought it meant. He found the keys in the ignition, grabbed them, and circled back to the trunk and opened it.

On one side of the trunk sat a big, olive drab canvas duffel bag with zippers. All the way on the other side was the alligator suitcase. Right in the middle was the footlocker Francis had been hoping to see. He opened it and scanned the assortment of weaponry.

He took a pass on the automatics. He understood you put the bullets in the handle, but after that he wasn't sure enough of his ability to mess with them. He'd been a pretty crappy marksman with the revolver, but at least he'd loaded it several times while trying it out and felt comfortable with that much. He swung out the cylinder. Loaded. Good. He clicked the cylinder back into place and set it aside for a moment.

Then he dug deeper into the footlocker for the shotgun. He opened a box of shells, tried to load, but his hands shook, palms sweaty. He took a deep breath, let it out slowly. His heart beat so fast he felt it in his stomach and all over his body. He pulsed with nervous energy. His face felt like it was burning up.

He took one more deep breath, then thumbed in the double-aught shells one by one. He snatched a canvas bandolier out of the footlocker, filled it with more shells, and then slung it over his head and across his shoulder.

The idea of wading back into the fog and pumping buckshot in random directions was a nonstarter. Francis needed a plan. He could—and probably should—save himself.

I could just take off.

He discarded the notion immediately. He was going back for Emma. Case closed.

He cracked the barn door open a half inch and peeked out into the fog. A shape slowly resolved as it came. Another second and details snapped into focus. It was one of Cavanaugh's flunkies, the bald one. He had a pistol out and walked straight toward Francis.

Francis backed into the barn, shut the light off, positioned himself, and waited.

And waited.

For a second, Francis wondered if the thug had wandered off somewhere else, but a moment later, the barn door creaked open. He eased in, gun up, squinting into the shadows.

Francis leaped forward and slammed the butt of the shotgun against the side of the guy's head. He grunted and went down but began muttering obscenities immediately. Francis hadn't put his full strength into the blow, was squeamish about cracking the guy's head open, but he swung again harder, striking the man at the base of the skull. This time he went down and stayed down.

Francis grabbed the man's pistol and flung it across the barn. He searched the guy's pockets in case he had another gun. He didn't, but Francis did find something he thought might be useful. He put it in his pocket.

He dragged him by the ankles to a spot between the truck and the tractor and tossed the tarp over him that had previously covered the Pontiac.

Francis took stock of the other things in the barn, and slowly a terrible plan came together, but it was the best terrible plan he could think of on short notice.

"Where is it?" Cavanaugh asked.

The girl lay bound on the bed, stabbing Cavanaugh with eye daggers.

"Once I get it, Middleton wants you gone," Cavanaugh said. "You know that, right?"

Something in her face shifted. Yeah, she'd known, but it was something else to hear it. Few people can hear *we're going to kill you* and not feel it. This was when Cavanaugh needed to drive his point home. *You've got one chance to save yourself, little girl.*

"So this is a foregone conclusion," Cavanaugh said. "You're dead. And there's not one thing you can do about." A slight shrug. "Unless maybe . . . there is?"

Her eyes narrowed.

"You're listening now, huh? You give me what I want, and I let you go. Simple."

"Why?" she asked.

"So you can live, you dumb shit," Cavanaugh told her. "Aren't you listening?"

"I mean, why do *you* want it?"

"You convinced us it was valuable," Cavanaugh said. "Valuable enough to take it for ourselves and sell it to the highest bidder and tell Middleton to piss off."

"I don't believe you'll let me go," she said.

"Believe what you like, but if you don't help, and we rip this house apart and find it, I'm going to remember you didn't help. In any case, we're about to go from the conversation part of this to the coercion part. All roads lead to the same place. How long of a trip is up to you. And maybe after you tell us where it is, you might have some ideas how to sell it. The more useful things you think of to tell us, the longer we keep you around. These are all things to ponder."

"Loosen this up." She lifted her hands, indicating the cord around her wrists. "My hands and feet are going numb."

"Tough shit."

"I'm serious. They're going numb."

"You're going to wish all of you was numb in a minute." He took a small pocketknife from his pocket and opened it.

Cavanaugh bent over her, brought the point of the little blade to within an inch of her eye. "I need you to talk. Don't really need you to see."

She turned her head away, tried to scoot across the bed, but he grabbed her by the face, brought her back to meet his gaze. He lay the flat of the blade against her cheek, the cold metal making her flinch.

Then he put the tip of the blade through her nose ring, gave it a gentle tug. "Or maybe this needs to come out. What do you think about a little amateur surgery?"

She froze, waited to see what he'd do.

Cavanaugh folded the knife and returned it to his pants pocket. "Maybe we'll work up to that. Let's start out the old-fashioned way."

He cranked his hand back, then brought it down hard, slapped her face with a loud *pop* of skin on skin. The girl's eyes filled with tears, but she stuck her chin out, teeth grinding, expression defiant.

"Where is it?"

She said nothing.

Cavanaugh grabbed a fistful of her shirt, pulled her halfway into a sitting position, and slapped her back down again. The left side of her face flared an angry red.

"Where is it?"

"I don't know," she said. "It's gone."

"Wrong answer."

This time he punched her square in the mouth, just a light pop but enough to bloody a lip.

"You can make it stop," he reminded her. "Just say the word."

She spit at him. Blood and saliva ran down the side of his nose.

"Fucking bitch."

He punched hard this time, getting his shoulder into it, catching her right across the jaw and spinning her head around. She went limp all over as if someone had unplugged her, fell back, arms flopping lifelessly.

Ernie looked in the mirror above the sink and dabbed at the scratches with cotton balls. They came away pink. He put rubbing alcohol on the next cotton ball and continued to dab. It stung. A lot. He hissed in breath and dabbed until he figured the wounds had been sanitized enough.

He turned his head side to side, examining the scratches from different angles. They weren't as deep as he'd thought at first. He hoped they wouldn't scar.

He unzipped and started pissing. He thought he heard some noises coming from the room down the hall and figured Cavanaugh had started in on the girl. He hoped Cavanaugh knew what he was doing. Middleton paid well, and up until this current job tracking down the girl, it had been easy work. Ernie just wasn't able to get fully comfortable with this. He liked to keep things simple. Follow orders. Collect a paycheck. Cavanaugh had made a good case, and Ernie had agreed to go along with the plan, but doubts still nagged him.

Ernie shook, zipped up, and flushed.

He opened the bathroom door and—

A guy was standing there. A shotgun rested lazily on one shoulder. For a tenth of a second, Ernie thought it was one of the new guys. It wasn't. Recognition hit him like a rubber band snapping back.

It was Berringer.

Ernie's hand flashed into his jacket for his pistol, but he was too slow.

Berringer jabbed something into his chest. There was a buzzing crackle and a blue flash, and in a blinding moment, every part of Ernie's body was on fire. His teeth vibrated in his head.

The room tilted violently, and Ernie realized he was stumbling backward, legs like noodles. His arms flailed, looking for something to grab on to. Gravity beckoned. The back of his legs hit the bathtub, and he tumbled backward, grabbing on to the shower curtain as he went down. There was a *pop pop pop pop pop pop* as the curtain ripped loose from each of the rings. His tailbone hit the bottom of the tub hard, the curtain falling down on top of him.

He tried to push the curtain off him. His arm felt like lead. He could barely lift it, but with a huge effort, he pushed the shower curtain aside.

Just in in time to see Berringer leaning into the tub. Ernie uselessly tried to turn away, but Berringer jabbed the stun gun into Ernie's neck. Another crackle and a blue flash.

And then everything went dark.

20

Francis left the one with the shaggy mustache unconscious in the bathtub. He slung the shotgun over his shoulder by the strap before backing out of the bathroom. The shotgun had been a poor choice for inside the house. Even with the stock folded, it was cumbersome in doorways and narrow halls. In any case, he wanted to keep one hand free for the stun gun. He didn't want to shoot anyone. He wasn't a killer.

Still, he pulled the revolver before heading down the hall.

He paused at the bedroom door, cocked his head to listen. He definitely heard movement coming from within, then a man's voice pitched low. Francis twisted the doorknob, not making a sound.

He took a deep breath, let it out slowly.

Francis shoved the door open, rushing into the room in the same motion.

Emma lay on the bed. Cavanaugh leaned over her, shaking her by the shoulders, but his head came up when Francis entered. Cavanaugh's expression shifted from annoyed to suddenly worried when he saw the revolver in Francis's fist.

"Take it easy, kid," Cavanaugh said.

Francis lifted the revolver, pointed it at Cavanaugh's face. "Get away from her." He thumbed back the revolver's hammer. He kept his hand with the stun gun low and behind his leg.

Cavanaugh stood straight and took a step back from the bed. "Take. It. Easy."

"Go over there." Francis waved the revolver to a spot across the room. In order to get there, Cavanaugh would have to walk right past him, and then Francis would put him down with the stun gun.

Cavanaugh moved slowly. "You're in way over your head, kid. If I were you, I'd want to talk this over so everyone can get out of this in one piece. I got a bunch of guys outside. Shoot me in the head, yeah, sucks for me, but it doesn't help you. They'll hear the shot and swarm in here, and then you're done. The girl too."

"Just keep moving."

When Cavanaugh passed in front of him, Francis brought the stun gun up fast. Cavanaugh had been ready, grabbed Francis's wrist. With his other hand, he grabbed the pistol, pushed it away.

Francis tried to pull away, but Cavanaugh stepped in, brought a knee up hard into Francis's groin. Pain flared in his testicles, and it took every bit of Francis's willpower to resist the need to drop and curl into the fetal position. His face went hot, nausea rising up.

They bounced around the room, holding on to each other, each trying to get the upper hand. They banged into the desk and the dresser, knocking over baseball trophies. Their legs tangled, and both went down, Cavanaugh ending up on top.

Francis tried to bring the stun gun up, but Cavanaugh had the angle and put all his weight into holding Francis's arm down. But this meant the hand holding the revolver at bay was in a weaker position. Francis began to twist his hand, and slowly the barrel swung even with Cavanaugh's left eye.

"Shit!" Cavanaugh let go of Francis's other arm so he could push the barrel of the revolver away.

Francis jammed the stun gun under Cavanaugh's chin and thumbed the trigger.

Zap.

Cavanaugh went rigid a split second, then fell limp across

Francis's body. He groaned but didn't move. Francis pushed him off, then zapped him again.

"Fucker!"

He zapped him a third time. Cavanaugh lay still.

"Sh-shoot . . . him," came a weak voice. "Shoot . . ."

Emma lay still on the bed, one eye open but glassy. "Kill . . . kill him."

Francis ignored her and lurched to his feet. The ache in his balls was going to slow him down, but it was already beginning to ebb.

He unbuckled the belt around Emma's ankles, then untied the cord around her wrists. "Can you stand? Can you walk?"

She muttered something unintelligible.

The urge to simply wait and rest nearly seduced him. He hurt, and Emma was obviously in no shape to go anywhere. Maybe he could just lie down next to her, just for a few seconds.

But there were still men out there with guns, and soon they'd lose the fog.

"Emma, please. Come on."

He put one of her arms around his neck, lifted her off the bed. Part of her must have been listening, because she tried to stand for him but nearly collapsed when her feet hit the floor. She groaned and flopped back on the bed.

"Can't . . . can't feel my feet."

She fought hard to stay conscious, eyes trying to focus on him.

Francis retrieved the shotgun, slung it over his shoulder, stuck the stun gun into his back pocket. "Easy, Emma. I've got you."

He bent and gathered her up, shifted her weight, then heaved her onto his shoulder in a fireman's carry.

Thank God she's thin. I need to start working out.

He wrapped one arm around her bare legs to hold her steady, revolver up in the other hand, and headed down the hall. By the time he made it to the kitchen, his legs already felt weak, partially because of the knee to the balls, partially because of Emma's weight.

If I put her down, I'll never get her up again.

He opened the kitchen door and stuck his head out. The fog was still thick. The others were out there somewhere, looking for him. They would search the barn as a matter of course, but that's just where Francis had to go. Luck. He just needed a little luck.

He nudged the door open the rest of the way and headed out through the fog, ears straining to hear a voice or a footfall or any warning at all the thugs were nearby. He circled the barn to the smaller side door, paused to listen.

A sharp pain spread from his shoulder blades, and he shifted Emma's weight slightly. He'd need to set her down soon, but he forced himself to move slowly. He opened the door a couple of inches, stopped again to listen, then eased the door open the rest of the way and entered, pulling it closed softly behind him.

The lights were on, and he froze. He tried to remember if he'd shut them off or not. He had. He started backing toward the door but stopped himself. No, the lights being on was a good thing. It meant they'd been here and searched and left.

His eyes darted around the interior of the barn. He *hoped* they'd left.

Francis took the narrow path between the GTO and the tractor, circling around to the other side of the Pontiac. He opened the door. He bent, grunting, and gently lay Emma in the back seat. It was a relief to put her down. He rubbed his shoulder and neck.

Emma muttered something. She tried to lift her head, fighting to stay conscious, eyes blinking and trying to focus.

"It's okay now," Francis whispered. "We'll be out of here soon. Just sleep."

Wait, what did they say to do if somebody had a concussion? Maybe he was supposed to keep her awake. How did one even diagnose a concussion anyway? Something with eye dilating, Francis thought. He couldn't quite remember.

Because he was fucking useless.

Stop panicking, Francis told himself. *And keep moving*.

He reached in and buckled the seat belts around her as best he could. There wouldn't be time to do it later.

He circled back to the other side of the car and turned his attention to the tractor. Yet another thing he didn't know a thing about—starting a tractor. He hoped it wasn't complicated. He'd mowed his grandmother's lawn with a riding mower when he was in high school. It couldn't be more difficult than that, could it?

While he pondered the tractor, something else nagged at him. Something was . . . missing?

He looked down at the floor. The tarp was there. The bald thug wasn't.

Francis turned quickly to run back to—

The fist hit him square between the eyes. His vision filled with stars exploding like fireworks. He staggered back into the tractor, bruising his back on some jutting piece of machinery, then rolled away, trying to blink his vision clear.

He sensed the bald thug coming forward. Francis reached into his back pocket and came out with the stun gun. He waved it wildly in front of him, thumbing the trigger, the blue light spitting and popping. His ears rang. He blinked and cleared his vision just in time to see the bald one rushing him.

The thug slapped the stun gun away, and it spun off into the distant, dark reaches of the barn. The thug kept coming, barreled into Francis, and both of them went down. The thug ended up on top. Francis punched upward. The thug's chest absorbed it as if it were nothing.

One of the thug's hands took Francis by the throat. The other hand squeezed tight into a hammy fist. He raised it high. "You little fucking shit. Zap me with my own stun gun."

Francis tried to talk, to plead, but the thug's fist tightened on his throat.

The fist came down hard, and a whole new world of pain exploded in Francis's jaw. His eyes filled with tears. The man sitting on his chest was a blur.

"Little fucking cocksucker," the bald thug said. "Fucking kill you."

The thug squeezed harder, and Francis tried to suck for air and failed. His vision grew cottony around the edges, and he felt himself fading, slowly being drawn down into a cold blackness. He tried to pry at the fingers at his throat, but there was no strength remaining in him. As darkness closed in, his ears filled with a roaring like the blood in his body rushing to a single spot.

Francis shoved his hand down between his body and the thug's, fingers clawing, searching.

"You're going to die now, little man," the thug said. "And then we do whatever we like to your freaky little bitch girlfriend. That's what I want you to know. You'll be dead, hero, and nobody will save her. Is that what you think you're doing? You're not saving nobody."

Francis's hand closed around the butt of the revolver stuck in his waistband. He twisted it, and the thug felt the cold metal in his gut. The recognition of what he was feeling dawned in his eyes.

The gun went off, the report muffled by the two bodies sandwiched around it. Francis felt a burning force against his stomach as the revolver bucked.

I'm shot. Oh my God, I'm dead.

Francis realized the thug had gone limp on top of him. He pushed the body off and scooted away. The thug rolled back up against the tractor, and at first Francis thought he was dead. The thug blinked once slowly, an expression of disbelief on his ashen face. One of his trembling hands went up to the hole in the center of his chest, blood seeping between each finger.

Francis inched away from him, looking on in horror.

The thug worked his mouth to say something, but suddenly coughed once so violently it made Francis flinch. Blood erupted from the thug's mouth, dripping down his bottom lip and chin. His eyes met Francis's, pleading.

In the second Francis's brain spun, wondering what to do, it was over. He watched the light fade from the thug's eyes. Francis imagined he could almost see the life lift out of the man and drift away like a puff of smoke. The dead man's eyes looked like glass. And in that moment, it didn't matter if he was a good guy or a bad guy. In the single pull of a trigger, Francis had ended the man, something so final it was hard to believe. Of course it was self-defense, but Francis stood, weak and sweating, the feeling that something inside of him had shifted and could never shift back into place again.

He took three deep breaths and steeled himself. There wasn't time for this. Francis couldn't afford the luxury of self-reflection. Not now.

He looked down at the revolver dangling loose in his hand. He didn't want it anymore but knew he might need it. He picked up the shotgun where it had fallen and took both to the back seat of the Pontiac. He dumped them in the floor behind the driver's seat and paused to look at Emma.

She breathed easily, eyes closed, legs pulled up slightly. If it hadn't been for her face, she might simply have been napping

NO GOOD DEED • 175

peacefully. Her bottom lip was split, and the left side of her face swelled badly.

Francis went back to the tractor, climbed up into the seat. At first, he had no idea what he was looking at, but then it turned out to be as simple as he'd hoped. He thumbed the starter button and was relieved when the tractor cranked immediately. It made a thunderous rattling sound much louder than Francis had expected. He needed to hurry and get the thing out of there. He wanted to attract attention, but not to the barn.

He hopped down from the tractor and turned out the lights before throwing the barn doors wide. Back atop the tractor, he shifted into gear and headed out, the tractor's headlights impotently trying to penetrate the fog. He tried to remember what his environs looked like without the fog and pointed the tractor toward what he was fairly sure was the widest part of the pasture.

Francis leaped from the seat, hit the ground, and rolled. He sprang back up, looked to see the tractor still on course, its shape slowly being swallowed by the fog, only the fuzzy glow of the headlights still visible.

Francis cupped his hands around his mouth and yelled, "There he goes! He's getting away!"

For a long, tense moment, Francis thought he had accomplished approximately dick.

Then suddenly shouts back and forth through the fog. Francis glimpsed dark shapes running after the tractor. More shouting.

Francis stood frozen, listening. Had it really been that easy?

The sound of gunshots sent Francis running back to the barn.

He climbed in behind the wheel of the Pontiac and cranked the ignition. The engine rumbled, and the vibrations felt like raw power. He shifted into gear, and the car erupted from the barn like it had been shot from a Howitzer.

176 • VICTOR GISCHLER

As he sped past the house, he saw the one with the shaggy mustache stumble out the front door, gun in hand. Francis mashed the gas pedal and shot down the narrow dirt road. If he could just remember the zigs and zags between here and the highway, he should be home free. He glanced back to check on Emma, saw she was still sleeping.

When he faced forward again, a large SUV loomed large in the fog directly ahead of him.

"Shit!"

Francis jerked the wheel and hit the brakes. The Pontiac fishtailed and missed the SUV by an inch. There were two more vehicles parked behind the SUV. He realized this was where Cavanaugh and his goons had parked before slipping up on him through the fog.

The sun was up now, and soon the fog would burn off. Until then, Francis decided to drive on a little more slowly. He was desperate to put miles between him and the gunmen, but escaping only to wrap the car around a tree wasn't something he wanted to explain to Emma.

When his men had found the tractor spinning its wheels in a ditch on the other side of the pasture, Cavanaugh cursed and knew they'd been suckered. "These little shits are making us look like clowns."

Ernie sat behind the wheel. There was still a little fog, so he leaned forward, squinting as he drove. The other two vehicles with the rest of the boys followed behind. They were trying to hurry. If Berringer and the girl made it to the highway, then they could head off anywhere, and Cavanaugh would be back at square one.

"What year?" Cavanaugh asked.

"I don't know," Ernie said. "Sixties."

"Sixty-one? Sixty-two? Sixty-three?"

"Give me a fucking break, okay? I'm not a car guy. Late sixties. Sixty-eight or sixty-nine."

"You didn't see a logo? Ford or Chevy?"

Ernie shook his head. "I'd know it if I saw it again."

Cavanaugh pulled up a photo of a 1969 Camaro on his smartphone and showed it to Ernie. "That?"

"No. The front end looked more pointy."

"Pointy?"

"Yeah, I dunno. Pointy."

Cavanaugh showed him a picture of a 1969 Corvette.

"Jesus, I know a Vette when I see one," Ernie said. "Not *that* pointy. A muscle car."

Cavanaugh showed him a half dozen more photos, but Ernie kept shaking his head.

Then Cavanaugh showed him a picture of a 1968 Pontiac GTO.

"That's it," Ernie said. "I'm positive."

"What color?"

"Red."

"What kind of red?"

Ernie frowned at him. "Red red."

Cavanaugh sighed. "There's a whole spectrum, you know. A bright primary sort of red but also a red with some purple in it like a burgundy or something."

Ernie glanced at Cavanaugh like maybe he wondered if he were being put on. Then his brow wrinkled as he thought about it a moment. "A little darker. Like red with some cherry in it, maybe."

"Okay." Cavanaugh dialed the number into his smartphone. "We're going to find this Berringer son of a bitch and get him for what he did to Ike. We're going to feed him his own balls."

———

Bryant was eager to see how this would work. Middleton had ordered the new software to be completely uninstalled from Bryant's setup and relocated to the facility built into the new Sonoma house. So Cavanaugh's request might be one of the few chances remaining for Bryant to see the software in action.

He plugged *1968 or 1969 Pontiac GTO, cherry red or candy-apple red* into the search string for Berringer and the girl, then sat back and waited. He didn't need to add any other search parameters. The software knew what to do, and it was a pleasure to see the thing in motion. He'd had it put up on the big monitor so he could see everything unfold as the program went step-by-step through the process.

The software accessed multiple websites to get the average gas mileage for that year and make of automobile. Speed limits for the surrounding roads and highways. Numbers flashed across the screen as the software used the information to calculate a search radius.

Then a blur of photographs across the screen, vehicles with rest stops or highways in the background. Bryant could tell they were digital image captures from various surveillance cameras.

One of the images suddenly blinked, an accompanying bell, alerting him the computer had a hit. A picture-in-picture image of the Pontiac at a gas pump moved up to the corner of the screen. The man filling the car with gas had his back to the camera but could have been Berringer. They didn't get a credit card hit, so he must have paid cash. The image was from a truck stop on Highway 50 near Vermillion. The surveillance system saved its footage to the cloud, and the software accessed it with ease.

Another picture-in-picture image flickered into existence directly below the surveillance cam photo of the Pontiac. It was a Google Maps image pinpointing the exact location. A second later, another image appeared in the other corner of the screen. The Pontiac again, but this time a photo from a Nebraska State Patrol dash cam. To Bryant, it seemed the trooper was just parked on the side of the road, and the Pontiac had happened by.

The next image was again from Google Maps, showing the trooper's location as just over the state line on Highway 15.

They'd located Berringer and the girl, and had the direction in which they were traveling.

The entire process had taken ninety-seven seconds.

"Highway 15." Cavanaugh jotted it into his notebook. "Got it. Listen, if the computer gets another hit, let me know right away. Maybe you can work up some kind of intercept course for us. Right. Okay, thanks."

Cavanaugh hung up and then grinned at Ernie. "I think we got the little bastard."

21

Middleton's automatic kitchen brewed coffee and toasted him a bagel.

"Meredith Vines is at the front door, Mr. Middleton." The computer's dulcet voice seemed to come from midair.

"Let her in," Middleton said. "Computer, make a note." He refused to call the system *Adam* and still intended to change the voice as soon as possible. "Whenever Miss Vines is here, she's to be let in automatically. Just announcing her is all you need to do."

"Yes, Mr. Middleton," the computer said. "I've updated Meredith Vines' profile."

Meredith found him in the kitchen a minute later, and he poured her a cup of coffee.

"Bryant says a complete extraction of the program from his system should be complete in the next seventy-two hours. Maybe sooner," Meredith told him.

"How did he take that?"

"He wasn't thrilled," she said. "He didn't say anything, but I could tell."

"He's a valuable asset," Middleton said. "He doesn't have to worry about his job."

"Marketing is screaming," Meredith said. "The words *indefinite delay* have them pulling their hair out. They want to know why they can't get their package together for potential buyers. Care to share what you're thinking?"

"Who are the most likely buyers for the new software?" Middleton asked.

"Governments," she said. "Fortune 500 companies. Research universities."

"If a government buys it, what's half the value?"

"That other governments *don't* have it," she said.

"Let's say the federal government buys it," Middleton said. "They'll want exclusivity. Otherwise, they won't pay top dollar."

"We've crunched those numbers," Meredith reminded him. "Selling it to everyone nets us more even at a greatly reduced price."

"When everyone is special, then no one is."

She blinked. "What?"

"A line from a movie I like," Middleton said. "Every government intelligence agency will need it to keep up with every other intelligence agency. But they'll all negate each other then, won't they? And then this amazing thing we've created will be a big nothing."

"Sure, but after the company has made a gazillion and a half dollars."

"Money isn't everything."

Her eyes narrowed, pinned him hard. "What supervillain scheme are you concocting, sir?"

"I keep it."

"You keep it."

"Yes."

"For your own personal plaything?"

"That's not quite how I'd put it."

Meredith shook her head, eyes rolling. "The board will *love* this."

"I don't mean keep it forever," Middleton said. "We do a press release saying that we're tweaking it. In the meantime, I'll use it myself. It will make us money with market analysis alone. There are easily a hundred other applications. By the time we're ready to sell, we'll already have the gen-two version ready to go. We market the old one, keep the new one for ourselves. We'll always be one step ahead of the rest of the world."

Meredith sipped coffee, brow furrowed, thinking. "It's really taking the long view, but we might be able to sell the board on that." She yawned, rubbed an eye with a thumb.

"Are you okay?" he asked. He'd noticed that her eyes were red, dark circles underneath just beginning to form.

"Just . . . long hours."

"You're not still driving back and forth from San Mateo, are you?"

"That's where my apartment is," she said.

"You know I'm transitioning to working at home full-time," Middleton said. "Perks of being the boss. But the fact is, I need you. You're my right hand. The house is huge, and I had an office built for you, but really, it's a suite of rooms. One could easily be a bedroom. If we work late one night, there's no reason to risk a long drive if you're half-asleep."

That teasing smile quirked to her face. "My goodness, are you asking me to live with you, Mr. Middleton?"

He knew she was just messing with him, and yet he literally flinched, stomach fluttering. He'd seriously meant the proposal as strictly work-related, but her offhanded joke had ripped away the veil over his emotions. She watched his reaction, and all the humor drained from her face.

"No . . . I . . . I would never . . ." Why couldn't he make his words work? His mouth felt so dry. The more he tried to object, the more obvious it was that yes, he'd like nothing better than for her to be near him always, that every time she went away, his life was reduced to time spent waiting for her to come back again.

Meredith set her coffee cup on the counter. She looked at Middleton. He looked back.

She took three slow steps to close the distance between them. He didn't dare move. She lay a slim hand on his chest, palm flat over his heart. It beat so hard, and he knew she felt it. She tilted her head and very slowly lifted herself on tiptoes until her lips brushed his as softly as a whisper.

Middleton went dizzy, felt light, as if he might float up and out of his own body.

Meredith pulled away and said, "Am I fired?"

"You are so *not* fired."

They kissed harder.

The Pontiac GTO blazed across Highway 84 through brown Nebraska pastureland. The landscape had widened considerably in the last hour, an occasional stand of trees or farmhouse humping up on a small hillock breaking the monotony.

Francis had spent enough time in Manhattan that it had nearly erased the memory of wide-open spaces. Ohio had plenty of farmland, but so much land stretching between the horizons felt strange instead of familiar.

Francis had taken random highways, keeping generally south and west. He'd hoped to throw off any pursuit. He hadn't wanted to stop for gas, but with the needle nearing E, he hadn't any choice.

Now, he yet again had to force himself to ease off the gas pedal. It was as if the Pontiac had a mind of its own and *wanted* to go fast, but Francis equally wanted *not* to get a speeding ticket.

Sometime soon he'd need to stop and see to Emma, but he still wanted to put more miles between himself and Cavanaugh and all his goons.

A pickup truck passed him. The truck's sudden appearance startled him. It wasn't the first time this had happened. Francis was concerned about going the speed limit, but apparently the locals weren't. The truck sped ahead and left him in the dust.

Francis adjusted the rearview mirror to see down into the back seat. Emma still slept peacefully. Seeing her this way, it was difficult to imagine her with that hard edge. She seemed the sort of person who eternally had her fists up against whatever the world might bring. There was a soft prettiness about her now, a surprising vulnerability, and whatever Francis felt for her before doubled at that moment. He realized that whatever happened from here forward, he wouldn't undo what had brought him here. He'd still take the suitcase in the alley. He'd still follow the girl into peril.

He shifted the rearview mirror back into place, just in time to see another car coming up fast. At least this time he'd spotted it ahead of time so it wouldn't frighten the crap out of him when the car whipped past. Francis drifted to the edge of his lane to give the other driver plenty of room.

Francis glanced back again. The car approached at top speed, rapidly filling the rearview mirror until—

The car slammed hard into the back of the Pontiac.

The GTO fishtailed all over the road, and Francis wrestled with the steering wheel to get it back on course. The right tires went off the shoulder, kicking up dirt and rattling the car violently.

Francis yanked the Pontiac back onto the road just in time for the car behind him to fly up and slam him again.

The Pontiac spun, the world in the windshield distorting into a muddle of light and color, tires squealing. The smell of burned rubber filled the car. Francis went rigid, knuckles white on the wheel, and waited to die.

When the car lurched to a stop, Francis faced the opposite direction back east. He saw the other car in the rearview mirror. It had blown a hundred yards past him when he'd gone into the spin and was now making a three-point turn in the middle of the road to roll back through its own cloud of dust and get after Francis again.

Francis cracked his knuckles, then gripped the wheel at ten and two, his jaw set.

Then he mashed the GTO's gas pedal flat.

For a split second, the tires spun in place, rubber burning, and then an instant later, the Pontiac rocketed down the highway, Cavanaugh's car shrinking rapidly in the rearview mirror. Francis thought this might be how a bullet felt being shot out of a gun. He'd had the car up at a pretty high speed a few times, but this was his first go at taking it flat out. The acceleration pressed him back into the leather seat. His entire body hummed with the GTO's power.

The Pontiac ate up the miles, the scenery on each side of the road melting into a blur. Francis thought the car might actually take flight at any second. At this speed, Francis was afraid even to twitch. He wanted to glance down at the speedometer, but he didn't want to risk taking his eyes off the road. Sweat trickled down his back. Just a little longer, just until he could find a place to turn. The more distance and zigs and zags he put between himself and Cavanaugh, the better.

Francis couldn't understand how they'd found him in the first place. He was literally in the middle of nowhere. And they'd found him *fast* too. A pang of hopelessness made his gut clench. Was there no place they could go? Nowhere to hide?

No. He'd bested these assholes already. He'd do it again.

He hoped.

Francis passed back through an area with more trees. It had stood out when he'd come through before because the rest of this area was just brown fields stretching forever. The road took a long lazy bend toward the south, and if he remembered correctly, there was some kind of little crossroads on the other side. He eased up slightly on the gas pedal going into the turn.

At these speeds, the Pontiac guzzled unleaded like Kool-Aid. Francis had no idea where the next town might be, and the idea of running out of gas this far from—

There was a tractor in the middle of the road.

Not just a tractor. It was pulling a trailer stacked twelve feet high with square bales of hay. A couple had fallen as the tractor had tried to make the turn at the very crossroads Francis had been gunning for. An old man in faded jeans and a work shirt stood over them, seemingly in no hurry to rectify the situation. His head came up at the sound of the Pontiac's engine, eyes going to the size of dinner plates. The old man could not have looked more frightened if the grim reaper himself were the GTO's hood ornament.

A jolt of alarm went through Francis at the sight of the blocked road, and he slammed the brakes too hard. Tires squealed, the back of the GTO fishtailing and clipping one of the hay bales as it slid past. The car bumped front wheels and then back as it left the humped-up asphalt and spun halfway around in the semi-tall grass, finally coming to a stop in a cloud of brown dust.

Francis sat for a stunned moment, still gripping the wheel and breathing hard, heart thumping against his insides. Going from full speed to a sudden stop was an odd sensation.

"Hey, boy," called the old man. "You okay?"

Francis ignored him, turned the key in the ignition.

Nothing.

Shit shit shit shit shit.

He took the key out, put it back in and twisted again. The engine didn't even cough. At the edge of his vision, he saw the old man hobbling toward him. Francis kept turning the ignition key, hoping something different would happen.

Come on. Come on.

The old man was right at the driver's-side window now. "Hey, boy."

Francis heard the distant engine and didn't have to look to know it was Cavanaugh. He looked anyway. The sedan was coming around the long curve.

Francis slammed the dashboard with a fist. "Start, you piece of shit!"

The old man knocked on the window. "You're in drive, boy."

Francis rolled the window down. "What?"

The old man pointed at the gearshift on the steering column. "You need to put it in park first."

Francis shifted into park and turned the key again. It cranked immediately.

"Thanks," Francis told him. "Sorry if I startled you."

The old man took a step back, flipped a two-finger salute. "Good luck."

Francis cut across the corner of the field, heading for the road that went south. The ground wasn't as flat as it looked from the road, and the Pontiac swayed and bounced. A quick glance back showed Cavanaugh following his path down the gentle slope from the road. The old man waved as the sedan with the thugs rolled by, kicking up dirt.

The slope back up to the other road was steeper, and Francis felt and heard the Pontiac scrape bottom. The sedan made it up the slope with less trouble, and in an eyeblink, both cars were flying south down the narrow county road. The sedan swung around to pull up next to him.

Francis was about to mash the gas pedal again, but the road curved in and out of an area of low hills and scattered farmhouses. He couldn't rocket away like he did before on the straightaway, and he wasn't a good enough driver to outmaneuver the other car.

So when the other car came around the back and started to pull alongside, Francis jerked the wheel. The Pontiac veered toward the other car. Cavanaugh was doing the same thing, coming right back at Francis.

Both automobiles met at the dotted yellow line down the center of the road, the scrape and crunch of metal on metal sounding like the end of the world. The cars bounced off each other, both going off the road, then careening back and meeting in the middle to collide again.

It took all Francis's focus to steady the Pontiac and keep it on the road.

He chanced a glance at the other car and saw the passenger-side window roll down. Cavanaugh held his little silver pistol and was aiming it out the window not ten feet away, and now Francis was going to die.

Something stretched out from the car at the farthest limit of Francis's peripheral vision, and Francis realized it was Emma's arm reaching out the window behind his seat, her slender fingers curled around—

Cavanaugh's eyes shifted, going wide with alarm—

Three sharp cracks of thunder exploded behind Francis's left ear. He flinched and swerved. Three new holes bloomed in Cavanaugh's door, and they hit the brakes, swinging back behind the Pontiac.

Francis's left ear rang, felt like it was stuffed with cotton.

Emma climbed over the seat, the smoking revolver in her hand. She clicked the seat belt into place.

"You could have grabbed me some pants." She still wore only panties and a T-shirt.

"We sort of left in a hurry," Francis said.

Three loud pops drew Francis's attention to the rearview mirror. Cavanaugh was leaning out of his window, his little automatic spitting fire at them. Francis ducked his head, his shoulders hunching up. He swerved back and forth across the blacktop, trying to make the GTO a difficult target. More pops chased him down the road.

Emma unbuckled her seat belt again. "Don't crash."

She rolled down the passenger-side window, leaned out, and fired the revolver back at Cavanaugh. Cavanaugh's car mimicked the Pontiac's evasive maneuvers. The two cars roared down the highway, bullets flying.

They came out of the hilly area, the road curving into low ground and another crossroads. But here there was a scattering of buildings, a mom-and-pop gas station, post office, and feedstore. A collection of old clapboard houses spread out in a circle from the crossroads, some little rural community God had dropped out of the sky and into the middle of nowhere.

"You've only got one shot left!" Francis shouted over the engine racket and the wind howling past.

"Two," she said. "I've been counting."

Francis thought briefly of the man he'd killed, those wide eyes staring at nothing. "One."

"Fuck." She climbed halfway out the window, her butt resting on the edge of the door.

"Are you nuts?" Francis shouted, trying to grab for her. "Get back in here!"

"I got one shot, Frankie."

"Francis!"

The little gas station ahead sat at a gentle bend in the road. Francis slowed the GTO but not enough. The car slid, tires screaming, the GTO's back end coming around.

Emma's hand flailed inside the car looking for something to hold.

"Emma!" Francis's hand shot out to grab hers, only just preventing her from flying out of the car.

She hung on tight. Francis steered the Pontiac through the curve one-handed. Sweat soaked his shirt at the neck and under his arms, panic jolting his system with adrenaline.

Please please please.

He made it through the curve without losing control of the car or letting go of Emma. Cavanaugh's car hit the turn right behind them.

Emma extended her shooting arm, closing one eye tight, sighting along the barrel of the revolver. She held her breath. Let it out slowly.

And squeezed the trigger.

The pistol bucked in her hand, and Cavanaugh's front passenger tire blew.

The sedan slid into the curve just as the Pontiac had before, but with the blown tire, it slid halfway around and went off the road, its back end sweeping into the single gas pump at the mom-and-pop filling station. A crack and crunch of metal and glass, and the pump went over, banging against the cement. Gasoline fountained up from the new hole in the ground.

Francis watched the calamity unfold in the rearview mirror.

Two people fled from the filling station—a middle-aged guy and a freckled girl who looked like a teenager. A second later, Cavanaugh and the henchman with the shaggy mustache stumbled from the sedan, paused a moment to take in what was happening, then started running.

They got clear a second before the whole thing went up. Francis felt the Pontiac shudder with the explosion, fire and roiling black smoke reaching into the sky.

Emma climbed back into the passenger seat, refastened her belt. "We'll need to ditch the Pontiac."

Francis forced himself to breathe more slowly. He nodded. "Right." He forced his grip on the steering wheel to ease. His fingers ached. All of him was sore. He let out a long, ragged breath.

"And we'll need a store," she said. "I packed another pair of jeans, but I don't have shoes."

"Right. A store. Okay." Francis glanced in the rearview mirror one more time, the fiery orange glow shrinking behind them. "Where do we find a store?"

"Go west, young man."

22

They spooned under the comforter in Middleton's king-sized bed.

Middleton realized he'd dozed. How long? Not more than a few minutes, surely. He remembered what had happened with an easy smile. The kissing had gotten earnest, then had become frantic, each of them pulling at the other's clothing. They'd moved to the bedroom, and Meredith had pulled him down on top of her, legs wrapping around him, both of them so eager, months of wanting this finally coming to fruition.

In spite of some fumbling on his part, it had been energetic and glorious. And extremely brief.

He pulled her closer, nuzzled his face into her neck. She made a low kind of purring sound. She wiggled herself back against him, and he slipped a hand under the comforter and cupped a breast. Everything about her was so soft. She was perfect.

She kept wriggling herself back against him until he took the hint.

When he'd grown ready again, Meredith reached back and guided him in. He pulled her close, and they found a slow rhythm.

"Yes," she whispered. "That's . . . nice."

He paused.

"What is it?" she asked.

"Do you . . . have you taken precautions?" It occurred to him that it was an extremely tardy question.

"The pill."

"Oh. Good. Is that because . . . I mean are you . . . ?"

"I'm not seeing anyone else," she said. "I started in college. Seemed like part of the independent woman thing."

"Oh. I never thought to ask. Obviously, you could have been seeing somebody. I mean, why not?"

"It turns out my boss is a real slave driver, and I don't really have time for a social life."

Middleton laughed.

"Weren't you in the middle of something?" she reminded him. He resumed.

Every time his instinct was to speed up, he forced himself to maintain a steady, slow pace. He wanted to prolong the moment. He wanted it to last forever.

She took his hand from her breast, slid it down her belly to a spot between her legs. Middleton understood what to do. He wasn't completely without experience, and had a working knowledge of the necessary mechanics. Still, it had been a while. Perhaps he could make up for being rusty with raw sincerity.

With two fingers, he massaged tight little circles, matching the rhythm of his thrusting hips.

He sensed her getting close and picked up speed.

She went rigid, legs trembling, her head going back. Her mouth fell open, no sound coming out, and squeezed her eyes closed tight. He finished with her.

They both went slack again, breathing heavily.

They lay there for several minutes, not talking, just dreamily enjoying the afterglow. Then she scooted over to the edge of the bed, reached for the smartphone. She looked at the screen and frowned.

"Fifty-eight. Shit."

She swung her legs over the side of the bed and bounced up, began circling the room, grabbing her clothes off the floor.

Middleton sat up. "Fifty-eight what?"

"Emails." She stepped into her panties, looked around. "Where's my bra?"

"On the chair." Middleton pointed. "Is something going on? An emergency or something? How long were we in bed?"

"Not that long." She waved the smartphone at him. "This is *standard*. You realize I'm the gatekeeper between you and the rest of the world, right? If I don't start answering these emails soon, they'll send out a SWAT team and search dogs." She shrugged into the bra. Hooked it in back.

"Don't sweat it," Middleton told her. "I happen to know you're on the boss's good side."

She sighed, sat on the bed, and pulled on her stockings. "Okay, we need to talk about this."

"You don't need the stockings," he said. "Your legs are perfect."

"I'm serious," she said. "You need to listen to me."

"Uh-oh."

Meredith shook her head. "Not uh-oh. Nothing uh-oh. We just need to . . . compartmentalize things." She shimmied into her skirt.

"Compartmentalize." Middleton said the word out loud, hoping he'd understand her meaning better. He didn't.

"We've just got to keep things separate. This thing, whatever this thing is"—she gestured back and forth between herself and Middleton—"it can't overlap with work. I still need to do my job, and not have this"—she gestured at the bed—"somehow become my *new* job."

Middleton sat up straighter in bed. "No, oh, I mean, of course. I never meant—I hope you don't think—"

"I know, I know." She slipped on her blouse, began buttoning. "I just needed to say it. I've always wanted to be *professional*, you know? I mean, I *am* professional. I'm good at my job, I think. Aren't I professional?"

"You are."

She held up the smartphone and headed for the door. "I have to start answering these. Tell your kitchen to make me some more coffee."

Cavanaugh sat across the table from Ernie in a nearly empty cowboy saloon called the Bull Market Beer & Grill in Valentine, Nebraska. Even a casual observer would have recognized at a glance that the two men were beaten down and defeated. They slumped in their chairs, not speaking.

At last, Ernie said, "I don't think we're doing this right."

Cavanaugh waved him away. "Not yet. Just . . . not yet."

They sat and waited.

The beers finally arrived. The place had just opened, so it was taking a while to get things cranked up. A waitress left menus in case they wanted food later.

Cavanaugh sipped beer. It was cold and yellow.

When they'd set out after Berringer and the girl, they'd kept generally south and west on Bryant's suggestion. Once over the line into Nebraska, Cavanaugh had sent the guys in the other two cars down different highways to cover more ground. Fortunately, one of them had only been two minutes away, and after a quick call, they'd come to scoop up Cavanaugh and Ernie and take them away. On their way out of town, there had still been no sign of the local cops. Score one for being in the middle of nowhere.

One of the new guys entered the saloon and came over to Cavanaugh's table. "The SUVs are all gassed up. What now?"

Cavanaugh sighed, then gestured at the empty tables across the room. "We're figuring it out. You and the boys grab a table, get some burgers or whatever. Just have the girl send the check over here."

196 • VICTOR GISCHLER

"Okay," he said and left.

Cavanaugh and Ernie finished their beers. Cavanaugh waved the girl over for two more.

The beers arrived. They sipped.

Ernie raised an eyebrow. "Now?"

"Go ahead."

"Look, maybe we made a mistake, huh?" Ernie said. "If we'd just disappeared the girl like we were supposed to, we wouldn't be sitting here licking our wounds like a couple of chumps."

"We're supposed to find the paper anyway," Cavanaugh said. "We had to make her tell us. Nothing would have been any different."

"Maybe I'm just superstitious," Ernie said. "I feel like if we just did the job we were paid for, none of this would have happened. I appreciate what you said about a big score, but I think we got off track."

"Do the job we're paid for?" Cavanaugh asked.

Ernie sipped beer, shrugged, nodded.

"And how long can we do that? You got a retirement plan? You got a 401(k)?" Cavanaugh didn't wait for a reply. He already knew the answer. "How do you feel right now?"

"What do you mean?"

"How do you *feel*?" Cavanaugh said.

"Like shit."

"Elaborate."

"I feel embarrassed," Ernie said. "I feel like we should have wrapped this up by now, but fucking amateurs keep dicking us."

"And?"

"And what?" Ernie said. "I said I feel like fucking shit, okay? My neck and back hurt. My *face* fucking hurts. I've been in two damn car wrecks in as many days. I am fucking *tired*."

Cavanaugh was nodding along. "What you mean is you're old."

"Fuck you."

NO GOOD DEED   •   197

"Take it easy," Cavanaugh said. "I don't mean drool-your-oatmeal old like you can't control when you piss, okay? That's not what I'm saying. I'm just saying too old for this bullshit we're doing. You and me both. I spent prime years in stir making toilet bowl moonshine. You hear me? I mean, those years are fucking gone, right?"

"Jesus, who are you talking to?" Ernie said. "I know. Of course I know. I lived that shit too."

"Then okay, you know what I'm saying," Cavanaugh said. "Are we still going to be doing this same shit in ten years? Twenty?"

Ernie didn't reply. The look on his face was enough.

"And it's more than that," Cavanaugh said. "Everything's *changed*. Guys like us used to be something. We had respect. Now guys like Bryant sit in a comfy, air-conditioned room pushing computer buttons. We're just monkeys doing the grunt work. We're working for the computer. We get our hands dirty. We get the bruises."

"I thought working for Middleton would be easy," Ernie said. "Lean on people. Get their minds right when needed."

"Exactly," Cavanaugh agreed. "But now it's the computer that leans on people. Intimidating people used to be a professional thing. Now it's just like paying your electric bill online or some shit. And Ike is dead. *Dead*. Some fucking cubicle asshole killed him. What kind of world do we live in where a guy like that can take out a guy like Ike? Everything is upside down."

"So what do we do?"

"What I said before," Cavanaugh told him. "We get *out*. We say to hell with all this shit and get set up somewhere. I got my eye on Costa Rica. But that takes money, and this is our best chance right here and right now. I know we've hit a few bumps."

"'A few bumps,' he says."

"I know this hasn't been clockwork," Cavanaugh pressed on. "But this is our score. This is our ticket out of working for a computer and some kid billionaire. And God bless Ike, wherever he is now, but the fact is now we'd only be splitting the take two ways. We get this paper with the techno crap on it and cash out. Then we're our own bosses again. Then we get our lives back."

Ernie thought about it. "Okay. What happens next?"

"First thing is we stop chasing across flyover country like dumbasses," Cavanaugh said. "I'm pretty sure I know where the girl is going. We'll get ahead of them. We'll be cutting things close, but we'll make it work."

"And the girl and Berringer?" Ernie asked. "What do we do with them?"

"We do with them what we were always going to do with them," Cavanaugh said. "No loose ends."

Ernie shrugged in that way Cavanaugh knew meant it was a shame, but it is what it is. Ernie was always the pragmatic one. "Then how do we find a buyer once we get our hands on this thing?"

"I've been mulling that over," Cavanaugh said. "I think the best buyer is going to be Middleton himself. He obviously doesn't want anyone else to have this thing, and we know where he is, so we don't have to track him down. And we sure as hell know he has the money to spend."

"He won't like it."

Cavanaugh grinned. "The beauty is that he doesn't have to like it. What's he going to do? Call in his muscle? That's us. We tell him to pony up or we take the paper to another buyer. He can call it a severance package if he wants."

Ernie nodded, drained his beer, and smacked his lips. He thought about it a moment. "I'm good with it."

"Okay, then. It's decided. We do this." Cavanaugh picked up a menu. "First, we get a burger, and then we do this."

23

Francis had parked the Pontiac around the side of the Walmart near the Garden Center, stacks of potting soil bags and mulch and fencing and huge wooden spools of cable partially blocking them from casual observers driving by on the main road.

Francis emerged from the Garden Center with a plastic shopping bag in each hand and found Emma waiting for him, sitting on the hood of the Pontiac, bare feet dangling. She'd put on jeans and changed into a Drive-By Truckers T-shirt.

Francis set the bags on the hood next to her.

She held out her hands. "Give."

He took a shoe box from one of the bags, gave it to her. "I thought it best to keep it simple."

She opened the box and took out a pair of white canvas shoes. She wiggled her pink toes into one of them, pulled at the laces to loosen them.

"I got you socks too."

"I don't want socks." She put on the other one, tied the laces.

"Don't your feet get sweaty?"

"You're not the boss of my feet, Frankie."

"Francis."

From the other bag, he took a roll of paper towels and a bottle of hydrogen peroxide. He splashed some of the hydrogen peroxide on a folded paper towel and dabbed at her split lip.

"Hey!" She flinched away. "What the hell?"

"It'll get infected."

"I can do it." She grabbed the paper towel from him and dabbed.

Francis held up a finger at her eye level. "Keep your head still and follow my finger with your eyes."

"Would you like to know what you can do with that finger?"

"You're not at your most charming right now," Francis said.

"And you're not a medical doctor right now or ever."

"A doctor did this to me once when I was hit in the head with a baseball," Francis said.

"That explains a lot."

"Ha-ha." Francis held up the finger again. "Just follow it with your eyes."

He moved the finger back and forth, and she followed it with her eyes as instructed.

She said, "You should have shot him like I told you to."

"Just keep looking at the finger."

"They always come back," she said. "Only one thing stops them."

"Have you ever shot anyone?"

"No," she admitted. "But I would. Because it's that kind of world."

"Don't be so eager. It's . . . not like you think it is." Francis dropped the finger, leaned in, looked closely into her eyes. "Yeah, I don't know what I'm doing."

"Surprise."

"I guess if you fall over or pass out or puke or something, we'll know you have a concussion," Francis said. "How do you feel?"

"My head hurts."

Francis went back into the shopping bag and came out with a large bottle of generic-brand ibuprofen. He opened it, shook two out, and handed them to her.

"Water?" she asked.

"Better."

The last thing in the shopping bag was a six-pack of Coors Light. He handed her one. She cracked it open and washed down the pills.

"Give me another one of those," she said.

He didn't bother pointing out she hadn't finished the first and handed her another can.

She held it against the black-and-blue part of her face. She closed her eyes and sighed, some of the tension seeming to leak out of her. "How'd you get hit with a baseball?"

"I played in high school," Francis said.

"I can't picture it."

"Are you saying I don't strike you as the athletic type?"

"You do not. What position did you play?"

"Right field."

"They put the people who suck in right field, don't they?"

"Hey, I know, let's change the subject," Francis said. "You said something before about ditching the car."

"They've seen it," she said. "It's a big candy-apple-red flag." She guzzled the rest of the beer, then popped open the can she'd been holding against her face.

"I guess we can park it some out-of-the-way place," Francis said. "But then we're stuck for transportation."

Emma took a big gulp, burped. "I have an idea about that."

Gunn sat at his temporary desk in the NSA's San Francisco offices, sipping a Styrofoam cup of bitter, black coffee. When the local agents had heard Gunn and his team were coming, they'd cleared them some space. Gunn and his people had set up shop and gotten to work. He was still steamed about underestimating

202 • VICTOR GISCHLER

the girl, and all the agents buzzed about their tasks like angry hornets to make up for it. Gunn was in a whip-cracking mood.

An abrupt knock at the door.

"Come in," Gunn said.

One of his agents entered, one of the new men, and Gunn realized he'd forgotten the man's name or, more likely, had never learned it. They were all nearly interchangeable anyway, dark suits, muted red ties, gleaming wing tips. This one had sandy-brown hair cut short and neat, pale, bland features, eyes an unmemorable brown.

"What's your name again?" Gunn's tone made it sound like it was the agent's fault Gunn didn't know his name.

"Terry Boston. I was added to your detail just before we came west."

"What options did you find for us, Boston?"

"The security around the entire vineyard is pretty tight," Boston said. "And even more so in the environs around Middleton's new house. If I knew what sort of operation we were considering, I might be able to focus our efforts better."

"You need to be ready for multiple contingencies, and you need to be ready to move fast," Gunn told him. "But I don't foresee assaulting the place or anything like that. For now, we simply want to watch. As soon as possible, I want eyes and ears on that main gate."

"We've been doing drone flybys," Boston reported. "At a high enough altitude that I doubt we're being noticed. The resolution on the high-definition pics is more than adequate."

"That's not good enough," Gunn said. "I don't want to miss something in between the drone's back and forth. I want to know everyone who goes in and out of the gate. What's across the street?"

"Nothing," Boston said. "We thought if there'd been a parking area or something we'd have a food truck standing by."

"A food truck?"

"Mediterranean," Boston said. "Gyros and lamb kebabs and so on. One agent serves while the men in the back of the truck monitor the video and audio feeds."

"One supposes such a food truck would be suspicious if parked somewhere that there were no customers," Gunn said.

"One supposes," Boston agreed.

Gunn cocked an eyebrow at Boston, suspecting the man was being cheeky, but let it go. "Pull up the county utility records, then come back with ideas."

"Yes, sir."

Boston left the office.

Gunn sipped coffee. It had gone cold. He set it aside.

He pondered his mission parameters. On paper, he was meant to observe and conduct himself strictly within the confines of the law. But Gunn worked for the NSA. That meant something a little different. He wasn't some local cop. He wasn't even one of those squares over at the FBI. It wasn't Gunn's lot to sit around and wait for bad guys to do something so he could arrest them. If something needed doing, then Gunn needed to do it, law be damned.

Gunn was responsible for nothing less than the security of the nation itself. If he had to step over a few lines—and on a few toes—so every American could sleep safely at night, then so be it. He was playing a long game. In the end, he'd win.

America would win.

And the more rules Gunn broke, the more he felt proud he was defending the American way. Somebody had to get their hands dirty for the nation. Gunn was the man. And if it all blew up in his face, Gunn would take the fall. He was good with that, had always understood it was part of the job.

Boston knocked, then entered again. "Phone lines run along the road that passes in front of the main gate to Middleton's property."

"Is there a space to set up without blocking traffic?"

"There is," Boston said.

"See to it," Gunn ordered. "And alert the appropriate person at the phone company. When we're up and running, I want a feed to a monitor right here on the desk."

"Yes, sir."

"Have you retrieved the girl's personal effects from . . ." Gunn checked the file on his desk. He'd forgotten the name of the facility. "Whispering Meadow?"

"We're working on it," Boston said. "We're getting the usual patient privacy resistance, but it's perfunctory. We should have those materials soon."

"Tell the forensics team to finish with them as fast as they can, and then bring the items to me," Gunn said. "I want to eyeball them personally."

"Yes, sir."

"Are you the junior agent on this detail, Boston?"

"Yes, sir."

Gunn took a money clip from his pants pocket, peeled off two twenties, and shoved them across the desk to Boston. "Get doughnuts for the team. And coffee that doesn't taste like battery acid."

Eli Corning loved that show *American Pickers*, where the two guys found old junk in people's attics or wherever and fixed it up and resold it to yuppies who wanted retro stuff in their houses. Eli liked the idea of salvage and making a buck on what other people thought was trash. That's why there was an old Indian motorcycle in his barn. It didn't run, but there were some good parts there. There were also some Amoco and Sunoco signs he'd taken off some gas stations that had gone out of business. He'd learned from the show that heavy iron stuff was usually a winner and had a couple of old water pumps and weather vanes. Eli was in his early thirties and had just started collecting. Figured he'd eventually retire on the stuff, and he always kept an eye out for a deal.

Which was why he was looking at the beat-up Pontiac GTO and thinking about the trade the girl and the guy were offering and wondering what the catch was. It was some kind of unwritten rule that things too good to be true usually were, right? Anyway, that's what Eli's dad had always told him.

The girl and the guy had pulled up next to the barn about twenty minutes ago while he was outside fussing with the riding lawn mower, trying to get the thing to turn over. They'd come right to the point, and Eli had liked the Pontiac right away.

Too bad about the damage. He circled the car, hands on hips, sucking his teeth, and giving the vehicle another good look. The back end was fine, really. Just needed to replace the bumper. The side was different. He could likely buff out the scratches along the rear fender and fix that himself, but the door was crunched pretty good. That would need to be replaced too. And that meant time spent stomping around in junkyards or paying top dollar for one online.

Still, the rest of the car was total cherry.

"Let me get this straight." He talked to the girl. Pretty clear she was in charge. "You want to trade me straight up. Your GTO for that truck."

He jerked a thumb over his shoulder at the blue 1984 Chevy

Silverado. Or at least it *had* been blue at one time. Now it was sort of bluish with rust and a faded white driver's-side door from when he'd replaced it about five years ago. It was covered with the dings and scratches of three decades of farmwork.

But it ran like a top. He could hand-to-God certify that. He kept the oil changed and did all the maintenance himself.

"You fix the door and replace the bumper and that's a thirty thousand–dollar car at auction," the girl said. "What's the Silverado worth?"

Not so much, Eli thought. Which is why he was wondering what the catch was.

He leaned into the driver's-side window of the GTO and took a look at the interior. Pristine. Damn, this car was giving him a boner. He glanced into the back seat, saw the shotgun on the floor.

Huh.

Eli cleared his throat and asked, "Does anyone happen to be looking for this car?"

She looked him straight in the eye and said, "Not if I'm not in it."

Well. Okay, then.

It would need to be painted anyway, so he'd change the color. Maybe some crazy lime green or something. He could totally pimp the fucker out.

"You got the pink?"

She took it out of her back pocket and showed it to him. "Already signed."

He looked at it, nodding. So if somebody did come looking, he could show them the pink slip, claim he didn't know anything was . . . untoward. Everything square and legal as far as Eli Corning was concerned.

"I got the pink for the Chevy in the house," Eli said. "Wait here."

———————

Francis tossed the big canvas bag—which he now understood contained a tent—next to the footlocker in the back of the pickup truck, then slammed the tailgate closed. He glanced back over his shoulder to see Eli closing the barn door. He'd driven the Pontiac in there to keep it safe from the elements, Francis supposed.

"Do you think this is going to be okay?" Francis asked.

Emma tossed her backpack through the open passenger-side window onto the truck's bench seat. "What do you mean?"

"How do we know he won't say anything? You could tell by the look on his face he smells something fishy," Francis said. "What if he's down at the swap meet and old Rufus says, 'Hey, did you hear about that GTO roaring around with the girl hanging out the window in her underwear shooting at everybody?'"

"Why do you think he's hiding it in the barn?" Emma said. "He won't mention that car to a soul until Nebraska has completely forgotten we were ever here. Then when he's fixed the thing up and is finally ready to show it off, he'll make up some story about where he got it."

"Or he's in there right now on his cell phone calling the sheriff."

"Or that." She tossed him the keys. "You drive."

"You want me to drive?"

"I think you've proven yourself."

24

Middleton pressed the elevator call button, the giddy anticipation plain on his face. He didn't care. Nobody was around to see his grin. Meredith was neck deep into her emails. He let her work. He wanted this for himself, this first time to step into his new command center. The little kid welled up inside him. His personal *Sanctum Sanctorum*, as Doctor Strange would say.

The elevator arrived, and Middleton stepped onto it. He'd insisted on a full-sized elevator instead of one of those tiny things they usually put into residences. It was also an obscene expense to install an elevator in what was predominantly a one-story dwelling, simply to serve a relatively small area on the second level, but it wasn't like Middleton didn't have the money. If he started buying things like the Elephant Man's bones, then he'd worry. And anyway, the only other way up was a very narrow spiral staircase, so a full-sized elevator was essential for hauling up all the various furnishings and equipment.

Middleton considered piping music into the elevator, but the ride up was only thirty seconds. He supposed he could tie it in to the sound system for the rest of the house, then if he were listening to a song, it would continue uninterrupted when he got on and off the elevator.

It struck him suddenly that the house had become his new plaything. It had gone from haven to toy. Middleton felt different. Better. Like the world offered him things to enjoy instead of worries looming ever in front of him. Obviously, the dramatic shift in his relationship with Meredith was responsible. Life was good.

The elevator doors opened. He took one step, and that triggered the lights. They came up slowly to full brightness.

Middleton stood a moment to admire the place.

The huge room was a perfect circle. The walls rose and curved gradually into a dome ten feet overhead. Medium-sized circular windows like portholes ringed the entire room. Beneath the windows, a narrow shelf also ringed the room, plug-in stations for computers ten feet apart, a stool at each station. The arrangement gave the room the vibe of a futuristic coffee shop. Middleton figured he would eventually have meetings here. His intent was that this room would be the center of his empire.

But for just a little while, he planned to keep the room to himself.

A railing separated the outer circle from the inner circle. Three steps led down to the sunken area. An elaborate desk wrapped two-thirds around the inner circle. Simply to call it a desk would be an understatement. The focal point of the monitor display was a one-hundred-inch screen, a half-dozen thirty-two-inch screens arranged around it and various smaller monitors filling in the gaps. It was like Bryant's setup but on steroids.

Middleton eyed the chair. *No, not yet. I'll save that for last.*

"Computer, open the windows."

The internal shutters slid to one side, and fresh sunlight poured in through the portholes.

He strolled the outer circle, pausing to look through each window. The portal over the house's front door overlooked the road that came into the property and the vineyard beyond, the rows and rows of grapevines. The portal on the opposite side of the room offered a wide view of the lake and the undeveloped woodlands.

Middleton had wanted seclusion, and that's exactly what he'd gotten.

His eyes slid back to the chair, and the grin sprang back to his face. The child within strained at the leash, and Middleton finally set him free.

He skipped down the three steps to the sunken area. He stood in front of the chair a moment. Middleton reached out to touch the soft leather. He wouldn't admit it, but he'd modeled the seat after Captain Picard's chair on the bridge of the *Enterprise* from *Star Trek: The Next Generation*. Not to gloat, but this chair was even better. Middleton had been very precise with his requests, and now he was so eager to try the chair, he felt like a kid on Christmas.

He sat.

He wriggled his butt until he found the most comfortable position.

Various controls had been built into the armrests. The small joystick on the left armrest could be controlled with the flick of a thumb. Middleton gave it a go, nudging the joystick to the left. The chair scooted along the track to the left, following the same semicircle of the desk.

Middleton giggled with glee.

He nudged the joystick back the other direction until the chair centered itself back in front of the gigantic one-hundred-inch TV screen.

Middleton explored the buttons on the other armrest. The chair unfolded itself from sections underneath until it became a recliner, lifting his legs and tilting him back. He looked up at the big TV and thought, Wrath of Khan *is going to look totally kick-ass in ultra-high definition*. Captain Picard could suck it. Middleton's chair was a hundred times better.

Middleton realized that his life was perfect. The philosophers claimed such a thing impossible, and yet here he was. Living proof it could be done. Money couldn't buy happiness, but it had gotten him close.

And Meredith Vines had brought him the rest of the way.

"Am I disturbing you, Mr. Middleton?" As always, the computer voice seemed to come from midair. Middleton was impressed with whomever had installed the sound system. He'd not yet been able to detect where the speakers had been installed in many of the rooms.

"What is it?"

"You have a call from a Reggie Bryant," said the computer. "Shall I put him through?"

Middleton hesitated. Couldn't it wait? Couldn't he enjoy a day to himself?

"Yes, put him through, please," Middleton said.

"Mr. Middleton?" Bryant's voice.

"I'm here, Reggie."

"I thought it best to bring you up to speed on current developments," Bryant said. "I take it we're on a secure line."

"It's secure," Middleton confirmed. "Go ahead."

"I've heard from Cavanaugh," Bryant said.

"Oh?" Middleton fended off a stab of guilt. The task Middleton had set for Cavanaugh was unpleasant—not something he relished at all, frankly—but it needed to be done. Middleton couldn't stomach the threat of her always hanging over his head. "I hope to report that matters have been concluded."

"I'm afraid not."

A leaden feeling crept into Middleton's belly. He pushed it down. There was no reason to assume the worst. "He's made some progress, I presume."

"I'm afraid not," Bryant said. "It appears to be a one-step-forward, two-steps-back sort of situation. Cavanaugh suggests that continuing to chase her in this manner is not the best allocation of resources."

"Allocation of resources." Middleton said the words out loud to see if they tasted as stupid as they sounded. "He asked for more men, and I approved the funding. We're paying them in a way that can't be traced back to us, right?"

"Cash payments through the usual channels," Bryant said. "There's no problem there. It's just Cavanaugh's ability to get the job done that's in question."

"How does he want to handle it?"

"Cavanaugh feels he knows where she's heading and that putting himself in a position to intercept her is the scenario most likely to produce results."

"She's coming all the way back to California?"

"That's what Cavanaugh implied."

Now the anxiety rose up hard and wouldn't be pushed back down. "That's cutting it a little close, isn't it? A little close to home."

"Agreed," Bryant said. "It would seem to undermine the whole reason for sending Cavanaugh after her in the first place."

When his wife had escaped, Middleton knew what she'd wanted, knew she would resurface again. He'd wanted her handled far away from him, wanted no part of her fate attached to him. It would be reported to him in clean, clinical terms that the problem had been attended to. At least that had been the plan. A growing dread made him feel sick. There was an acrid taste in his mouth, and his tongue felt thick. He tugged at his shirt collar, felt like he wasn't getting enough air.

"Maybe Cavanaugh's wrong about her coming back," Middleton said. "Maybe she's just running."

"No."

Bryant had been too quick with the denial.

"You put it through the software, didn't you?" Middleton asked.

"It knows," Bryant said. "It knows everything."

The forensics guys gave the items the routine going-over, and when they failed to turn up anything useful, they handed the box over to Gunn. He signed for the items and took them back to his room at the Hyatt Regency.

He dropped the box on the bed. Soon he would focus his complete attention on it, but first, it had been a long day, and Gunn had a short list of evening rituals to help him decompress.

He undressed, hanging his suit in the closet. It could be worn one more day before going to the cleaners. He draped his tie on a separate hanger and placed his wing tips side by side on the closet floor. He stripped off his shirt and dress socks and put them into a plastic laundry bag and stuffed the bag into one of the dresser drawers. It disturbed Gunn for some reason to think housekeeping might come into the room and see his dirty clothes strewn about. He liked his dirty laundry hidden away.

After splashing some water in his face and patting dry with a towel, he changed into a T-shirt and shorts, slipped into white ankle socks and running shoes, and rode the elevator to the workout room on the first floor. He ran exactly two miles on the treadmill at a moderate pace.

The time on the treadmill was usually good for thinking. He put the girl out of his mind until later and concentrated on Middleton. He didn't actually concentrate too hard. When running, he preferred to let revelations drift in of their own accord. If Gunn couldn't make things work out with the girl, then he'd have to figure another way to approach Middleton. The NSA had planted a few people inside Middleton's company at various levels, and so far, they'd produced a smattering of useful information, but he couldn't remember hearing anything from them recently. He made a mental note to put Boston on it in the morning.

When he finished running, he returned to his room and kicked off his shoes. He grabbed the ice bucket and walked down the hall in his socks, found the ice machine, and returned with fresh ice. He stuck a bottle of Cutty Sark into the ice bucket. It was substandard scotch, but all the corner convenience store could offer.

He stripped, hid his workout clothes in a different dresser drawer, then stepped into the shower. He let the hard water spray him as hard and as hot as he could stand it. Now he tried not to think anything at all and succeeded for a few minutes. Mind blank, the shower steamed around him.

After the shower, he dried and put on sweatpants and a CIA T-shirt that was traded to him after an interagency basketball game. He poured the Cutty into a glass, decided it still wasn't cold enough, and dropped in a few cubes. He sipped again, winced. So, okay, better than no scotch at all. Gunn considered ordering a better bottle from room service. No. Keep it off the government tab, and anyway, this wasn't a vacation.

He sat cross-legged on the bed and pulled the cardboard box toward him. A white sticker on the side, WHISPERING MEADOW. MIDDLETON, EMMA, followed by a patient ID number.

The box didn't contain much, but Gunn went item by item, giving each its due. He'd decided the NSA had been neglectful in its approach. In a world of computer hacking and high-tech surveillance, it would be all too easy to overlook basic detective work. The NSA had satellites that could identify a suspect in an Iranian terror training camp from orbit, but that didn't mean simply poking through a box of seemingly banal personal possessions might not uncover something telling.

Gunn wanted to touch this girl's stuff, to get a sense of her, find something to serve as the foundation for a hunch.

A pair of faded jeans. Gunn went through the pockets but didn't find anything. He looked at the labels, some off-brand. A flimsy pink T-shirt with GIRLS KICK ASS written in glitter. A small stack of books and magazines he set aside for last.

Gunn sipped scotch, swirled the ice cubes in the glass, and dug deeper into the box.

A handheld Nintendo 3DS with a handful of games, mostly Pokémon related. A half-empty pack of spearmint gum. A chain and a small silver locket. Gunn opened the locket and recognized the picture inside from the file. There was nothing here he didn't already know—or could guess—about the girl that wasn't in the official profile.

He finished the scotch, decided against refilling the glass.

Gunn returned to the books and magazines.

The first magazine was an issue of *Southern Bride* with an elfin-looking redhead on the cover in an elegant wedding dress. The magazine surprised Gunn, didn't fit with what he knew of the girl. Everyone had a hidden side, he supposed. The other magazine was an issue of *Maximum PC*, which was more in keeping with the girl's profile. The first book was a copy of *Harry Potter and the Goblet of Fire*, a bookmark tucked between the pages about halfway through.

Gunn opened the second book and felt a surge of interest.

It wasn't a novel or a book at all, but rather one of those leather-bound journals with blank pages inside. The first half of the book was filled with the girl's tight, precise scrawl. Jackpot. If anything might reveal some hidden insight about the girl, it would be her personal journal.

But he felt disappointment as he began to read. Her first entry explained that she only wrote a journal at the insistence of her therapist to help "put her feelings into words." It was clear she didn't think much of journaling. Gunn turned pages, read similar entries. The food at the facility was bland. The staff "phony polite." The tile in the common-area restrooms the same "institutional green" as a Soviet bus station's. It was clear she didn't want to be there—big surprise—and the entries all blended into one long complaint. Frankly, it was boring, and Gunn almost set the journal aside.

But he kept reading, his proclivity for completion pressing him on.

Slowly the girl opened up, revealed in fits and starts her resentment for wrongly being placed in such a facility. Musings on past events in her life. He was nearly to the final entry when something caught his attention, not further personal revelation but rather something concrete that spurred Gunn to action.

He looked at the clock. It was late.

No matter.

Gunn picked up his phone and dialed. Agent Boston picked up on the third ring.

"Boston? It's Gunn."

"Yes, sir."

If Gunn had woken him, he couldn't tell. Boston sounded alert and ready.

"I want you to put together a second surveillance team," Gunn said. "Attach a swoop-and-grab team and have them standing by."

"That will stretch our available resources." No criticism in Boston's tone. He merely related information.

"Stretch them."

"Yes, sir," Boston said. "You have a lead?"

"Call it a hunch."

25

The dead man lay against the tractor, eyes closed, flesh looking rubbery and fake in the cold light. The bald thug had been alive one moment, and then a *pop* of gunfire, and then he'd coughed blood and sagged as deflated as whatever made a sack of flesh a human being seeped out of him.

And then . . .

. . . his eyes popped open.

The thug blinked, struggled to sit up. His mouth worked open and closed as he tried to gurgle something, blood so dark it was almost black, gushing over his bottom lip, dripping on his shirt. He reached, clawing, blood now streaming from his nostrils and eyes.

Fear. Shock. Revulsion.

The thug lurched forward, bloody hand grabbing for—

Francis sat up in the darkness, shivering, sweat sticking his T-shirt to him.

As always when he was away from home, it took him a few seconds to remember where he was. Emma lay next to him, both of them tucked into two sleeping bags zipped together. They'd driven out of Nebraska and into Colorado until Francis's back and shoulders ached and he could no longer sit behind the steering wheel. They found a spot off the beaten path in the Arapaho National Forest to pitch a tent, a flat area overlooking a still lake. It was a warm time of year, but at this altitude still cold at night. Francis and Emma had happily huddled together for warmth. It was a pristine patch of wilderness fit for a picture postcard, but the ground was hard, and the bathroom was a tree.

But Emma had insisted. She'd dismissed the idea of a hotel and hadn't even wanted to check into the official Arapaho campsites, deciding instead to take a random fire road. They'd parked the truck out of sight and pitched the tent with their remaining strength and had fallen immediately asleep. Off the grid and on the down low, she'd said.

Francis recalled all this in a flash, his heart still fluttering from the nightmare.

"What is it?" Emma's soft whisper in the darkness.

"Bad dream."

"Tell me."

He lay back down, thought about it, then told her, letting it all spill out in one long breath, the struggle with the bald thug in the barn, the fight for the gun and it going off, how the man's face broke out in surprise in a single twitch. He'd coughed blood and had gone slack, and then that had been the end of him.

Francis felt lighter for having told her. He wouldn't quite call it a confession, knew the thug would surely have killed him, but Francis was still glad to have talked it out, like he'd puked out some poison that had been making him ill.

She didn't say anything. Just scooted toward him, putting a hand on his chest.

"I don't think I can get back to sleep," he whispered.

She kissed him softly on the cheek, her warm lips lingering. She kissed down to his ear, nibbled the lobe.

Emma's hand drifted lower from Francis's chest and under the waistband of his boxers. She found him ready. She covered his mouth with hers, and they kissed hard as she worked him. She ducked into the sleeping bag to tug his boxers off.

Her head popped back up, and she said, "Did you buy what I told you? At the last stop for gas?"

He had.

Francis fumbled in the dark for the little paper bag, found it, and opened the box of condoms inside, handed her one. She ripped it open with her teeth, her other hand still on him. She took it out of the package and rolled it down along his length. She pulled him on top of her.

"You get to do the work," she said.

He was more than happy to oblige.

She was ready and eager, and he glided inside, soon finding a rhythm. Her arms and legs went around him, pulling him into her, nails digging into his back toward the end as their breaths caught and they finished together in a blinding explosion of pleasure.

And Francis had no trouble getting back to sleep.

Middleton sat on the edge of his bed. He wore black silk pajamas and had sprayed himself with expensive cologne. He'd forgotten the name. Something French. His sat with his head down, elbows resting on his knees, his toes kneading the plush carpet. He felt all tight inside, wound up.

"*Ahem.*"

He looked up and saw her leaning in the bathroom doorway.

"What's a girl need to do to get noticed around here?" Meredith teased.

She wore a gown that literally took his breath away. It was a subtle pink held up by two straps and going all the way down to her ankles. But it was fashioned of some gossamer material and hid absolutely nothing. She stood in bare feet, toenails painted red to match her fingernails.

"I'm noticing," Middleton said. "I promise I'm definitely noticing."

She crossed the room with a deliberate, almost painful slowness until years later she stood directly in front of him, his knees on either side of her legs. She caressed one of his cheeks with delicate fingers.

"You okay?" Meredith asked. "You seemed distracted when I came in."

"No," Middleton said. "I mean . . . let's not talk about it."

They agreed to meet when her workday was done . . . which was about three hours after everyone else usually knocked off for the day. He'd been waiting for her in the pajamas. Then waited for her to *slip into something more comfortable*, as they say. But she'd seen it in his face, could read him like a book. The large-print edition of a very simple book.

"We don't have to talk," she said.

Good.

He ran his hands down the sides of her body. The gown was so sheer it might as well have been a hologram. She pulled him to his feet, wrapped her arms around his neck, and they kissed. His hands roamed. They kissed harder.

She pulled away, her eyes met his, and a mischievous smile bloomed, a wicked gleam in her eye. Her hands went to the ties on his pajama bottoms, tugged them loose.

Slowly she sank to her knees.

Middleton's eyes went wide. Yes. *Thank you.* This was what he needed.

Anything to distract him from his wife. It wasn't fair. All he'd built, the world he'd created for himself. *She* was the one who'd decided it wasn't working between them. *She* was the one who'd changed when everything had been fine. Why should she make demands, intrude, interfere? Now she was trying to take away what was his. He'd been forced to take drastic steps. He took no pleasure in it. In fact, it made him ill whenever he tried to imagine the gruesome details. No, he would *not* feel guilty. And yet it ate away at him. The acid in his stomach churned, and all he could do was think about—

"What's the matter?"

He looked down. In spite of her attentions, Middleton was quite clearly failing to rise to the occasion.

"Oh, I . . . uh . . ." Middleton felt his cheeks and ears burn. He began to tug on himself. "Just . . . wait, I can do it. Just wait."

"It's okay."

"A minute. I just need a minute." His breath became short, that all-too-familiar panic feeling creeping up on him.

She stood, leaned in, put her cheek against his, her arms going around him. "*Shhhhhh*. It's been a long day." She held on to him. "I'm tired too. Exhausted."

A sob welled up in him, and it was silly the pride he felt at forcing it back down. That would be too much to break down and cry in her arms. He hugged her back, gratitude flooding him. He hung on to her as if she were a rock in the middle of a raging river.

"Yes," he agreed. "A long day. A long week."

She pulled up his pajamas for him, tied them. "These are nice. I like silk."

"Yes."

She eased him down onto the bed. He curled, drawing his knees up to his chest. Meredith scooted in next to him, draped an arm over him, and pulled him close. He sighed. She stroked his hair. They stayed like that for a long time. She'd stay as long as he needed her. She'd hold him close to her. Thank God for her. Thank God.

The lights faded ever so slightly. It was the house computer sensing them in bed, lying so still, but without a command to turn off the lights. So it was decreasing the illumination gradually, easing them into the night.

Middleton thought about his father so long ago in hospice. The cancer had left the old man a husk. Middleton was maybe thirteen at the time. He stood at the end of the bed, his mother and uncles and aunts gathered around to watch the light leave the old man's eyes. *We're here, Arthur,* he remembered his mom saying in a hushed tone. *We're all here.*

Middleton tried to imagine how it must have looked from inside his father's head, looking out through his eyes at those gathered to watch his passing. The pain had been so very intense at the end. Arthur Middleton had floated on a cloud of painkillers, his bed a magic carpet that would deliver him to the great beyond.

Middleton lay there, with Meredith nuzzled against him, and watched as the computer house gradually took the light away. Is this what it looked like to his father, the world growing dim slowly and slowly and slowly, easing him finally into total darkness?

He hoped he wouldn't dream.

The boat was a distant dream, but she sure was pretty.

Ron Kowolski had finished the fantasy novel he was reading. A pretty good one about a girl with magical tattoos that gave her special powers. Lots of good sword fighting and wizard action. He'd need to hit the library soon for a new stack. He usually gave fantasy novels two chapters, maybe three, to decide if he'd keep reading.

In the meantime, he paged through an issue of *Salt Water Fisherman,* occasionally glancing up at the security monitors. The other three guards in the blockhouse played Monopoly in the break room.

Ron looked at the magazine ad for the boat with naked longing.

At twenty-eight feet long, the Boston Whaler 280 Outrage was perfect. A good size for just him or maybe one other beer-drinking buddy. Twin outboard motors. Yeah, he could see himself out there on the ocean, a cooler of cold beer, reeling in a big one.

Yeah, right. Maybe if a huge sack of cash falls from heaven.

He resigned himself to a future of pier fishing.

Ron did his usual scan of the monitors. Nothing around the vineyard or the old house or the big house. Nothing on the roads. All quiet in the land of Richie Rich.

Something on the main gate monitor caught his attention. It looked like a truck or maybe a van, but at this angle, he could see only the tires and lower half. Technically, anything beyond the gate wasn't Ron's headache, but he took his job seriously. Nobody should be parked over there.

He reached for that camera's remote and maneuvered it, the picture on the monitor swinging up to show the rest of the vehicle. It was a van, the phone company's logo clear on the side. So nothing fishy. A repair truck. This time of night seemed odd to send these guys out, but if Ron Kowolski could get stuck with shitty hours, then so could phone company employees.

He went back to his magazine, drooling again over the Boston Whaler.

26

Francis felt like he was on some bizarre honeymoon.

The old truck ate up the miles west. Francis always drove. Emma never volunteered to take a turn, and Francis didn't ask her. For her, the long ride seemed like downtime. She talked little, stared out the window at the passing scenery. It wasn't quite like meditation, but her face seemed peaceful in a way he hadn't seen before. Sometimes she'd reach across the bench seat and hold his hand for a little while.

At the next gas stop, Emma purchased a bar of soap and a bottle of cheap shampoo. If she had a secret plan to find a shower, she wasn't sharing. As far as Francis knew, the plan was to camp again. Even if they hadn't been in hiding, he had the feeling Emma didn't want to be around people. She also bought cheap hot dogs and buns, a bag of salt-and-vinegar potato chips, a twelve-pack of Coors Light, and a Styrofoam cooler with ice.

They were camping. They were a couple. Everything was good and normal.

But something weighed on her, and it seemed like she was taking a break from it. Part of the odd honeymoon again. She needed to ignore it—whatever the *it* was—wanted only to enjoy Francis's company, the wind on her face when she rolled down the truck window, the sights of the mountains and the forests as Colorado turned into Utah.

"I want to stop earlier tonight," she said. "I don't want to keep pushing until we collapse. I don't want to put up the tent in the dark."

"Okay," Francis said. "You know a place?"

She did.

They soon found themselves passing through Fishlake National Forest. Again, they avoided the designated camping areas, and Emma directed him to an unmarked dirt road.

"You've been here before?"

"Dad took us camping," she said. "Starting when we were six and eight years old until we were about fifteen. All over. State and national parks, mostly. He said people always wanted to go to Paris or whatever, but we had such great, beautiful places in our own country, and our own people didn't even know about half of them. I guess my sister got the travel bug from him."

"Not you?"

She thought a moment, then shrugged.

The narrow road took them through the forest, limbs overhanging the road, possibly a sign the road hadn't been used in a while. Fine by them. Privacy was what they wanted.

The forest split open to reveal a huge lake glimmering blue before them. The dirt road continued on around the lakeshore to the east, so Francis took the truck off road west, weaving a path between tree trunks, keeping the lake in view out the passenger window. He stashed the truck in a copse of trees, feeling confident it wouldn't be easily spotted.

He climbed out of the truck, stretched.

Emma did the same. "There's still plenty of daylight. Let's get the tent set up."

Francis stifled a yawn, nodded. "Right."

He grabbed the big canvas bag from the truck bed and followed

Emma to a flat patch of ground she'd designated tent-worthy. They unpacked it, spread it out, and began inserting the thin, flexible poles that would hump the tent up into a dome. By the time Francis had circled the tent, pounding the final stakes into place, he looked up to see Emma gone.

I see how it is. Leave the man to do all the hard work.

But he didn't mind, really. There was something satisfying about the erect tent, the synthetic fabric pulled tight. Like a well-ironed shirt. Like a properly tied necktie without the thin part hanging down lower than the fat part.

I am a dork.

He shrugged. So be it.

Francis saw her come out from behind the truck. Emma stood completely naked, back straight, white skin brilliant in the sunlight. She held the bar of soap in one hand, the shampoo bottle in the other. She strode toward the lake like some earth goddess, the wilderness seeming to surround her, to make her its center.

He would never get used to her, he realized. She would always be new to him, startlingly beautiful, a puzzle, a fantastic bewilderment.

Emma paused, glanced back at Francis over her shoulder. She nibbled her bottom lip, a wicked gleam in her eye.

Francis dashed for her.

Emma shrieked laughter, running to get to the lake before he could catch her. Francis shed clothing as he went, tossing shoes over his shoulder. He left a trail to the water's edge.

She splashed in just ahead of him, still laughing. When she was hip deep, she dove in, kicked, and shot below the water and surfaced again ten yards away. Francis jumped in and swam after her, the water cool but not the cold shock he'd feared. They circled and splashed each other, playing like otters.

When the laughter trickled away, they drifted into each other's arms, kissed, the green world wide and bright around them like they were the only two people on the planet. The made love unhurriedly but directly and without frills simply for the release.

She soaped Francis, then shampooed his hair. He returned the favor, and they emerged from the lake, fresh and clean and wet, and realized they didn't have towels.

It didn't matter. Nobody was there to see them, and they went about their business until the air dried them. Francis felt part of some hippie commune as he gathered firewood buck naked. It was with a bit of relief when he dried enough to slip back into jeans and one of Dwayne's Harley-Davidson T-shirts that Emma had packed for him.

So. Francis wasn't cut out to be a nudist. Another thing he'd learned about himself.

His eyes slid to Emma, now wearing cutoff denim shorts and a yellow tank top. He smiled and watched her. She was still barefoot, hair damp and slicked back. She squatted on the ground, stacking the firewood in a tepee, a ring of stones making an impromptu fire pit. Emma was delicate with it, placing each stick so as not to disturb the others. Her face was peaceful, focusing on the mundane task, no tension in her, that hardness in her eyes Francis had seen so many times now gone.

She looked up, caught him watching her, and smiled. Not the quirk of lips he knew so well, the wry smile edged with sarcasm. This time it was warm and effortless, and at that moment Francis knew he'd lost himself to her and there was no coming back and that was just fine.

"Go pick your stick," she told him.

Francis blinked. "Wait. Do what to my stick? Are you saying a rude thing?"

She laughed. "For your hot dog, dink."

They cooked hot dogs on sticks and ate and drank beer. Francis circled the area one more time for firewood before the sun sank. They built up the fire and drank more beer and talked about the least important things they could think of. Emma told him every knock-knock joke she'd ever heard, and they were all terrible.

Since it was warm, they dragged the sleeping bag out of the tent and lay together looking up at the stars. She took his hand and cradled it to her chest, and a few hours slipped lazily away from them. Unasked questions loomed in their future, would insist upon them in the morning light, but without speaking both agreed to pretend there was no tomorrow. They were tired and buzzed from the beer but fought off sleep for as long as they could.

At last they surrendered and dragged the sleeping bag back into the tent, falling down the endless dark hole of sleep, holding on to each other, chests rising and falling as if breathing together, heartbeats in sync.

They awoke with the light and silently went about the business of breaking camp, a light mist on the lake, dew on the grass. When the truck was packed, they headed back to the dirt road, then eventually to the highway again, resuming the trek west.

Francis couldn't bring himself to start in on the questions that needed to be asked. His heart wasn't in it. He felt leaden.

They crossed into Nevada, their green world giving way to brown.

"I'm hungry." It was the first thing Emma had said in an hour.

It was a little early for lunch, but they hadn't had any breakfast.

"Okay," Francis said.

They stopped at a place called the Silver State Restaurant in

Ely just off US 50. They sat at the counter. She had a cheeseburger and fries. He had a BLT and a salad. Francis thought maybe now was the time to start asking questions, but they both set about their meals with mechanical determination—bite, chew, swallow, repeat.

Thirty minutes later, they were back in the truck, heading west again.

When they reached the open, dusty nothingness beyond the city limits, Francis said, "I think we need to talk."

"I know," Emma said in a small voice. "I know we do."

"I'm not trying to pressure you about it," Francis said. "Really, I'm not. It's just that we're running out of America. California's next. I want to know how to help you. I want to know everything."

She looked out the window, saying nothing. Tumbleweeds and cacti.

"There's nothing you can say that will change how I feel about you," Francis said. "We've come too far for that. So if you're afraid, don't be."

She looked back at him, face unreadable. "Not here. Not out in the desert."

"Then where?"

"There's a place I used to love," she said. "Do you like doughnuts?"

"Of course," Francis said. "What am I, a commie?"

"Then that will be our reward," she said. "I'll tell you anything you want. We'll save it all for the end."

"To the end, then."

27

Bryant held the external drive in his hands, looking at it with wonder. It was the only place on the entire planet the new program existed in its complete form.

And Bryant held it.

Not that the program couldn't be reproduced. It would be foolish to think Bryant could walk out his front door and be crushed in the street by a moving van or something, the external drive irrevocably damaged and the program lost to eternity. The corporation was not about to let a decade of research and development go up in smoke though sheer ineptitude.

It had been Middleton who'd insisted that the major components of the program be stored separately, different officers in the company holding passwords to access those components. Should some calamity necessitate a reassembly of the software, the entire board would need to be convened for all components to be accessed. Bryant wasn't surprised, really. Middleton was one of the most paranoid men he'd ever met. It would be easy for him to imagine any and all of his employees from vice president on down to the lowliest college intern stealing the information and selling out to a competitor.

Which, Bryant realized, was exactly what he could do now. The information in the drive he held was literally worth millions of dollars.

He glanced over his shoulders at the tech crew. They would spend the next few hours scrubbing all the computers at his station, making sure no trace of the software remained. And although they didn't say it, they would also make sure Bryant hadn't hidden a copy of the software in some file or saved it to the cloud. They'd already examined his smartphone and personal laptop.

He glanced down at the drive in his hands again. He could do it. He really could. Just walk right out with it.

A knock on the door.

He opened it. Two of the corporate security guards. Blue blazers with the corporate logos over the pockets. Muscles bulged under the jackets. Bryant knew they were armed. These weren't mall cops. They were pros. Not thugs like Cavanaugh and his goons, but formidable in their own button-down way.

"Hello, Mr. Bryant," one of them said. "We're here to escort you to Sonoma. We have a limousine outside."

Bryant raised an eyebrow. "Oh? I was just going to drive myself."

"There are those who might take the drive from you," the guard said. "We wouldn't want you hurt if that happened. We're here for your safety."

Bryant nodded along with the man's words, thinking, *Yeah, and to keep me from getting lost along the way. Middleton doesn't trust me any more than he trusts anyone else.*

In a way, it was why Bryant had been picked. He had unique qualifications that made him the perfect liaison between Middleton and Cavanaugh. Or, to broaden things, the liaison between Middleton's legitimate business ventures and the seedy shortcuts he sometimes took to accomplish things expediently. Not only did Bryant possess the technical know-how Middleton found useful, but Middleton had Bryant over a barrel.

About eighteen months ago, Middleton's people had caught Bryant embezzling. By no means was Bryant a Goody Two-shoes, but he'd certainly never set out to become an embezzler. But there were the gambling debts, and he kept getting deeper and deeper into the hole, and, well, one thing led to another.

It was actually a pretty good deal. Middleton paid him an obscene amount of money, and because he held the embezzlement over Bryant's head, there was a weird trust there that wouldn't exist if Bryant had simply been another honest citizen.

However, that trust did not extend to letting Bryant walk out of the building unguarded with the corporation's greatest achievement.

At least Bryant could ride in a limo.

"We need to hit a drive-through on the way," he told the guards. "I'm starving."

Middleton sat on the edge of the indoor pool and watched Meredith swim. He admired her athleticism. Something he lacked. And she didn't just float around. There was nothing recreational about it. She'd done ten laps, had good form. Middleton was content to watch. She made a lithe and graceful shape, cutting through the water in a sleek, black one-piece.

Middleton sat with his khakis rolled up to his knees, bare feet on the first step in the shallow end.

Meredith made the turn at the other end of the pool, kicked off from the wall, and glided underwater an impressive distance before surfacing, kicking hard, arms rotating in and out of the water, head coming up every few lengths for a breath.

She reached the wall near Middleton and hoisted herself up, dried her hands on a towel. She picked up her smartphone, scrolled.

"Bryant is on his way," Meredith said. "He's with the security detail."

"Good," Middleton said. "I'll feel better when it's done."

In fact, Middleton felt better already.

His initial embarrassment at the botched sex with Meredith had evaporated. He'd slept like a baby. She'd held him all night. Meredith was everything Aaron Middleton needed and desired. The news of Cavanaugh's failure to handle his formal marital situation had rattled him badly. It was the most egregious of loose ends.

But Meredith was the cure for any malady. This was not the time to despair. It was a time to rejoice. Emma would be taken care of, and then he could launch his new life. With Meredith by his side. The life he deserved.

"Let me be up there with you when he installs it," Meredith said. "I've heard so much about this software. I'd like finally to see it in action."

He began to tell her that of course that would be fine.

But Middleton stopped himself. He wasn't even sure why. An instinct or a superstition. Was there still some kind of distrust there, a last enclave of vulnerability within him that he was protecting? More likely some childish selfishness. He wanted to play with his new toy all on his own, nobody looking over his shoulder.

"Let me get the kinks out," Middleton said. "Then I'll put on a show for you."

The slightest hesitation, perhaps Middleton had even imagined it. Then she grinned. "You're the boss."

"Did you tell the board I wanted a meeting?"

"First of the month," Meredith said. "I don't think you can Skype this one. My advice is to put on a tie and go down there."

"Do you think they'll go for it?" Middleton had asked her this question at least a dozen times. He thought his idea to work on a next-gen version of the software a good one. That way, the corporation would always be one step ahead. Never mind that the plan also allowed Middleton to keep the program to himself for the time being.

"Above my pay grade." She grinned. "Ten more laps."

She launched off the wall, backstroking toward the far end.

Middleton thought about what he would say to the board. He was sure he could convince them. Yes, short-term profits would take a hit. Stockholders would kick. But he could sell them on the long-term potential—although he wasn't particularly fond of the word *sell*. He didn't consider himself a salesman, some cheap huckster. Middleton had a passion for this project and for the corporation. Conveying this passion to the board would win the day.

They'd see it his way. They had to. No more wishy-washy worry about it.

And if not, he already knew ways to convince people who didn't want to be convinced.

28

The old truck clattered across the Nevada desert. US 50 took them through the little towns, and at last, they hit Interstate 80 at Fernley and took it through Reno and across the state line into California.

The sun went down, but neither of them suggested making camp. The honeymoon was over. They felt a pressing need to get on with it now. Mostly it was Emma, but Francis could feel the urgency radiating off her, and it infected him. Stops were infrequent and quick, a gas fill-up, an unappetizing service-station egg salad sandwich, in and out of the restroom.

They passed through Sacramento, and when they made their final stop just outside of Vallejo, Emma took over driving.

"Easier than your having to follow my directions," she said.

Fine with Francis.

They hit Berkeley just after 11:00 p.m., and Emma exited the interstate. She drove past the campus, looking at it with nostalgia.

"Man, it seems like a long time ago." She leaned over the wheel, looking up at the buildings through the windshield. "I can't even tell you what it was like to come here, a girl like me from Podunk, USA. It was crazy and wonderful, like the world was showing me what it could be for the first time."

"Do you miss it?"

"I miss things about it," she said. "I miss feeling like everything was new."

236 • VICTOR GISCHLER

She turned down the main drag, passing coffee shops and book-
stores and the occasional pub. She almost missed the turn down
the side street she was looking for.

"Been a while," she said.

A block later, she parked on the street in front of a place called
Atomic Doughnuts. The entire interior of the place was visible
through huge glass windows. It was brightly lit. Booths and a counter
and all the décor meant to look retro like from the 1950s.

"Come on," she said. "This place will change your life."

They got out of the truck, and Francis glanced into the bed.
"What about that?"

Emma followed his gaze to the footlocker full of guns. "Yeah.
Probably should lock that up."

They put the footlocker into the front seat and locked the
doors. Emma stuffed the keys into the front pocket of her jeans.

They walked into the doughnut shop. College kids sat at various
tables, hunched over textbooks, nursing cups of coffee.

"I like sitting at the counter," Emma said. "I always did when I
used to come in here."

"Fine with me."

They took two stools, and a guy came to take their order. He
had a full, perfectly trimmed beard, gold hoops in each ear, curly
brown hair under a watch cap. He looked directly at Francis.

"I don't know what to get," Francis said.

The bearded guy didn't look like he had a lot of patience with
this.

Emma leaned in, took over. "He'll have coffee and a raspberry
filled." She looked at Francis. "Trust me."

"And you?" Beardo asked her.

"I'll have a raspberry too," she said. "But also a cream filled."

"Right."

"And a chocolate with sprinkles and a blueberry."

"Will that do it?"

"And a double fudge."

Beardo hesitated. "We good?"

"And coffee."

Beardo nodded and left to fetch the order.

Francis looked at her, raised an eyebrow. "Hungry?"

"I'm making up for a lot of lost time."

Beardo brought the doughnuts and set them on the counter. He returned a second later with two cups of coffee.

Emma took half the raspberry in one bite. She moaned, eyes rolling back in her head. "Oh my God, I've been waiting for that for so long." She finished the doughnut in two more bites, then went after the blueberry.

Francis looked down at the doughnut and coffee on the counter in front of him.

Emma noticed he wasn't eating. "Problem?"

"Egg salad."

"I *told* you not to eat a gas station sandwich."

Francis rubbed his stomach, stifled an acrid burp. "I feel gross."

Emma twisted on her stool, looked back through the big glass window. "Try Jerry's across the street. Get some antacid or something."

"Yeah. Okay."

Francis slipped off the stool and left the doughnut shop.

Jerry's was a narrow storefront wedged between a florist and an aromatherapy salon. Magazines, soft drinks, snacks, cigarettes, batteries, aspirin, all the world's bright and varied sundries. The bored oldster behind the counter looked up from his copy of *Road & Track* long enough to sell Francis a bottle of water and a single pack of Alka-Seltzer. He took his purchases outside, stood in the doorway of the store, and crumbled the tablets into the bottle.

He watched them fizz, then guzzled the water until the bottle was empty. A long, searing belch pushed up and out of him. He felt better.

He watched Emma through the doughnut shop's big window. She chomped into the last of her doughnuts. Even from across the street, the raw glee on her face was clear. He hated to ruin her moment, but time was up. They needed to talk about what she intended to do and why. Emma had a score to settle with her husband. Depending on what she told him, Francis would try to help, or he'd try to talk her out of it.

But no matter what, he wasn't walking away.

Two men in dark suits entered the doughnut shop.

Francis thought nothing of it until they approached Emma. One of them gestured toward the door. He couldn't hear what they were saying, but the gesture looked like *Come with us, please.* It all unfolded in the big window like a show on a huge TV screen with the sound on Mute.

Emma started to stand, face open and cooperative, like she was more than willing to go along with them. Her little fist suddenly came up hard into one of their guts. He doubled over, and she shoved the other one aside, dodged away as he grabbed for her. She leaped up on a stool, jumped to the counter. Everyone in the place was watching now as she ran along the counter, knocking off cups and plates, the guys in the suits following and still trying to grab her.

Francis's hand went to his front pocket. Emma had the truck keys.

Shit.

He had to go to her. Francis took two steps into the street and was brought up short by the sound of slamming car doors. His head snapped around to look.

A black sedan parked on his side of the street four car lengths down. Two men in similar dark suits came toward Francis.

"Sir," one of them said. "Can we have a word, please?"

Francis turned slowly as if he hadn't heard them and went back into the sundries store.

"Is there a back door?" he asked the oldster.

"It's just for deliveries."

Francis headed down the back hallway past a restroom and a bunch of storage boxes.

"Hey, idiot," the old guy called after him. "Didn't you hear me?"

Francis walked faster.

He emerged from the back door into a dark, narrow alley. Trash cans and locked back doors on the wall across the way. A ten-foot-high chain-link fence blocked one way, so Francis turned the other way and jogged.

The two suits exploded out the back door right behind him.

Francis broke into a run.

His head spun. What was happening to Emma? He needed to help her, but he needed to escape first.

He erupted from the alley, not breaking stride as he sprinted across the street. The blare of a horn, and a little compact slammed on its brakes, tires squealing, the front bumper missing Francis's leg by three inches. He paused in the wash of headlights to look back. The two guys were still coming fast.

The driver stuck his head out the window, screaming insults, but Francis was already running again. There was some kind of club ahead of him, and Francis entered.

It was crowded, college-age people. The interior was dark, and it took a second for Francis's eyes to adjust. Everyone wore black, hair falling down in front of people's eyes, black lipstick, piercings, and tattoos. A goth club. If Francis had been hoping to blend in, he could forget it.

He hunched down, trying to make himself small, and waded into the crowd. When he glanced back, he saw the two suits standing in the doorway, scanning the crowd. One of them brought his wrist up to his mouth and muttered something. Francis noticed the wires hanging from their ears.

Francis kept low and found the hallway back to the restrooms. There were no other doors or exits. He entered the men's room and shut the door behind him, slapping the cheap bolt lock into place. It wasn't much of a restroom. A single toilet and a sink. It didn't matter. His eyes went to the little window.

The *very* little window.

He was relieved when it opened easily. He had to stand on the toilet to look out. The space between the building he was in and the next wasn't wide enough to legitimately call it an alley. He leaned out and looked both ways, saw the blur of headlights at the far end of the narrow space. Good. He could get back to the street. Or at least some street. Once he'd ditched these guys, he'd bend his mind toward how he could possibly help Emma.

A banging on the restroom door sent his heart into his throat. He ignored it and braced his hands on the windowsill, making ready to hoist himself up. The banging on the door became more insistent.

Francis failed the first attempt to hoist himself, foot almost slipping on the toilet seat. He caught himself.

The banging on the door was so loud now it rattled the hinges. He thought maybe they were kicking it. They were definitely coming through at any moment.

He hoisted himself again, made it, and wriggled through the small space. It wasn't easy. He had to put one arm through at a time.

He wasn't huge by any means, but his shoulders were just too wide to fit.

This time the banging was accompanied by a sharp crack. The door wouldn't last much longer.

When Francis wriggled down to his hips, he got stuck, the top of his jeans catching. Francis heard the door smashed inward, hinges clanging on the cement floor. Men shouting.

He panicked, tried to push himself through with a big heave, his belly and lower back scraping. Hands grabbed his ankles. He twisted and kicked, his heel connecting with something solid. A grunt and the hands let go.

It was enough to dislodge him and knock him through, and for a long second, he floated in the air, facing upward at the dark, narrow space between buildings. Falling backward was a strange sensation. An endless plummet that felt like it would go on for—

He hit hard, the air slammed out of him. His legs pointed straight up the side of the wall. There wasn't enough room in the cramped space for him to spread out. His mouth worked for air.

A head poked out of the window, one of the slick-haircut suits who'd been chasing him.

"Stay right there, sir."

Fuck you. Francis wished he'd had the breath to say it out loud.

He righted himself, gulped oxygen, and hobbled away.

"Sir!" The voice behind him. "Sir!"

Francis was almost breathing normally again by the time he came out on the street. He didn't recognize where he was. A glance back showed the guy trying to come out the window after him, but he was a lot bigger than Francis and couldn't fit. Francis picked a direction to run when a black sedan came around the corner and screeched to a halt, blocking his way.

He turned to run the other way.

A black SUV roared into view, blocking him that way.

Francis froze, eyes flicking right to left, seeking an escape route.

Shit shit shit shit.

Suits and haircuts spilled out of the two vehicles, forming a quick semicircle.

"Come with us, sir," said one of them. "There's no point making this more difficult."

Francis could have sworn the man speaking to him was the same guy who'd told him to stay put through the window. All these guys looked like they were made in the same factory.

Francis spotted a slight gap between two of the guys and ran for it.

The two guys slammed into him from either side, and all three of them went down. More came to pile on top. Francis thrashed, tried to twist loose. A forearm against his neck. One of his arms twisted behind his back.

"Don't struggle, sir."

"Go to hell!" Francis had hoped to sound tough, but it came out desperate and afraid.

He heard a crackling sound and in the farthest periphery of his vision saw the flash of a familiar blue light. Francis remembered zapping the one with the mustache in the bathroom, the expression on his face.

Oh, hell no. No no no no—

The guy stuck the stun gun into Francis's ribs, and Francis contorted with what felt like a million volts running through him. Darkness closed in from every side.

So that's what that feels like.

29

Boston was waiting for him when Gunn walked in.

"Tell me," Gunn said.

"Berringer is in interrogation room A," Boston said. "The girl in B. We're going through the truck now and all their belongings."

Gunn thought about that a moment, then said, "Okay, I'll give Berringer a go first. Mostly because I want the girl to stew awhile longer. But I'll expect a report on what you find in the vehicle before I start with her. I want to go in knowing everything."

"I anticipate no difficulty with that," Boston said.

Gunn gave Boston a curt nod, then entered room A, a file folder tucked under one arm.

Berringer looked up, raw anxiety plain on his face.

Gunn paused to take in the room. It was like nearly every other interrogation room he'd ever been in. A metal table. A chair on either side. The suspect cuffed and chained to the table. The only thing missing was the quintessential two-way mirror. It had been replaced with multiple cameras that would record the interrogation from various angles.

Gunn sighed, sat in the chair opposite Berringer, and opened the file folder.

Berringer cleared his throat. "Okay, so, yeah, look, I know I have a lot to explain, but if you just hear me out, I promise all this—"

Gunn held up a finger, eyes never leaving the folder. "A moment."

He kept Berringer waiting as he read the file folder he already knew by heart. He nodded as if mulling over the information, closed the folder, and set it on the table in front of him. He steepled his fingers under his chin and fixed Berringer with a hard stare.

"Who are you, Mr. Berringer?" Gunn asked.

"Uh." Berringer glanced nervously around the room as if the answer to the question might be hanging on the wall. "Francis Berringer?"

"Humorous, Mr. Berringer," Gunn said. "Very humorous. Do you know who I am?"

"The police?"

Gunn laughed. "Oh my, no. You should be so fortunate. The police would read you your rights, meaning that you had some. My name is Harrison Gunn. I'm chief field operative for the National Security Agency, and I'm in no way concerned about your rights, or in fact your safety and well-being in any way."

"Aren't there laws or something?" Berringer asked.

"Most assuredly," Gunn said. "But the laws are not here. I am. So if I were you, I'd stop worrying about laws and rights and start worrying as much as humanly possible how you can be useful to me."

"This is all a huge misunderstanding," Berringer said. "I mean, it's crazy, but I can totally explain."

"Then explain who you are," Gunn said. "And I don't mean your fucking name. How did you hear about the algorithm? What put you onto the girl? Tell me who you work for."

As he spoke, Gunn watched the kid. Berringer had gone pale, expression looking sick. If it was an act, then it was a *good* act.

"I promise you I'm not being coy here," Berringer said. "But I'm honestly not sure what you're talking about."

Gunn sighed, opened the file folder. "You are nobody, Mr. Berringer. In the context of my world, you are an utter and complete nothing."

Berringer swallowed hard. "I'm . . . sorry?"

"You don't compute," Gunn told him. "We've encountered deep-cover operatives before, but the life I'm looking at here"—Gunn gestured to the file—"is such a perfect and absolute nothing that it strains credibility. What are the odds that such a nothing should intercept the subject of my agency's investigation and pursuit, a subject that just by coincidence carries perhaps the biggest technological advance of the decade?"

"Okay, I mean, I guess from your point of view the odds would be pretty long," Berringer said. "But see, the thing is, I was walking along, and this suitcase was in an alley on some garbage. I know this sounds dumb, but I noticed the suitcase because of the panties. I mean, not because of the panties, but because everything was so new and—"

"Long odds indeed, Mr. Berringer." Gunn had interrupted on purpose, because Berringer was squirming, and he liked to see people squirm. "According to the statement you gave one of my agents, you rescued the girl after she'd been taken captive by some thugs." Gunn glanced at the file folder again. "That's your word. *Thugs.*"

Berringer shrugged apologetically. "I mean, I don't know the proper term, but these guys, I mean, if you'd seen these guys—"

"And with all your skills as a . . ." Gunn consulted the file again. "With all your skills as a purchasing agent, you pursued these thugs and effected the girl's rescue."

"Ah, okay, I can see how that might seem odd, but see, this cabbie—"

Gunn pressed on. "And then later at the girl's temporary residence in South Dakota, these thugs struck again. You subdued at least three of them and then created an elaborate diversion with a tractor before escaping at high speed in a stolen muscle car."

"Okay, now come on." Berringer wiped sweat from his forehead. "You make it sound like I'm James Bond or something. Seriously, it wasn't like that. I mean, things just happened, okay? It just . . . happened." Berringer's voice rose alarmingly at the end, almost a screech.

Gunn closed the file folder and sighed. "Mr. Berringer, I believe you."

"But you've got to listen. I tried to tell you—Wait. What?"

"Your story checks out," Gunn said. "As hard as it is to believe, you are indeed the complete nothing you appear to be."

"Oh." Bewilderment seized Berringer's features and wouldn't let go. "Thanks?"

"We've checked you out top to bottom, ran your fingerprints, everything," Gunn said. "And my own instinct is that you did indeed stumble into this whole affair as ineptly as you've described. You've been impossibly stupid and lucky, Mr. Berringer."

If Berringer was offended, he kept it well hidden. He actually seemed to brighten. "Then we're done here? I can go?"

Gunn laughed hard. Not part of the act this time. He really did find Berringer's wide-eyed stupidity hilarious.

A knock at Gunn's office door.

"Come."

Boston entered, grinning.

This was exactly what Gunn had been waiting for. He felt 99.9 percent certain that Berringer was the dupe he appeared to be, but the girl was another story. She seemed so obvious in her methods and motivations that Gunn was suspicious. He didn't want to interrogate her until he knew he was holding all the cards.

Gunn eyed Boston expectantly. "You have it?"

Boston handed over the folded wad of butcher's paper. "It looks legit."

Gunn doubted Boston had the expertise to determine such a thing. Nevertheless, he was excited. He took the paper, unfolded it on his desk, and smoothed it flat. The algorithm. Gunn admitted to himself he was no more an expert than Boston, but he felt sure this was it. They'd finally hit the jackpot.

"Give me the details," Gunn said.

"There was a footlocker full of weapons," Boston reported. "And a tent. We're pretty sure they were hiding out off the grid the last few days. The paper with the algorithm was actually found in an alligator-skinned suitcase. It was filled with women's clothing, all new with the tags still on. There were an inordinate number of panties."

Gunn's ears perked up at the mention of the suitcase and the panties, part of the story Berringer had tried to tell him. Gunn was now convinced the kid did not work for some foreign agency. Nobody could fake such raw innocence and blatant dumb luck. But he was going to keep him in custody anyway just in case, at least until he'd finished with the girl.

Gunn carefully refolded the paper with the algorithm and handed it back to Boston. "I'm going in there and get started on her. Wait for my cue, then bring in the algorithm."

The girl's room was not significantly different from Berringer's. She sat cuffed to the table, didn't look up when Gunn entered.

Gunn looked her over, thought a moment before taking his seat. He decided to approach her differently from how he had with Berringer. No definable reason. He simply trusted his instincts.

"Berringer said he found the suitcase in an alley on some garbage," Gunn said.

She sighed. "I thought Aaron's men had me cornered. I tossed the suitcase down a garbage chute. I got away, but it wasn't there when I came back later. I thought it was all over right then. When Francis emailed me, he'd found the suitcase, it felt like . . . a miracle." She looked up at him briefly, profound fatigue in her eyes, then looked back down again.

He fished the little key out of his jacket pocket, leaned across the table, and unlocked the handcuffs.

She rubbed her wrists. "Thanks."

"I'm hoping I can trust you while we work things out," Gunn said. "You broke an agent's nose during the apprehension at the doughnut shop. I'm hoping to avoid further unpleasantness along these lines."

"Do you plan unpleasantness along different lines?"

Gunn offered his trademark grin. All teeth and no warmth. He sat, opened her file, and pretended to look at it. He already knew everything there, even better than he knew Berringer's.

"That all depends, I suppose," Gunn said. "You've been very busy indeed. Let's see, grand theft auto, resisting federal agents, and you've apparently hacked at least eleven ATMs for over three thousand dollars in cash. I presume this was to fund your recent capers. Too smart to use a credit card and leave a trail, aren't you?"

Again, she kept her eyes averted and said nothing.

"Except then you did use Mr. Berringer's credit card just once, didn't you?" Gunn said. "Clever girl. You figured we must have had a line on him by then. Stupid of us not to consider you'd jump ship in Minneapolis instead of making the connecting flight. A bit embarrassing for the agency and for me personally, all this standing there with egg on our faces in LAX waiting for you to deplane. Except then you didn't."

The hint of a smile flickered at the corners of her mouth.

"You see, it didn't occur to us you might do that," Gunn said. "Especially since I know you have something so important waiting for you in California."

Any hint of a smile vanished.

"And then there is the footlocker full of weapons," Gunn said. "One wonders what dire enterprise you had in mind."

A long hesitation, and then she said, "There are worse people than you after me."

"Then it's fortunate you've fallen into my hands instead of theirs," Gunn said. "I think we're in a position to help one another. I doubt that can be said of Middleton's henchmen for hire. Yes, we have our suspicions about how Aaron Middleton conducts his affairs. It only matters to us insofar as it gets us what we want. This isn't a law-and-order issue; otherwise, your recent escapades would have you in the slammer for a good long stretch, and we'd be discussing a plea bargain for your cooperation."

The girl remained silent, but her eyes were attentive. Gunn figured she was willing to listen.

"We've been gathering information a long time," Gunn told her. "Long before you escaped from Whispering Meadow."

She shivered slightly at the mention of the mental health facility.

"I've spent a lot of time piecing this information together," Gunn said. "So I'm going to tell you a little story. All you have to do is listen, but when I'm finished, you can tell me what I got wrong."

Her eyes came up to meet his again, and her nod was so small, Gunn wondered if he'd imagined it.

"Your marriage to Aaron Middleton started out with so much

hope," Gunn began. "You were just in from flyover country, ready for a bigger, exciting world. Middleton wasn't a billionaire yet, far from it, but there was an exciting promise in him that captured your attention. You got married and proceeded to do the things married people do. It seemed to go well for a couple of years."

Gunn looked at the girl. He didn't get confirmation of his story, but he didn't get denial either, so he we went on.

"But then Middleton's success caused problems," Gunn continued. "Most people think strife in a marriage comes from money problems or a spouse cheating, and they do obviously, but people fail to take into consideration that sudden success can cause problems too. Am I close? How about helping me fill in some of the gaps?"

She didn't say anything for a long time, and Gunn was tempted to prod her. He was patient instead. Sometimes silence would simply become intolerable, and an eagerness to fill it would get him where he wanted to go.

Finally, she took a deep breath and said, "He started to get really paranoid. At first, it was just like he was being careful, you know? Not scary, just him reacting to a new situation."

Gunn nodded along, encouraging.

"But it eventually got weird, and then it got scary," she said. "He didn't trust anyone. Everyone was out to use him for something. Everyone wanted to take what he had. That some of those people really did exist made it worse. It was like proof of everything he suspected. Everyone became a potential enemy. Even me. He was losing it fast. He even knew it on some level because he saw a doctor and got a prescription for anxiety medication. It helped a little at first, but in the long run, it didn't matter."

"Let me guess." Gunn felt on safe ground that he knew the rest of the story. "He was the one going off his rocker, but he was also the one with all the lawyers and the money and the influence. It would have been simple for his people to come up with a reason that *you* were the problem and then zing you're off to Whispering Meadow for group therapy and basket weaving. What did Middleton's pet doctors come up with?"

Gunn already knew the answer, but it was important to keep her talking.

The hesitation was shorter this time. "Anger issues. Evidently, I was a danger to myself and others. More than that, I was declared . . ." A crack in her voice. This part upset her. She cleared her throat. "Unfit."

Gunn nodded, understanding. It was an unfair world, and he was a sympathetic ear. "They never even listened to my side of it," she said. "Denial only proved it, they said."

"Any feelings left for Middleton?" Gunn asked. "You're still married, after all."

Her eyes narrowed. If they'd been daggers, blood would have been squirting from Gunn's face.

"So we can safely declare that romance terminated," Gunn said.

Her expression was as flat and hard and cold as a tombstone. "Dead."

"So," Gunn said. "That just leaves the unfinished business."

"Yes."

"And you hoped the algorithm might be a bargaining chip."

Back to the stony silence, but her hard gaze met his and held it.

"I think this is where I should take up the story again," Gunn said. "Just to keep things moving along."

She didn't object. Gunn smiled, sincerely this time. He was enjoying himself.

"You no longer wanted Middleton, but he had something that was rightfully yours," Gunn said. "At least it was yours as far as you were concerned. You would be more than happy to be shed of the bastard, except he had this one thing that belonged to you. The one thing you couldn't live without. Am I right?"

She didn't contradict him.

"So you had a copy of the algorithm," Gunn went on. "And naturally Middleton wants to keep it out of a competitor's hands or the hands of some hostile government. So you offer a trade. He gets the algorithm. His invention is safe again. And you get back what you so desperately want. But there was a problem, wasn't there?"

"Yes."

"Tell me about it."

She sighed. "He sent his people. Said it was a meeting to do the trade. Obviously, they wanted to make sure I kept silent. Maybe also wanted to make sure I wasn't around to sell anyone a copy."

"And did you make a copy?"

She shook her head. "I meant to take it to a copy center, but one thing just kept leading into another. I've been sort of . . . swept away by all this." She leaned forward and put her elbows on the table, closed her eyes, and massaged her temples. "I'm just so tired."

"I can imagine," Gunn said. "Stupid not to make a copy, but we can remedy that right now." He came out of his chair, knocked on the door behind him, then sat again.

Boston entered, and the girl's eyes widened when she saw the folded butcher's paper in his hands.

"Agent Boston, please carry on as we discussed earlier," Gunn said.

Boston unfolded the paper on the table, smoothing it flat. He took out his smartphone and aimed it at the algorithm. "This scanner app has the highest resolution available."

He *clicked*, handed the phone to Gunn. Gunn looked at the image on the phone's screen and compared it to the image on the butcher's paper. "Good. Take a few more just to be sure."

Boston obliged.

"Let me know when they're uploaded," Gunn said.

The girl watched all this with open curiosity.

"It's done," Boston said. "Successfully uploaded to the secure mainframe."

"Good." He reached underneath the table and came back with a small metal trash can. He set it on the table. From his pocket, he took a disposable lighter. He lit the butcher's paper and dropped it into the trash can.

The girl shot to her feet. "No!"

The paper burned quickly and was nothing but ashes in a matter of seconds.

The girl sank back into her seat, looking stricken.

"I can't let you back out into the world with the algorithm," Gunn said. "It might fall into the wrong hands. But outside of this room, nobody knows what has transpired here. Middleton *thinks* you still have the algorithm, and that's good enough."

"Is it? Good enough?" All traces of defiance had evaporated. Defeat weighed on her shoulders, and she seemed to deflate before Gunn's eyes.

"I'm prepared to offer you a deal," Gunn told her. "A much better deal than you'll get from Middleton."

"Oh?"

"Our inside people tell us the complete software—not just the algorithm but the fully assembled package—is going to be installed in Middleton's new home office. Trust me, if we'd had the chance to snatch it without raising an alarm, we would have tried it," Gunn said. "But Middleton is a prominent billionaire, and if something were to go wrong, that's not the kind of thing the NSA would like to see in the newspapers. Oh, we'd come up with some story for the public, but those in DC who know how to read between the lines wouldn't like it. I've worked too hard to find myself on somebody's shit list now."

"What am I supposed to do about any of this?"

"All you have to do is whatever you were meaning to do anyway," Gunn said. "You have a cache of weapons, and Middleton has something you want. And as far as he knows, you still have your copy of the algorithm. I don't need to know the details. Would prefer not to, actually."

"Why?"

Gunn frowned. "What do you mean? Do you mean why you? Or do you mean why all this trouble in the first place?"

"All of it."

"We have a window of opportunity, and you're in a position to take advantage," Gunn said. "If you blow it, then the entire episode will simply be a tabloid story about a billionaire's wife who went off the deep end. She was in Whispering Meadow for anger issues, after all, so it's really not a surprise. But if you succeed"—and here Gunn smiled like a child giddy with his secret scheme—"if you happen to lay your hands on the external drive with the software and deliver it to me, then I can make all your recent antics go away—the auto theft, hacking the ATMs, all of it. As if it never happened."

"You can do that?"

"I can do that and more," Gunn said. "As for why the NSA wants to do all this in the first place, the answer is simple. Our government has been lagging behind for over a decade in cyber-security. A couple of years ago, there was a mass shooting in San Bernardino. When we tried to break into the shooter's smart-phone, the company who made the smartphone refused to help us.

The US government should not have to go crawling to an electronics company in matters of national security. Just recently, the Democratic National Committee was hacked by a foreign power. If I told you about the various cyber assaults on our country's power grid, your hair would stand on end."

Gunn leaned forward, lowered his voice ominously. "Enough. No more. The new algorithm will not only make our cyber defenses the best in the world, but it will finally allow us to go on offense in a credible way. Imagine a program that analyzes a suspect's actions, predicts what he will do, and allows us to apprehend him before he commits some horrible act of bloodshed."

"Is that legal?" the girl asked.

"Legal isn't my business," Gunn said. "America is. Even with the key algorithm, it will take our tech people three to five years to extrapolate the rest of the components. You grab the external drive with the complete software, then America gets that much safer that much sooner."

"In writing."

"In writing what?" Gunn asked.

"Clearing my record, all that stuff you said. I want it in writing," the girl insisted.

Gunn grinned. "I don't have the standard clandestine agreement boilerplate on me at the moment, but I'm sure we can accommodate you."

"And all that Whispering Meadow stuff," the girl said. "That's gone."

"As if it had never happened," Gunn promised.

30

They'd dropped him back in front of the doughnut shop and left him there. No instructions, no explanation, no nothing. Francis stood there not knowing what to do and feeling foolish.

There was a vague sense of relief at no longer being in federal custody, but Francis wondered if it were a trick.

He tried both doors on the pickup truck. Still locked, and Emma had the keys. He looked around, clueless. It was the wee hours of the morning, the street deserted. The lights were still on in the doughnut shop, but the place was empty.

Headlights appeared at the end of the street and came toward him.

A black sedan stopped next to the truck. A back door opened, and Emma got out. The door closed again, and the sedan floated away onto the night.

She looked up and saw him. "Francis!"

She rushed to him, arms going around him, pulling him in tight. He hugged back like he never wanted to let go.

When they finally released one another, Francis asked, "What happened? Why did they let us go?"

"They offered me a deal."

"Oh?" Suspicions rose up in Francis again.

She told him about the conversation between herself and Agent Gunn. It was all too obvious to Francis she was still holding something back.

Francis didn't care. "I'll help you. Tell me what to do."

"You do nothing." She fished the keys out of her pocket, circled to the truck's passenger side, and unlocked the door. "I'm going solo on this one."

"This again? We settled this."

"It's different now."

"How is it different?"

"Because Gunn burned the fucking algorithm!" She spun on him, heat in her voice, face tight with anger and frustration. "It's gone, okay? Everything's changed."

"Nothing's changed," Francis shot back. "You told me, Gunn said it didn't matter. As long as Middleton thinks you have it, that's good enough."

"Shut up! Stop acting like you know how to do this. You don't. You don't know anything!"

"Why are you yelling at me? I'm the only person on the planet trying to help you."

"Well, you can't!" she screamed.

"Tell me why!" he screamed back at her

"Because . . ." Everything seemed to go out of her, all the heat, the defiance, the anger, every breath. She sank against the truck. "It wasn't the algorithm I needed. I mean, yes, I was going to try to trade it, but that wasn't what was important. On the back of the paper were three codes. A parting gift from Marion Parkes. I kept thinking I should make a copy, but everything kept happening so fast, and . . ." She smashed a fist against the side of the pickup. "Stupid!"

"Three seven-digit numbers?"

"Yes. They were written in the upper-top corner of the—Wait. What? You saw them?"

"When you showed me the algorithm," Francis said. "I looked at the wrong side first by accident. The first number is eight-six-four-eight-five-one-eight."

She blinked. "No, it's not. I mean . . . is it?"

"Yes."

"You remember?"

"It's just a knack I have with numbers."

"Like photographic memory?"

"It's *not* photographic—this isn't really important. I know the numbers. Let's focus on that."

"What's the second number?"

"Nine-four-nine-three-two-nine-one."

"You're serious?" Her face made it clear she wasn't messing around. "You're certain these are right?"

"I promise."

"What's the third number?"

He hesitated.

Her eyes narrowed, and her features went stone cold. "Francis."

"I'm coming with you," he said. "I can help."

"How?"

"Any way you tell me to."

She turned, ducked into the truck's cab, and Francis heard her open the footlocker. When she turned back, she grabbed Francis by the wrist and held his hand up.

"Like this." She slapped the revolver into his open palm. "I need this kind of help. Nothing less. Straight down the line, no half measures and no guarantee of a return ticket."

Francis's fingers closed around the revolver. He leaned in and kissed her. She didn't react at first, but then her hand went to the back of his head, held him, prolonging the kiss. When they at last pulled apart, she brushed his cheek with her fingertips. Her eyes were so full of love and gratitude, Francis thought he might cry. Or maybe laugh. He wasn't sure how to feel. All he knew was there wasn't anywhere else on earth he wanted to be if it was without her.

"Give me the keys. I'll drive," he said. "You load the guns on the way."

Ernie pulled the sedan off the road and parked.

"What're you doing?" Cavanaugh asked. We're a quarter mile away."

Ernie motioned ahead.

There was some kind of service van parked across from the main gate.

"I figure we don't want them in the way if we have to move fast," Ernie said. "We can see good enough from here."

Cavanaugh looked up and down the highway before agreeing. "Yeah. Okay. We can see her if she's coming from either direction. Then we call in the others and we take care of all this shit in one go."

"You sure she *is* coming?"

"She's on a mission. She's coming," Cavanaugh said. "Anyway, she's got nothing else."

Gunn scooped the files off his desk and packed them away into his briefcase. They'd no longer need the San Francisco offices. Matters were coming to a head, and when it was all over, he didn't want to have to come back here. Gunn preferred catching a flight directly back to DC to revel in his triumph.

The full extent of that triumph remained to be seen. As it stood,

260 • VICTOR GISCHLER

simply securing the algorithm would be enough for a feather in his cap. But if the girl could actually secure the complete software package intact . . .

Well. Either she would or she wouldn't.

Boston entered. "I've told the watch point outside Middleton's gate to be on the lookout for the girl and to notify us immediately when she arrives."

"Good," Gunn said. "And you've found us a good candidate from the local sheriff's department. He's on standby?"

"We've got a man," Boston assured him. "He's en route."

"Excellent."

"The watch team wants to know at what point they intervene," Boston said.

"Intervene?" Gunn looked appalled. "You tell them not at all. We're on mop-up duty only. Our young lady is on her own. It's go time. If she happens to go belly up, we break camp and slip into the night like federally funded ghosts."

31

The ride to Middleton's place in Sonoma went fast with little conversation, Francis behind the wheel, and Emma dutifully checking the weapons.

They rolled up to the main gate. It was high and solid and iron. Francis stopped at the call box. He shifted the truck into park and looked at Emma. "Your husband lives here?"

"It's a vineyard," she said.

"You lived here with him?"

She shook her head. "This is new."

"So you don't know what's ahead?"

"Only vaguely. What Marion Parkes told me. He was suspicious of the algorithm and what could be done with it even before he realized his own life was at stake. He said he felt like he was part of some modern Manhattan Project. I didn't know what he meant."

"In World War II," Francis said. "All the scientists who worked on the atomic bomb—"

"I know *now*, dink." She scowled at him. "I Googled it."

"Sorry."

"The point is that Parkes was always suspicious of the project, and so he passed these codes on to me along with the algorithm. It wasn't maybe the grandest revenge, but he hoped whatever I did with the information would at least stick in my husband's craw."

"And now here we are."

"Roll down the window."

Francis rolled it down.

"The keypad," she said. "Put in the first code."

He typed it in.

A second later, there was a metallic clunk, and then the gates began to swing inward.

"Is that all it does?" Francis asked. "Opens the gate?"

"No," she said. "It does more than that."

Ron Kowolski snorted himself awake.

Damn, had he fallen asleep again? It was always tough to stay awake the last hour or two of a shift. How long had he been sitting there, snoring? He started to glance at his watch when something on one of the monitors caught his attention. Was that a pickup truck at the main gate? Before he could blink and look again, the screen went to static.

"What the fuck?" He came out of his seat and turned the monitor on and off. No help. He looked and saw that all the monitors had gone fuzzy with the same static.

Okay, wait, there was a thing for this. In case of a surge or something, he was just supposed to reboot the whole system. He found the button for that and pressed it. All the monitors went dark. A second later, the monitors flickered to life again amid the whir and hum of computers rebooting. The static on each monitor had been replaced with a test pattern.

"Shit."

Ron was going to have to call somebody. Was there a tech support number? He picked up the phone. No dial tone. Dead.

This . . . wasn't good.

He took his own phone out of his pocket and tried to dial the Vines woman. Nothing. He squinted at his phone screen. No bars. No Wi-Fi. It was all jammed, blocked, gone.

Okay. This was *bad*. He flipped open the plastic lid covering the red alarm button. He mashed the button flat with his thumb.

Nothing. No shrieking Klaxon. No flashing lights.

Huh.

He fished the keys out of his pocket as he went into the next room. The other three guys didn't look up. One of them had sacked out on the sofa. The other two watched an episode of *Pawn Stars* on cable. They were younger, beefy cops collecting some moonlighting cash.

Ron crossed the room to the weapons cabinet, found the correct key, and unlocked the cabinet. A row of AR-15s lined the inside of the locker, the drawer below full of ammo and magazines. Ron took one of the rifles, slapped in a fresh magazine.

"Alarm, guys."

One of the guys watching TV looked back over his shoulder. "What are you talking about, Ron?"

"There's an alarm." He took one of the vests hanging on the wall and began strapping it on.

"I don't hear nothing."

Ron sighed. "Just come get one of these fucking guns."

"The gate's not closing," Ernie said. "You sure that was them?"

"It was them," Cavanaugh said. "Call the others. We're going in."

They slowed the truck a bit as they passed the old mission-style house, but after eyeballing it a second, Emma said that couldn't be the place, so they kept driving.

They took the road up to the main residence but pulled off, parking halfway hidden in the trees. They stood in the darkness as

Emma strapped on a pair of shoulder holsters. She'd given Francis a holster for the revolver that clipped to his belt. He clutched the shotgun with sweaty palms, the bandolier with additional twelve-gauge shells across his shoulder.

"We're going through the trees to circle around back," she said. "Leave some space between us. Bunching up makes an attractive target. Don't rush, but keep moving, and when we get there, don't come out from the tree line until I signal clear."

"Have you had training for this?"

"*Call of Duty.*"

The woodsy area turned out to be easier to traverse than expected. Much of the underbrush had been cleared, and the lights from the house drew them on. Francis paused at the tree line as instructed and took a knee. Emma was easily visible in the moonlight ten feet away. She was taking a good long look at the back of the house before making a decision.

It was an odd-looking house, Francis thought, but clearly huge and expensive. Where a billionaire might live, he supposed. From this vantage point, he overlooked a large deck, a line of ten deck chairs in a neat row. Ten-foot-high metal shutters spanned the wall behind the chairs, and Francis thought he saw a door all the way to the right of the shutters.

A hand on his shoulder startled him.

"Easy," Emma whispered. "It looks clear, and I've spotted a back door. I think there's a keypad. Follow me."

"Wait." Francis took a deep breath, then let it out slowly. Another deep breath. Blew it out. He couldn't make the feeling that he might throw up go away.

She put a hand on his cheek. Her fingers were cool. "I've seen you murder a paint can with extreme prejudice. You've got this."

He chuckled. In spite of his racing heartbeat, and the sweat behind his ears, and the butterflies doing barrel rolls in his gut, Francis chuckled. He looked at Emma and nodded.

She led him out of the tree line and up the short set of stairs to the deck. Francis worried about his steps creaking, but the deck was built of thick, solid timber, and they made their way to the back door in silence.

The door was a dull burnished metal with simple engravings, modern and minimal. As predicted, a keypad hung on the wall next to the door.

Emma nodded at the keypad and whispered, "The house is on a different system. Put in the second code."

Francis typed it in.

Middleton stood in his bathroom and splashed water on his face.

He couldn't sleep and felt frustrated that installing the new software had hit a snag. Bryant had been in the saucer for hours— Middleton had taken to calling it *the saucer*—trying to make it all work. Apparently, when Middleton's former employee had designed the system for the house, he'd picked one that was completely incompatible with . . . well, with everything. Bryant was beside himself trying to understand why somebody of Marion Parkes's intellect would do such a thing. Bryant had said he could still install the software, but it meant uninstalling the old stuff first, and the whole process could take hours, and he would be back in the morning to check on it.

Middleton had said *Screw it* and had gone to bed.

Except his mind kept drifting back to what Bryant had done up in the saucer. How long would it take? Patience wasn't a virtue

Middleton had been developing the last few years. He dried his face, tossed the towel over his shoulder as he walked back into the bedroom.

Middleton looked at his empty bed. Meredith had gone to bed hours before he had. To her own bed in her own room. It would be selfish to wake her at this hour.

Selflessness was another virtue he hadn't been working on, but he let it go. He'd see her over breakfast. Bryant would install the new software soon enough. Middleton just needed to settle the hell down.

He put on his robe. He was already up, so why not start the coffee? Might as well—

Click.

What the heck was that?

Click. Click.

He opened his bedroom door, looked both ways. The clicks echoed down the hall.

"Computer, is there something going on?"

Nothing.

He quelled a stab of worry. The old system was uninstalling itself. Of course that was it. But what were all those damn clicks? He checked his bedroom door, twisted the bolt to the lock position. It immediately snapped back. Middleton blinked. All the doors could be locked or unlocked by the computer. What was it, a spring or a magnet? He didn't know, but it was definitely stuck in the unlock position now. Was that the click? Were all those other clicks . . . ?

Were *all* the doors in the house unlocked?

He grabbed the phone. No dial tone.

"Fuck!"

They were coming for him. Okay, a bit dramatic. Who exactly would *they* be?

Anyone who wants the software. They know it's here. Bryant maybe told somebody. They're making a play for it right now. Do something!

He went to his closet and pulled down a polished mahogany box. He opened it, and there in velvet was the pistol he'd purchased on a whim. Not something for combat. Something he'd simply thought looked cool. The Colt Model 1889 .38 revolver. Gleaming nickel with mother-of-pearl grips. He took the revolver and tossed the box aside. He swung out the cylinder, checked the load, then snapped it back into place.

Now for the saucer. He could hole up there and protect the software at the same time.

No. Wait. He needed to make one stop first.

Ernie parked the car at the beginning of the walkway up to the front door. The SUVs with the rest of the hired guns pulled up and parked behind him. Cavanaugh and Ernie got out of the car.

"Okay, I want to go in fast and take control of the whole situation," Cavanaugh said. "Priority is to find the girl alive. This time, we're not so gentle about making her give us what we want, and then we tell Middleton flat out he has to pony up *big* or we walk and peddle the goods elsewhere."

"What about Berringer?" Ernie asked.

"Shoot that little prick on sight," Cavanaugh said. "Shoot him square in his fucking face."

"Right."

"Sir. Please stand still and follow my orders to the letter."

Cavanaugh looked around. "Who the fuck said that?"

Ernie pointed.

Four men came out of the tree line about fifty feet away. They were well spaced, all with AR-15s raised and aimed at Cavanaugh and Ernie.

"Who the fuck are you?" Cavanaugh shouted.

"My name is Ron Kowolski, and I'm in charge of this security shift, sir."

"Fuck. Rent-a-cops."

"Sir, I need for you and your friend to take out any weapons you might have and place them on the ground."

"Yeah, I'm not doing that," Cavanaugh said. "I work for Middleton, for Christ's sake."

"*Sir*," Kowolski said. "Please *immediately* take out any weapons and place them on the ground *now*. We'll sort out who you are after that. We are in a lockdown situation and are proceeding to secure Mr. Middleton's safety."

Jesus, this was all Cavanaugh needed. He wasn't about to let a rent-a-cop take him into custody. That would ruin everything.

The rest of Cavanaugh's men got out of the SUVs. Most had pistols in hand.

The three men with Kowolski shifted their aim to cover them with their AR-15s.

"You men need to stand down *right now*," Kowolski said.

"Wait a minute!" Cavanaugh shouted. "Everyone just calm the fuck down!"

Absolute silence stretched. Everyone looked at everyone else, holding breaths, fingers on triggers.

Cavanaugh took a deep breath, then yelled, "Light 'em up!"

He threw himself across the hood of his car, rolled to the other side, and dropped behind the vehicle just as a hell storm of gunfire erupted.

The car window glass shattered and rained down on him amid

the chatter of automatic rifle fire and the *pop, blast, pow* of multiple handguns.

Ernie elbow-crawled around the car to join Cavanaugh. "Jesus Christ!"

The sedan shook, metal *tunks* across the hood as it was raked with lead. Shouts and screams as men died.

"We've got to get the fuck out of here!" Cavanaugh shouted over the gunfire.

"You convinced me," Ernie said.

"When I signal, you run like hell for the front door."

They'd found themselves in a huge indoor pool area after coming through the back door. They moved through the house quietly, Francis simply following Emma. She knew what she was looking for.

He hoped.

The hallways within the house were weird, curving around at odd angles and branching off unexpectedly.

Francis felt like he were aboard some alien spaceship.

They eventually found themselves in an entry foyer with a soaring ceiling and a crazy-ugly chandelier looming above.

"We've come around to the front of the house," Emma whispered. "Where now?"

"I . . . don't know," she said.

Ah.

She looked back down the hall. "Maybe one of those turns back there—"

Both their heads snapped around at the sudden burst of gunfire outside. It kept going, sounded like all hell was breaking loose just beyond the front door.

"What's happening?"

"Go," Francis said. "Do what you need to do."

"What?"

"The house is huge. Go find what you need to find. Finish your business with your husband. Anything that comes through that front door"—Francis pumped the shotgun—"is my problem."

She searched his eyes a moment, then reached out and grabbed his face, pulling him into a hard kiss. She released him, nodded once, then turned and jogged back the way they'd come.

Francis was alone.

The gunfire still raged outside.

Wow, this was a terrible idea.

He wiped his sweaty palms on his pants.

Francis glanced down at the safety on the shotgun. What had Emma told him? *F* for forward. *F* for fire.

He thumbed the safety forward.

The gunfire seemed to be ebbing. Whatever they were deciding out there was close to being over. Francis held the shotgun up and ready. Okay, he definitely planned to defend himself, but at the same time, he wasn't eager to shoot anyone. His hands shook. He'd yell *Freeze* or *Hold it*, give them a chance to drop weapons or maybe—

The front door slammed open.

Francis fired, the shotgun kicking hard, barrel spitting flame.

He was shooting before he'd even recognized it was Cavanaugh coming through the door. The shot had gone high, buckshot peppering the wall over the door.

You can't just point it, idiot. You've got to aim.

Francis pumped in another shell, but Cavanaugh had already leaped aside. Another thug filled the doorway. Francis squeezed the trigger. The buckshot slammed into the thug's chest, and he was lifted off his feet in a spray of blood and knocked back outside.

Francis pumped again, shot the next thug coming through, who spun and died half in and half out of the house. He was pumping in the next shell, when Cavanaugh began shooting at him with the little pistol.

Francis flinched back to the sound of the *pop pop pop*, the shots exploding plaster on the wall an inch from his face. Francis backed around the corner.

More goons came through the door. He recognized the one with the mustache.

Francis aimed the shotgun at the ceiling and fired. The chandelier came down hard on the mustache, shattering on top of him and slamming him unconscious to the hard tile.

Cavanaugh and the other thug were still shooting. Smoke and dust filled the foyer.

Francis dove to the floor, rolled out, and the thug fired over his head. Francis aimed the shotgun along the ground and pulled the trigger. The thug's ankle exploded, and he went down in a puddle of his own blood. Francis pumped and fired again, blew half the thug's head away. He rolled back out of Cavanaugh's line of sight just as three bullets whizzed past his nose.

He pushed back up against the wall, breathing hard, heart flailing against his chest. The sudden silence was eerie and unnerving. He thumbed fresh shells into the shotgun, marveled that his hands were rock solid now, no hint of a single tremor.

"Berringer?" Cavanaugh's voice. "Come out and let's talk about this. What do you say?"

You should have killed him. Francis heard Emma's voice in his head. *They just come back if you don't kill them.*

If Francis got his chance, he'd take it.

"We can work this out, Berringer. We can all walk away from this. Let's talk about it."

Francis scooted to the corner, went low, and barely peeked around the corner. A quick look, then pulled back. It was enough to see that Cavanaugh was up and in a crouch, slowly coming toward his position.

Francis could jump out and start shooting.

And just as easily get shot.

He risked another glance around the corner. Cavanaugh was getting closer.

Another figure appeared in the open doorway, a middle-aged man in a security guard uniform. One of his arms hung limp and bloody, but he held a pistol in the other hand and raised it at Cavanaugh. "Hold it!"

Cavanaugh spun and shot, and the guard went down holding the fresh wound in his thigh. Cavanaugh turned back, but Francis was already out of his hiding place.

He fired the shotgun, buckshot hammering Cavanaugh's shoulder. Cavanaugh went spinning and stumbling. Francis pumped and fired again, knocking Cavanaugh up against the wall. Cavanaugh slid down, leaving streaks of garish red against the white. His mouth worked, blood foaming out.

Cavanaugh looked at Francis with raw hatred. "You . . . fucking . . . little . . . son of a—"

Francis pumped and fired one last time.

He tossed the shotgun aside and went to the fallen guard. The man trembled, desperately holding his thigh wound, dark blood seeping between fingers.

"Easy," Francis said. "Stay calm."

He took the bandolier from around his shoulder and removed the remaining shells. "I'm going to use this as a tourniquet, okay? I'm going to tie it tight, so brace yourself."

He tied it tight. The guy grunted but didn't protest.

"I've got to go, but that tourniquet is on there good, okay?" Francis said. "Somebody will be along. You've got to hang tough."

There was fear in the man's eyes, but he nodded.

Francis hoped it was true that somebody would be along. He didn't know what else to tell the man.

He rose and fled into the depths of the house.

32

The girl stood in front of the elevator door, knowing with keen instinct it would take her where she needed to go. Aaron was above her, waiting. He had taken so much from her. It would be impossible to get it all back, and she wasn't even going to try.

But there was one thing at least he certainly didn't deserve to keep, and that was the one and only reason she was here.

Her name was Emma Middleton, but before, when her life had been entirely her own, she'd been Emma Klondike, which she'd hated because it made people think she was an Eskimo lesbian. Anyway, that was one of the stupid things she'd thought in high school when people made fun of her name. Never mind that high school kids made fun of everything.

She hit the elevator call button and flicked the safety off one of the automatics. She was frightened but strangely calm. No matter how drastic her current choice of action, it was a relief not having to second-guess herself, knowing there was no other choice.

She would feel bad if something happened to Francis. A pang of dread rose up in her, and she smashed it down again. She had a job to do. Nothing else.

The elevator door opened, and she stepped aboard.

The ride up was so brief that panic seized her suddenly. This was it. This was what she'd come so far to do, and in a second, the elevator door would open again, and both the idea that what she'd been seeking would be on the other side and the idea that it wouldn't be there terrified her equally, but there was no more time to dwell on it.

The door opened.

"Mommy!"

Emma's heart leaped.

"Mommy!" The little girl tried to run to her, but Aaron Middleton grabbed her from behind.

"Not so fast, Mable," he said. "Remember what I told you about Mommy. She's been sick in her head, and it makes her not always act in a safe way. We need to hold her here until the doctors can come get her and help her." In one hand, he held an absurd-looking revolver.

But she could barely see him, barely registered he was talking. All she could do was look at Mable, auburn hair falling in tight curls around her shoulders, apple cheeks, bare feet with pink toes. She wore a *Frozen* nightgown. How long since she'd seen her? Held her. Emma's eyes glazed with tears.

"Mommy missed you, honey."

"Are you sick?"

Emma shook her head. "Mommy's better. I would never hurt you."

"Well, that's really for the doctors to decide," Middleton said.

She scowled at him. "Can we please drop the bullshit, Aaron?"

"You left me, then tried to take my daughter from me," he said. "Did you really think I wouldn't take action?"

"Please," she said. "You have so much. Just let me take her. I'll never ask for anything. I'll never bother you again."

"She's my daughter too."

"Please." Emma took a step toward him.

He lifted the revolver. "Don't."

276 • VICTOR GISCHLER

"Are you going to shoot me in front of my daughter?"

"I'll do what I have to do."

"Don't shoot Mommy."

Aaron shushed her. "It's okay, Mable. Just let Daddy handle it."

"Mr. Middleton?"

Emma and Middleton both turned to see the woman coming up through the spiral staircase hatch.

"Meredith, I hadn't meant for you to see this," Middleton said.

"Who's this?"

"An . . . unwanted visitor," Middleton said. "Could you go back downstairs, please?"

"I can't do that."

"I know this seems odd," Middleton said. "I promise to explain it all later, but I really do need you to please leave. Trust me, I have this in hand."

"No." Meredith lifted a small automatic pistol and pointed it at him. "I mean, I really can't do that."

All the blood drained from Middleton's face. "But you're supposed to be on my side."

Meredith put a hand up in a calming gesture. "See, that's the thing. I am. Oh, Aaron darling, I promise I am. That's why I need you to put the gun down so we can fix this instead of making it worse. And think of Mable. Let's not have a bunch of guns going off with her here."

Emma took another step forward. "She's right. Listen to her."

Middleton swung the gun back toward Emma, pulling Mable closer to him at the same time. "Don't tell me what to do."

Meredith eased toward him. "Please, Aaron."

He swung the pistol back to Meredith. "Who are you? Who do you work for?"

"I love you, Aaron," Meredith said. "That's the truth."

"You're tricking me."

Emma took another slow half step. "Just let me have Mable."

Middleton swung the gun back again. "Back off. I need to think. Just fucking stay still."

The elevator chimed.

Everyone froze.

The door opened, and Francis stepped out. He saw the man pointing a gun at Emma and went for the revolver on his belt.

Middleton lifted the revolver and fired.

Mable screamed.

Francis screamed too, grabbed his bloody shoulder, and went down.

Emma's eyes shot wide. "Francis!"

Meredith fired.

The bullet struck Middleton in the chest. The betrayal so plain on his face.

Emma dove for Mable, who was still screaming and screaming and screaming. She pulled the little girl to the ground, covered her body with her own. *Just let nothing happen to my daughter. Just not her. Anything but that.*

Middleton turned toward Meredith, pure disbelief at the hole in his chest. He raised the pistol, face shifting to anger and rage.

Meredith shook her head. "Don't, Aaron. Please."

He fired.

And fired and fired and fired and fired.

He was still clicking on empty when she wilted limp to the floor like something discarded, a pool of blood spreading rapidly from beneath her.

Middleton had gone bone white, face covered with sweat. He

turned very slowly, swaying on his feet and aimed the revolver at Emma. She clutched Mable crying to her chest, not letting the little girl look.

Middleton squeezed the trigger.

Click.

His hand fell to his side, the revolver clattering to the floor.

Middleton looked around, dazed. "I . . . I'd just built a house."

He took one watery sideways step and tumbled down the stairs to the lower level, coming to a stop up against his special chair. Then he closed his eyes, and that was all for Aaron Middleton.

Emma clung to her daughter and sobbed and kept right on sobbing, not even noticing at first all the people crowding into the room.

"Her first!" shouted a paramedic.

Emma looked up, wiping the tears from her eyes to see them attending the woman who'd shot her husband.

"Get her on the board. Get her down to the van. We're losing her. Come on!"

Hands lifted Emma up, took her across the room. She was holding her daughter still, who buried her face into her mommy's neck.

It was Gunn. In his other hand, he held an external drive. "You did well. I know you've had a hard time. I just wanted you to know I'm as good as my word. You'll have everything you need in writing."

What was he saying? She couldn't focus. She held on to her daughter with both arms.

Men swarmed the computers in the room, a flurry of activity. She didn't care. *Mable.*

"The sheriff's report will say you came to take custody of your daughter as per court order," Gunn said. "It's all been signed by a

judge and backdated. It's all legit. When you came to take custody, your husband didn't react so well. The result was tragic but
unavoidable."

"Francis!"

Emma broke loose from Gunn and ran to where the paramedics worked on Francis. They had his shirt cut open, tubes running
into his arms. She took one of his hands in hers.

His eyes opened, and he smiled at her weakly. "What . . .
happened?"

"You got yourself shot, dink."

"Did we win?"

She nodded, laughing, tears dripping from her face onto his.
"We won."

"We've given him something for the pain, so he'll probably be
out of it soon," said one of the paramedics. "Stay with him. We'll
be right back with the stretcher."

She leaned low and whispered into Francis's ear. "Francis. I need
the third code."

"The . . . what?" He was fading fast.

"Francis!"

A vague groan.

"Francis Berringer, I love you, you stupid, clumsy dink, but if
you don't dig down deep and give me that third code, I'll fucking
shoot you in the other shoulder."

EPILOGUE

The next six weeks were interesting.

For starters, it came to Emma's attention that California was a community property state. A small army of lawyers and accountants descended upon her from Middleton's corporation. Smelling a buck, another small army of lawyers and accountants leaped into the fray to defend her honor.

Utter lawyer-apocalypse was averted when Emma made it clear she wanted no part of her husband's corporation, and if they could just show her where to go to cash out, she'd happily remove herself from the equation. Naturally, the board of directors found this decision acceptable.

Even after being appropriately gouged by lawyers and accountants and state, federal, and local taxes, Emma found she was now worth several hundred million dollars. She sat down with her new checkbook and immediately showed Francis again the depth of her character.

The checks were in the mail the next day. But to Francis, it was the personal notes that added that little extra touch.

Marcus Clay was a junior at St. Cloud State University in Minnesota. With his check for $25,000 was the brief note *I heard your car was stolen from the airport. Maybe get a better one with this? Take care and study hard.*

To the old couple who'd lost their mom-and-pop filling station, she'd written, *I hope we can leave a different impression the next time we pass through your town.* Probably they'd had insurance, but the check was big enough to completely rebuild.

Ron Kowolski did not receive a check. As an employee for Aaron Middleton, his gunshot wounds would earn him a nice monthly payment for the rest of his life, over and above his police retirement. But he did get a telegram from Emma that read, *You seem like the kind of guy who'd say he was just doing his job. But I still want you to know we appreciate you.* Ron had then been asked to step outside of his little house. His jaw dropped upon seeing the brand-new Boston Whaler 420 Outrage sitting on a trailer to be taken to the harbor of his choice, where a permanent slip would be purchased for him. The boat had already been filled with top-notch fishing gear.

Emma wrote checks like this late into the night, emptying half a bottle of Wild Turkey, the checks getting slightly bigger with each shot. Then she'd declared the slate clean and had gone to bed.

The next morning, she announced she was perfectly cool now with spending some of that money on herself. Fortunately, there were several high-end shopping districts in San Francisco that were more than happy to accommodate her.

Enid had nearly finished passing out the flyers.

Acting with the traveling show had turned out to be a bit of a drag. Sure, she had a good supporting role. She was *acting*, and that beat the shit out of waitressing every time. But she hadn't realized the actors were also responsible for setting up and breaking down the stage. Packing away the costumes and loading the trucks. She often found herself working a lot harder than she had back at the diner.

And now she was handing out flyers that advertised the show. *Ugh.*

This street was packed with boutique shops and rich people throwing their money around. Enid had given away most of the flyers in less than an hour, but she wanted to hang on to the last couple for a special purpose. This weekend's show was the last one, and Enid would need to find a new gig.

Unless she found a rich guy first.

But the problem was that the people with all the money were all so *old*. Most of the women coming in and out of the shops had had a lot of work done and still weren't fooling anyone. The few men she'd seen had either been a lot older or wearing red valet parking jackets.

Wait. Who was *that*?

She spotted him coming out of a shop, clearly young and hip, jeans and some kind of snakeskin boots and one of those western shirts with the overdone scrollwork and a really cool leather jacket. He was walking away from her, and she followed, wondering if he were a good candidate. She'd only got a glimpse of him from the side, but he seemed good-looking.

And then he got into a parked car close by. It was a perfect, bright red Ford Fairlane 500 Skyliner convertible. It was a gorgeous car, and Enid knew classic car restoration was a rich guy's hobby. Maybe he was some up-and-coming country music star.

She unbuttoned an extra button on her blouse and approached the car, flyer in hand.

Enid put her hands on the passenger-side door, leaning into the car in a way she knew would give him a glimpse down her blouse. She turned her smile up to full volume.

"Hey, you," she said. "I'm inviting people to the big show this weekend and—"

She looked at the man's face. Blinked.

"Francis?"

"Enid. What are you doing here?"

"Well . . . uh . . . the show. The run ends in Frisco," she said. "We're at the Orpheum."

"That's awesome," Francis said. "Congratulations."

Enid ran her hand along the side of the car. "Did you get a promotion?"

Francis laughed. "I quit that job."

"You found a better one, I guess."

He shook his head. "I'm sort of between things right now."

She thought about that a moment, smiled again. "Well, then, you have time to come see me in the show. You know, I was thinking we could catch up, maybe get a drink or something."

"Darling, *there* you are," came a new voice. "You know if you leave me alone in the shop, I'll lose track of time."

Enid turned to see her, stunning and young and obviously the source of the money.

"Pardon me, dear."

Enid stepped out of the way so the woman could put the shopping bags in the back seat of the Fairlane.

She wore an exquisite retro tea-length cocktail dress with a rich floral pattern of red and black. Her hair was the same bright red as the flowers on the dress. Lines up the back of her stockings, also very retro. Red gloves up to the elbows. Enid wondered if the Fairlane had been purchased specifically to go with the outfit.

"Now, darling, we discussed your talking to strange women on the street." She turned to Enid, offered a tolerant smile. "I'm always shooing pretty young things away from him."

"Oh, I, uh . . . I mean, I didn't mean to . . . uh . . ." This wasn't going as Enid had expected.

284 • VICTOR GISCHLER

"Enid is an old friend from New York," Francis said. "Her show is at the Orpheum."

"An actress. How exciting for you." The woman circled the car to the driver's side. "Scoot over and let me drive, will you, Frankie darling? You know I love to feel the rumble of the engine up my thighs."

Francis scooted.

She took Francis's face with one gloved hand and pulled him possessively into a long kiss. When the kiss ended a year or so later, she looked back and saw Enid still standing there.

"Ta-ta, Enid. It was nice to meet you," the woman said. "Have fun with your show. I'm sure you'll be just an enormous hit."

She cranked the engine, and the Fairlane moved easily into traffic. Enid stood and watched it go, wondering what exactly had just happened.

Francis found the image of Enid in the rearview mirror with her mouth hanging open to be vaguely satisfying, but really he just wished her well and planned not to think much about her in the future. It seemed impossible she'd ever been important to him.

He looked at Emma, who had a big satisfied grin on her face. "Laying it on a bit thick, weren't you?"

"Girls got to learn they can't come sniffing around my property." She gave his leg a squeeze. "How's the shoulder?"

"Hurts."

"Take the pills," she said. "That's what they're for."

Francis shrugged. "I feel like I want to wean off them."

Emma glanced at the $24,000 Cartier watch on her wrist. "We still have two hours before we pick up Mable. How about a medicinal glass of wine?"

"Can you get us in someplace?"

"If not, then I'll buy the joint."

Francis didn't know if she was kidding or not.

They'd found a special preschool for Mable, a place where she could play with other kids and all the normal things, but also sessions with therapists. She'd had a shock, but like most kids, she was more resilient than expected. More than writing checks, more than shopping, Emma had spent the bulk of her time with her daughter. It was hard to convince her to let Mable go for just the few hours a day to go to the preschool, but Emma had seen it was good for her.

Emma was a mom. Francis loved her for it. Loved her for so many reasons.

"Yeah, I could go for a glass of wine."

"It's not really economical to buy it by the glass," Emma said. "Better to get a bottle."

He grinned. She drove. She quite obviously enjoyed being the pretty girl in the convertible. He felt like they were in a really esoteric perfume commercial.

"Hey," she said. "Are you sure that you gave me the right numbers for the third code?"

"How many times are you going to ask me this?"

"But are you *sure?*"

"I told you I don't remember giving you the final code," Francis said. "I was pretty much out of it. But when you told me the numbers back the next day, yeah, those were the numbers."

In the end, it had all come full circle back to Marion Parkes. The final code commanded the software to turn on itself, to seek itself out wherever it might be stored, and erase itself from existence. Parkes was a crusader from the grave. Time would tell if the software was safe behind the NSA firewall, but Francis liked

286 • VICTOR GISCHLER

to think that one day Agent Gunn would log on to his computer back in Washington, DC, and find that all his hard work had gone up in a puff of cyber smoke.

It was a happy thought, but if it ever actually happened, Francis doubted he'd hear about it.

He could live with that.

"We should take a vacation," Emma said. "When she has her next school break. We should all go somewhere together."

"We could go white-water rafting."

"Don't be an idiot."

"But I'm so good at it."

"She likes *Frozen*," Emma said.

"You're thinking Disneyland?"

"I was thinking Norway."

Francis laughed.

She shot him a sideways look. "What?"

"I just love you."

She sighed, shaking her head. "I guess I love you too, dink."

ACKNOWLEDGMENTS

Special thanks as always to superfly agent David Hale Smith and his right hand Liz Parker and the entire crew at InkWell Management. Much gratitude to all of the folks at Tor/Forge/Macmillan who make books happen. Thanks and apologies to the stalwart copy editors. I promise I do know how to spell, but when I get in a writing frenzy, the typos come fast and furious. The usual gratitude to my family for putting up with me. I know it never looks like I'm working, but somehow the books get written, right? I'll get to those dirty dishes in the sink. Last but not least (to coin a cliché), this novel would simply not exist without the creativity and support of uber editor Brendan Deneen. Shine on, you crazy diamond.